CAN'T STOP THE FUNK

A "Cadillac" Holland Mystery

H. Max Hiller

INDIES UNITED PUBLISHING HOUSE, LLC

ISBN: 978-1-64456-133-1
Library of Congress Control Number: 2020936381

INDIES UNITED PUBLISHING HOUSE, LLC
P.O. BOX 3071
QUINCY, IL 62305-3071
www.indiesunited.net

For my own Miss Js;
Joyce and Jackie.
Thank you for your
patience and service.

Chapter 1

The FBI office in New Orleans waited five years to open an investigation into the police-involved shootings during the chaotic aftermath of Hurricane Katrina. The focus seemed to be centered on my nominal boss, NOPD's Chief of Detectives Bill Avery. Chief Avery signed off on the judgment of his own department's investigators when they consistently cleared every stressed-out officer responsible for any of the shootings. NOPD's police superintendent at the time selected the detectives who handled these most cursory of investigations. Avery was now under fire for not questioning their conclusions that all of the shootings were justified. The new police superintendent seemed a bit too eager to let Avery be NOPD's scapegoat for everything his predecessor mishandled during and after the storm ravaged the city and its already troubled department.

Chief Avery was my father's partner at NOPD until my father became Chief of Detectives when I was still in grade school. Avery assumed the position when my father retired to spend his days deep sea fishing. This connection his was how a permanent position for a State Police Detective at NOPD was created the very same day I

1

received my gold badge in Baton Rouge. The secret purpose of this unique arrangement was to facilitate my investigation into my father's abrupt disappearance while conducting rescues in the Lower Ninth Ward during the turmoil after Hurricane Katrina. My investigation left me in a worse position with the FBI's Special Agent in Charge than Chief Avery when it was unexpectedly solved a few weeks earlier. Bill and I shared a conviction that his problems were a direct result of my uncovering evidence an FBI agent was involved in murdering civilians, including my father, in the wake of the storm.

Bill Avery uses being my supervisor to justify having breakfast with me three or four times a week at Strada Ammazarre, the French Quarter bistro I co-own with Tony Venzo. Conducting business over breakfast at the restaurant is both a blessing and a curse for Avery. He gets to enjoy gourmet meals he couldn't otherwise afford, but his waistline is testament to the frequency of his visits. Chef Tony likes to sleep late and usually leaves preparing our breakfast to a cranky fire-plug of a Black woman I have always known as Miss J. She knew my father when he was a rookie officer patrolling the Florida Projects in New Orleans East. She helped my father deal with the Black Panthers, who literally ran the Florida Projects when he was a rookie officer patrolling in New Orleans East.

Bill's breakfast this morning was a gingered fruit compote, grits and grillades, hash browns smothered in onions and gravy, three chocolate croissants, and café au lait. I was happy with fried eggs and grilled andouille sausage. I also invited my Uncle Felix to join us for breakfast under the pretense of his 'just happening to be in town.' His compliments on the plate of eggs Sardou Miss J set before him were met with a smile that hid her indifference to such opinions. She doesn't need Felix's praise to know what a good cook she is. The Creole dish sets a pair of poached eggs atop an artichoke bottom and creamed spinach smothered beneath a blanket of hollandaise, and everything was indeed perfect.

Uncle Felix Deveraux is both a legend and a phantom in Louisiana politics. The best indication of his influence on a situation is the absence of any sign of his involvement. He is cut from the old-school "political fixer" mold and he is the guy you need to call when you are being blackmailed, or when you need someone blackmailed. There had been a brief moment in time when there was a plan for me to join his firm after college. That idea was scrapped when I was an underclassman at LSU. I took ROTC courses to pad my GPA and wound up in the Army. My uncle has never forgiven this betrayal.

The three of us made polite conversation between bites of food. It ranged from the recent re-opening of the Fairmont Hotel under its previous moniker of Roosevelt Hotel to my uncle's unsolicited endorsement of my dating one of the local State's Attorneys. Uncle Felix saw the potential for us to be a power couple, even though I was still having a difficult time even seeing us as a couple. What we absolutely did not discuss was anything to do with Chief Avery's legal troubles. I could have no part in any such discussion without becoming party to whatever scheme Felix hatched to save Avery. This meal provided a plausible explanation for our meeting if the FBI tried to connect me to any intervention my uncle made on my boss' behalf.

"I need to check on a couple of things," I said and excused myself. I left the two of them alone at the Chef's Table. The table seats six and is tucked into a niche in the sizable kitchen Tony had modeled on the Mafioso-owned trattoria in Sicily where he apprenticed. My family believes Tony is a chef I became friends with while on vacation, but the name we gave to our bistro translates from Italian to the English phrase "road kill." That is what I looked like after an ambush in Baghdad left me with a crushed skull and three bullet wounds. Tony saved my life that night, because he was part of the intelligence mission I was leading when we were ambushed. It had nothing to do with cooking. I am still bound by a security clearance contract which bars me from discussing my years as a Special Operations operator and my later work for any intelligence agencies. This also keeps Tony's and my mutual secrets safe.

I found Miss J alternately stirring three stockpots on the massive range in the prep kitchen. Two pots held traditional Italian sauces; the third was full of the day's fresh pot of gumbo. Tony's apprentices struggled to keep up with her demands for the ingredients required for each recipe. Miss J stands barely five feet tall and requires a foot stool to see inside the tall pots. I bit my tongue about the fluffy pink bedroom slippers she insists on wearing for comfort's sake. She had been with us for three years; I gave up on her changing her shoes a long time ago. Tony and I both understand how much more we need her than she needs this job. She also doubles as den mother to the staff, in both the front and back of the house. She defers slightly to Juaquin, our general manager, on matters of budget and purchasing. I sincerely believe that she is the first human being to intimidate Tony, and I have seen him make grown men piss themselves.

"Has Mister Bill got you working on anything for him?" Miss J asked when we were alone for a moment. I could smell the garlic and basil simmering in the pot of red sauce. I would smell like a pizza delivery boy all day if I lingered here too long.

"No. He's got bigger problems than keeping me busy right now."

"Can you go talk to my sister? Esther's all upset that someone wants to buy our house. They made offers on all the houses them Make-It-Right folks built." I could tell she was upset. I also knew there was not going to be an easy way to say buying houses is not a crime.

"I'd be happy to," I assured her. It took me a moment to realize that the look she gave me was her way of silently questioning why I wasn't already on my way to see Esther.

"You two okay?" I asked my boss and uncle on my way past their table. I grew up envisioning Uncle Felix as being a cross between a slick-haired used car salesman and the Devil; the one you'd meet at a crossroads around midnight to sell your immortal soul. I still think he cultivates that impression.

"Better than I have been." It was the first time I had seen Chief Avery smile since Michael Conroy, the head of the local FBI, personally informed him he was under investigation. I began to consider the size of the debt I was going to owe my 'devil' uncle as I walked to the garage on Decatur Street.

Chapter 2

The Lower Ninth Ward has always been the city's poorest and least racially diverse neighborhood. Prior to the storm, it was home to the marginally employed, and very poorly paid, faceless Black workers that keep the city's various service industries running. They make beds, wash dishes, dig ditches, stock shelves, and do whatever it takes to put food on their tables. The children of these hard workers don't always want to work so hard for so little money. This attitude led to drug dealing and escalating crime in the neighborhood in the years proceeding Hurricane Katrina. Gang turf battles had killed or wounded hundreds of people. The de facto moat formed by the Industrial Canal made it possible for the city's white minority population to consider the problem of the brutal Black on Black violence to be contained. To be perfectly honest, it allowed many of them to imagine a day when the Lower Ninth Ward might finally kill itself off.

Katrina physically flushed everyone from the neighborhood. This gave rise to both a new hope for the community and a shaming of those who wanted to keep its law abiding and hard-working residents from ever returning. Repatriation was the big issue in the previous mayoral election, and it was front and center in the current election as well. A new mayor would be elected in less than three months. The vast majority of homes lost to the storm were family owned, but poorly insured. It took efforts by groups like Make It Right and the Musician's Village to get the rebuilding process started. It also took activists and loudmouths like Esther and Lionel Batiste to keep it moving.

The new home Miss J, Esther, and Lionel Batiste stay by on Deslonde Street is built like a fort against future storms. The thunderstorm I drove through to get to their house seemed determined to test the flood walls the Corps of Engineers insisted on patting itself on the back about. They rebuilt every section of flood wall Katrina breached within a year, and were proudly proclaiming they were "just as good as" the ones that had failed so spectacularly. I was driving the bistro's Ford Raptor pickup truck because my low-slung Cadillac coupe doesn't have the ground clearance to handle even the city's normal street flooding. This storm was expected to last for days and was already making a mess.

The Batistes' living quarters are twelve feet above ground level and built atop thirty five foot deep pilings. Only a place to park their ancient Crown Victoria and a storage shed are at ground level. The primary construction materials are storm-resistant masonry and steel. The metal roof is lined with solar panels. A lot of attention went into every aspect of its durable construction, but almost none into making it look like the shotgun house it replaced.

Lionel Batiste opened the door a crack when I knocked.

"Your aunt asked me to come talk to you about someone trying to buy your house." My explanation lessened the scowl on Lionel's face.

"It's all good. Let Cooter in," Esther shouted from behind him. "We don't keep the only good NOPD cop in the city standing in the rain."

"I work for the State Police, not NOPD," I explained to Lionel. I stepped past the lanky twenty-five year old and looked around the open-concept interior. The Batiste's interior decorating appeared to have been handled by one of the local buy-on-credit furniture stores that advertise on late night television. A heavy sectional sofa and glass and bronzed-metal coffee table faced the living room's black metal TV stand and flat panel TV. The dining room table had metal legs and chairs with plastic cane-look seat backs. The art on the walls only qualified as "art" because the pictures were in metal frames. Each room reflected the Batiste family's tastes and budget, but the decorating hardly conformed to what the architect likely had in mind.

"That's supposed to be better?"

I felt confident in assuming he had a bad history with the police in the past. A disturbingly high percentage of the city's young men have criminal records full of misdemeanors simply because they caught some cop's eye the wrong way.

"Not really. I just want to be sure you hate me for all the right reasons." I hoped a combination of sarcasm and honesty might get me through the interview.

"Cop's a cop," Lionel muttered and let me past. I finally understood why we had never spoken when he dropped by the bistro to see his aunt. He had absolutely nothing to say to me.

Esther Batiste was in the kitchen. She is a heavy-set woman in her sixties, with Type-2 diabetes and kidney problems. She pointed to the counter separating the dining room from the kitchen. I took a seat on one of the tall wooden stools while she rummaged around in a stack of papers next to the refrigerator. Lionel sat down at the dining room table behind me. He positioned himself so I had to turn to address him, but where I could sense he was staring at me.

"This is what they sent us." Esther handed me a large envelope. She flashed her son a reproachful look. My taking the time to come here and listen to their concerns obviously did nothing to change Lionel's opinion of policemen in general.

I studied the large white envelope before I emptied its contents on the counter top. It was sized so the contents could lie flat, which made them seem a bit more formal and intimidating. The logo beside the return address was a square red box with the letters CSA and the words 'A Holding Company' in bold white letters. It was likely a shell corporation. The return address was printed on the envelope with an elegant, dark gray font. The address was on the forty-third floor of a building in Mobile, Alabama. I had been in Mobile in the past year and could remember no building anywhere near that height. This was likely a letter-drop address meant to further conceal the actual nature of CSA.

The contents of the envelope weren't much help. There was a very cleverly written letter of introduction about the company and its mission. Even the company's mission statement failed to explain their real purpose. CSA Holdings billed itself as a real estate investment group looking for opportunities to develop not just homes but entire communities. I wondered if they were buying here to be able to show a loss to offset some far more lucrative development's profits.

The holding company's cash offer was two hundred and sixty thousand dollars for the Batistes' home and lot. It seemed like a great deal of money for a three bedroom home in this part of town. It also sounded like a once in a lifetime opportunity for the family to move to a much nicer part of town. It did not seem like an intelligent investment for experienced real estate investors to make. I could see nothing to be gained by the holding company in making an offer to buy the Batiste's home, much less their entire neighborhood.

"What do you think?" Esther barely let me put the packet back together before she wanted my opinion.

"I think it is the best offer you will ever get if you want to sell."

"Well, we don't." I knew this without Lionel's telling me so.

"Your sister told me that the company wants to buy all of the houses the Make-It-Right Foundation built."

"That's right. Everyone on this street got one of these," Esther confirmed. "They all came to me, to see what we should do."

"What did you tell them?"

"To do nothing at all. I wanted to find someone who could find out what these people are really after."

"Is anyone else buying renovated houses in this neighborhood?"

"Yes, but that's some other company." Esther said this as though she understood there were implications in the fact that the offer made on her home was only made on the homes the Make It Right Foundation had completed. There were only sixteen homes on this street. Three more were under construction. Brad Pitt's pet project had a long ways to go to get to the hundred and fifty houses he once promised. Still, buying just the finished homes at the price being offered was going to cost CSA well over three million dollars.

"Can I borrow this?" I pointed to the packet. "I need someone better at the business end of things to give me an opinion. I'm with you, though. It doesn't make any sense for someone to spend this much money to buy these houses."

"You don't think they're worth that much?" I managed to step on another trap in Lionel's mine field.

"I think they are worth far more than that to the families living in them. I also think the same amount of money spent on the other side of Claiborne would buy a lot more places. If they really want to buy a community, and not just houses, they should be spending the money somewhere over there."

Lionel couldn't find a way to attack that tactful response.

"Did you ever find out what happened to Ralph after the storm?" Esther changed the subject on me. Ralph is my father's name.

"I found someone that said he died pulling folks out of

the East right after the storm. I don't think we'll ever find his body." This was my practiced response to the question. What I actually discovered was that he was shot by a private security contractor who later joined the FBI. The combination of me exposing the agent's crime, and his death shortly thereafter in a suspicious car accident, had me made an a problem for FBI Special Agent in Charge Michael Conroy. I was sure that Chief Avery's current problems were related to all of this. "I remember he always said the Batistes were his favorite 'Angry Black Women'. Supposedly, you two could raise a ruckus when you felt you needed to be heard."

"True dat!" Lionel finally found something to agree with me about.

"I guess I should be glad that I'm not the one making you mad about trying to buy your house." I tried to joke.

"Lionel and me be mad already," Esther said. She waved for me to follow her around the corner to the living room.

The wall usually reserved for family pictures had been transformed into what looked like a situation room from my military days. White boards dotted with post-it notes and handwritten comments covered the wall. A piece of plywood set atop a pair of two-drawer file cabinets served as a desk. A computer, monitor, and printer competed for space with stacks of file folders. I looked over the materials without touching anything.

"What's all of this for?" I finally had to ask. All of the materials were about the immediate aftermath of Hurricane Katrina. There were newspaper clippings, official reports, Freedom of Information documents, and doznes of photos clipped from magazines and newspapers.

"Lionel's writing a book about the Convention Center. There's lots of books out there about white people during Katrina, but nobody wants to hear about the time Black folk spent in that place. It's time somebody stepped up to the plate and told the story. Nobody wants to know what they done to us then, and what they are still trying to do to us."

"What are they still trying to do?" I only meant to show I was listening.

"They want to get rid of everyone that ever lived here or

over in the Treme," Lionel was the one giving voice to this familiar story line.

"What makes you think anyone is still trying to kick you out?"

"They been buying up houses along the levee all the way back to the Quarters. They fix the houses up and sell them for a bunch more money than they paid for 'em. Folks can't even afford to rent a home down here no more."

"Who is this 'they' you keep talking about? Can you give me a name? Is it companies like this CSA Holdings or do you mean somebody specific, maybe somebody local?"

I figured one or the other of the pair had at least one name to spit on the ground.

"How about Alex Boudreaux?" Lionel was still doing the speaking. I was vaguely aware of the guy, and that he had been flipping houses by the score since the storm. I'd seen his name on the bistro's reservations list. My sister graduated a couple of years after him at Tulane law school. She thought him to be unusually greedy and shallow.

"You know the Government and City Council wanted to keep us from moving back here after the storm. People still be trying to keep us from moving back. Now the city started in to bulldozing people's houses if they ain't moved back yet." Esther was beginning to show her legendary anger.

"I do remember that being an issue." Most of the mayoral candidates in the election held just months after the storm advocated rebuilding the city on a far smaller footprint. The only candidate who wanted the whole city back was the incumbent mayor, and he was always going to be remembered for his 'Chocolate City' comments. Most of the current candidates for the office were dancing around the issue while promising to cut through FEMA's red tape and make them rebuild the city as promised.

"I think offering to buy our house is part of a bigger plan to get rid of everyone down here once and for all," Esther said in a calmer voice.

"I'll look into it, but I gotta tell you what I wanted to tell your sister. Buying houses is not against the law.

Paying too much for them definitely isn't."

"Maybe not," Esther said and nudged me towards the door. "But what ought to be illegal ain't always a crime, neither.

Chapter 3

The rain continued overnight, so I was still driving the bistro's pickup truck the next morning. There were now entire blocks where the water was over the first steps of the houses and I had to slow down for these residential no-wake zones. If someone really wants to make a fortune, they should come up with a GPS program that routes you around urban street flooding.

My sister is the best civil attorney I know and I was going to need her legal opinion on the contents of CSA Holdings' packet to determine what I needed to do next. Tulip's office is on the lake side of a long block of commercial buildings ending at Jackson Avenue. This stretch of Magazine Street has appeared in nearly as many movies as the late John Wayne. It remains little changed, architecturally, from its heyday in the 1930s. Sidewalk-wide overhangs with low iron railings serve as expansive balconies for the second-floor apartments above the row of small shops and cafes on the river side of the street. I stopped by a quick service joint across the street from my sister's office called Juan's Flying Burrito. I ordered a pair of overstuffed burritos and then waded across the street, which was curb-deep in filthy water.

"Just the man I didn't want to see. I guess it's still raining?" Tulip laughed as I squished my way into her inner office. I took off my waterlogged Merrell work boots and rain saturated socks before I sat down in a chair facing her desk. She pounced on the Veggie Punk burrito I handed her. My own burrito was stuffed with jerk-seasoned chicken. I let her take a couple of bites of food before I passed the envelope from the Batistes across her glass-topped desk. She eyed it warily.

"Take a look at this. Someone is trying to buy up the houses Brad Pitt built over in the Ninth Ward." I said by way of explaining my visit.

"You do realize there are more people involved in doing that than just Brad Pitt." She set her burrito aside and reached for the packet.

"Yeah, but I don't know any of their names."

Tulip ignored me as she flipped through the pages of legalese. She came to an abrupt stop and looked up. Her expression was a mixture of disdain and anger that I found uncomfortable to look at. I was just glad I was only the messenger.

"Did you see that the offer is only good until Christmas Eve? Could you have given me any less time to look into this?"

"I wasn't brought in on it until yesterday morning. It doesn't really matter anyway because I doubt any homeowner is taking the offer."

"Does anyone even know why the holding company wants to buy these houses?"

"According to their little packet there they want to build a better world or something. What caught your eye?"

"Well for one thing they are offering a lot of money to the people living in them, but they'd be paying considerably less than what it cost to build any of those houses."

"What?" I looked up from my lunch. I couldn't quite wrap my head around the idea that the house I had seen cost more than two hundred grand to build. It had three bedrooms and two bathrooms and the place covered less than two thousand square feet, even if you added in the front deck.

"They have famous architects designing the houses. Frank Gehry designed one, and his normal fee is higher than the price of the house they built. They are using the latest green building materials and techniques. Companies are donating their stuff just to be able to say they are part of what the Foundation is doing. What are they like inside?"

"Very modern. You would probably like one."

"What do you mean by that?" I hadn't meant to rattle the chip she wears on her shoulder.

"I was struck by the irony that people who had never known any place but New Orleans until the storm were evacuated to places that bore no resemblance to where they were from, were kept from returning to New Orleans for over a year, and then given a home that couldn't look any less like what they used to live in if you tried. I don't see a bit of New Orleans anywhere on that street. They look like houses on one of the canals over in Pass Christian. I'd move if I were them, just to get into someplace that feels more like home."

"It would cost you or me almost twice the price they are offering to build one of these places." Tulip was giving me information, not arguing with me.

"I assume the holding company is aware of that fact."

"Anyone with a magazine subscription is aware of all this. Those houses have been in just about every article about the city since the storm. The fact private money is doing what government money has refused to do is big news to some people."

"I've been busy," I grumbled. My nightstand is usually stacked with back issues of The Economist and Foreign Affairs Magazine. I'm used to dealing in theory rather than actual events. "So, what you're saying is that the guys at CSA are trying to get a bargain by offering what only seems like too much money."

"Well, they are offering more than any of those houses will ever sell for. Just because the Foundation spent so much money doesn't make the house worth a bundle. They are still only worth what they appraise for and what people in that neighborhood can afford."

"Now I am lost. Are they stealing the houses or what?"

"Not really," Tulip decided. "But, they will displace the people living in them and that will just about clear out the neighborhood all over again."

"Then this is a bad thing." I was rapidly losing track.

"It is in my opinion, and probably yours. This is not illegal, though."

"A wise woman has pointed out to me that something being legal doesn't mean it shouldn't be criminal."

My sister broke into a huge grin and began to laugh.

"That's Esther Batiste's battle cry. She has been using it for years. I don't know how many times she's been heaved out of the City Council for making a big scene or held in contempt of court. She even had a show on community access cable for a while before the storm. Stay on her good side."

"That's her envelope you're holding."

"I hate you, big brother," Tulip began sliding everything back in the envelope, but she didn't shove it across her desk. "Do you know the only difference between a case and a cause?"

"The letter U?"

"No. It's *you* personally." Tulip said, wagging her finger. Why can't someone offer to buy a house in a crappy neighborhood and not have you assume there must be some huge conspiracy behind it? I'll look into who owns CSA Holdings, but don't expect knowing that will tell you much more than you know now. Do I get to tag along on your date tonight?"

"Why would I want you to do that?"

"This is the Wednesday we get together to plan Mother's dinner." My sister and I alternate the monthly chore of having dinner with our mother while she gives a brutally opinionated critique of our lifestyles and career choices.

"I'll call Katie and cancel our dinner plans."

"You'll do no such thing. I'll join you two for supper and cut out before dessert. I'll even call Katie to let her know what's happening."

I shrugged and began pulling on my still soggy socks and shoes.

"I'd really like to think you have my best interests at heart," I sighed as I stood up to leave. "But I think it's safe to assume you're up to something."

"What a dreadful accusation." Her indignation was lost behind the sly grin she couldn't entirely suppress.

I had only been dating State's Attorney Katie Reilly for a few weeks and had yet to feel I had any control over the courtship. Katie's father joined NOPD in the same academy class as our father. Their career paths could not have been much different, but their friendship was always strong. The pair used to make an annual hunting trip to my father's hometown in the boot heel of Missouri. Katie's father retired there just after Hurricane Katrina. Katie also used to babysit my sister, despite the slim years between them in age. My father packed me off to military school before my hormones kicked in, so I had never given Katie any romantic consideration until I brought her a dog fighting case a couple of months earlier. The years we were apart favored her body more than they had mine. Mine had, in fact, been rebuilt on multiple occasions. My sister even selected my current face from a magazine when it needed rebuilt after my skull was caved in by the butt of an AK-47. Tulip also made sure Katie was waiting in the wings when my last romance collapsed, and the two of them had been driving this train ever since. I didn't mind in the least since the destination seemed to be worth the price of the ticket.

Chapter 4

I had plenty of time to kill before dinner. It seemed like a good opportunity to talk to Alex Boudreaux to see what he knew of CSA Holdings and their plan to buy up so many houses. I couldn't imagine two parties intent upon gentrifying the Ninth Ward not being aware of one another. I called his office and they let me know which project he was inspecting at the moment.

The Lower Ninth Ward, in the years before Katrina, was made up of single-family residences with five or six rooms laid out in what came to be known as a shotgun style. These long, narrow single-story homes are built on low brick pilings. There are variations to this style: There are camelbacks, in which someone adds a second story room instead of an entire second floor to an existing shotgun house. There are doubles, which are little more than two shotguns built side-by-side under one roof. The houses are built almost shoulder to shoulder, with nearly a dozen to a block in some places. Their builders set the homes apart visually with small touches of gingerbread trim, stained or leaded glass, and porches or three-step stoops. It's where the neighborhood watch idea started.

Most of these homes used to be painted in a range of bright colors to further set them apart, and contributed to comparisons of New Orleans to places in the Caribbean. Most of the homes still standing in the Lower Ninth Ward had not been painted since the storm. The watermarks of the long-since receded floodwaters served as a badge of honor for those who came back to rebuild their homes and lives. Every empty house reclaimed from the tall weeds and pea vines was a major victory for the community.

I found Alex Boudreaux working near the levee in the Holy Cross neighborhood, just blocks from the Batistes' home. The storm had added a new phrase to the local lexicon, "the sliver by the river." The sliver is a very narrow band of slightly higher ground that remained dry while the surrounding neighborhoods drowned. Alex wasn't the only real estate speculator exploiting this strip of houses, but he was far and away the most prolific house flipper in town.

Alex Boudreaux is the great-great-grandson of a Mississippi carpetbagger. His parents own a string of shopping malls and rental condos along the I-10 and US 90 corridors, and benefited very handsomely from the devastation of Hurricane Katrina because they were among the few who invested in flood insurance. The couple now controls most of the strip malls being built between Biloxi and Waveland. Alex struck out on his own upon graduation and made his own fortune in the gentrification business along the Redneck Riviera before capitalizing on opportunities in New Orleans after Hurricane Katrina.

He is a tall man in his late thirties with a carpenter's muscles. His sandy hair is cut short and his dark eyes make it hard to tell if he is faking it when he smiles. He may have left Mississippi, but he still speaks with a good-old-boy accent. The man was easy to pick out from his crew for other reasons as well. Alex hires a lot of felons on work release, so his work sites look very much like chain gangs. His crews wear denim uniforms to cover their tattoos and prison yard physiques from the neighbors. My partner and I have hired parolees in the past because they were usually very grateful for the chance and had an incentive to show up for work.

The Holy Cross neighborhood faces the towering Mississippi River levee and was never seen as a good candidate for house flipping until now. This had long been a place where families lived in their homes until the last member of the clan died; which was equally true about all of the Ninth Ward. The hurricane, though, created a trove of storm-damaged houses that could be bought for very little money.

"Quite the operation you have going here," I flashed my badge at Boudreaux and shouted over the sound of power equipment echoing under nylon rain shelters. Alex simply nodded and waved for me to follow him to a quieter place in the work site. It looked like his men were working on a row of houses simultaneously, and that every house was at the exact same point in its renovation. Whatever else I can say about the man, he has an efficient business model.

Today was tile day and the sound of so many wet saws was deafening. Alex had a third wheel-style camper trailer set up on the corner closest to the work site and we were able to find comparative quiet there. He could monitor the crews' progress through the camper's large windows. He pointed me towards the sofa and reached into the camper's icebox for cold drinks. I hesitated to sit down before I had a chance to look around. I saw floor plans for the new houses hanging on the wall and I studied them while my host busied himself with the drinks. The designs seemed to be based on the eradication of any sign of New Orleans.

"What can I do for you, Detective?" he asked once we were settled in. "Are any of my employees in trouble?"

"My visit has nothing to do with them. I'm looking into a company called CSA Holdings." I wanted to see his reaction to the name of the company. I was going to doubt his business acumen if he didn't bother to keep track of his competitors' offers and projects.

"Never heard of them," he lied and sat down across from me. He had taken a moment to answer. I might have believed he was racking his brain to try to remember if he had heard the name, but I didn't. His eyes briefly shifted from mine and that made me think he was already working on a better lie to use if I pressed him.

"I really thought you might have," I persisted. "You're both in the same business. They are based out of Mobile."

"What business is that?"

"Destroying neighborhoods. They're making offers on all of the new houses on the lake side of Claiborne."

"The ones Brad Pitt built?"

I nodded, but didn't say anything more. It was time for him to start showing me what he knew, and to let me know what he wanted to try to keep hidden.

"Why would they do that?" Boudreaux wondered. "There can't be any money in flipping those places. They wouldn't even make good rentals because nobody could afford the rent they'd have to charge."

"So, you really think that there's no money in flipping those houses?"

"I have a degree in this and I can assure you there is no money to be made in buying those houses where they sit." Boudreaux grabbed a notepad and pen before he came and sat on the sofa next to me. "Let me explain how to make money flipping houses in this part of town."

"Please do." I could tell him about my own undergraduate degree in economics later.

"I never pay more than thirty grand for one of these places. I pull everything I can out of the house that can be sold for architectural salvage. I usually recoup between three and five thousand dollars from doing that. The people moving into these places aren't really looking for genuine New Orleans houses anyway. They all expect level floors and square corners. We strip the house down to the studs and floor joists and then rewire and re-plumb. Then, we go back with central air and electric heat, new drywall, insulated windows, gourmet kitchens, and engineered wood flooring. I'll end up putting about seventy grand into each house, but we will have reconfigured them from shotgun layouts to a more open floor plan. We give every bedroom its own closet and bathroom. It's what people expect, even people buying old houses."

"So you put a hundred grand into every place you touch, minus whatever you get for the salvage. What do you sell them for?" I had already researched the answer to the question, now I wanted to hear his justification for doubling his investment. Nearby homes without this level of updating were listing for about eighty to a hundred grand. That was still a barely affordable mortgage for a family with two minimum wage incomes. The buyers Boudreaux targeted tended to be single and making a lot more money than that.

"Here's our secret." Boudreaux ripped the first page of numbers from his pad. It would be the second time in two days that I had my nose rubbed in the fact that everything that is just plain wrong is not necessarily illegal. "What determines the price you can sell a home for? The appraisal value and zoning. Banks won't lend any more money than the appraiser is willing to say a piece of property is worth. It doesn't matter how much money I put into any remodel, the appraisal is always based on the value of other homes in the neighborhood with similar numbers of bedrooms, bathrooms, and square footage."

"So how can you charge so much for a house?"

"That's where the zoning comes into play. Everything I remodel I have zoned as a commercial rental. I buy clusters of homes. That has been easier since the storm. The city and state own thousands of properties that were either abandoned or surrendered to the Road Home program. I renovate anything near viable parts of the neighborhoods. Then I rent them out. I always rent them on short term leases so I can raise my rents as the market allows, but I always set my rents to attract desirable tenants."

"Define desirable tenants."

"Young singles making about fifty-five to sixty-five thousand dollars a year. These are the people that can redefine a neighborhood's character. They can afford to support cafes, coffee shops, and retail shops that cater to their tastes and budgets. If I do my job right, the houses I am renting will spark other investors to develop nearby properties. It doesn't take much to create what appears to be a revitalization of these blighted areas. The value of my properties increases every time someone else upgrades their property. I rent my units until the market has turned around and then I sell my homes to people who plan to either go on renting them or to re-sell them in a few years for a profit. Selling my properties as commercial properties sets comps that increase the value of everyone else's homes as well. I can sell one of these houses today and it will nearly double in value in just a couple of years."

"But it's the same house. Nobody is doing anything else to improve them." This was merely my immediate observation. I wanted to object to everything about his business plan.

"The house is the same, but it will be a different neighborhood by the time they go to sell. I didn't come up with the system. I just learned how to work it. There are good things about this for everyone. Anyone else selling their home in the neighborhood can set a higher price than they would have otherwise. These higher property values are proven to attract new businesses to support the more affluent new homeowners. People already living here that choose to hold onto their homes get to enjoy those improvements, the same as their new neighbors."

"Until those new neighbors begin complaining about the condition of their poor neighbor's un-flipped house and the city starts pressing them for repairs they can't afford to make."

"Do you want to live next door to a trashy house, detective?"

"No. I also don't want to be the guy who squeezes a family that has lived in a neighborhood for generations out of their home."

"Every family moves on eventually. The families you're so concerned about will be able to sell their run down home for enough money to put a down payment on a really nice place somewhere else. It may be just down the street, but it may well be in another city."

"How much will you be asking for this house when you sell it?"

"Are you interested in investing?"

"Maybe. You seem to have been pretty successful so far."

"I'd make you a good deal on one. I'd let you have your pick of these places for one eighty. You can get two grand a month in rent out of it, and even more if you rent it by the week as a vacation place. You can re-sell it for two hundred and thirty grand a year from now."

"Who vacations in the Lower Ninth Ward?"

"Tourists have no idea where they are. They see a good rental deal and take it. The neighborhood benefits because those tourists will go home and say what a great time they had. Someone they talk to may be looking for a fresh start and they'll know to look here."

"Has that ever happened? Has anyone contacted you about buying one of your vacation condos after renting it for a week?"

"Not yet, but they have done so in the other markets where I've followed this plan. It takes a few years for the neighborhood to reshape itself."

"So you'll finance a home for me, priced at a hundred and eighty grand that I can sell for fifty grand more than I paid for it, after making another fifteen grand renting it for a year?"

"As many as you'd like. Now do you see why so many people want to invest with me?" Boudreaux grinned as he stood up. I didn't want any part of his offer, or in helping to destroy the fabric of the city. The city's tourist and hospitality industries need a supply of people willing to work for minimum wage, and they need to be able to afford to live here, too. Cheap housing has been part of the city's dirty secret social contract for decades.

"If that's too rich for you I also offer fractional deals. You can buy part of a house deal for just fifty grand. I put four or five people's money into one house and then they split the money when they sell it. Most of those investors just keep reinvesting and eventually can afford to buy a house or two of their own."

"It sounds faintly like a pyramid scheme." I meant this as more of a joke than he took it.

"Well, is there anything else?" Boudreaux was done trying to be polite and his attention was already on something at one of the distant job sites.

"No. Thank you for your time."

We parted ways with a hand shake, and he likely thought I would never bother him about CSA Holdings ever again. He would have been correct if I wasn't convinced he was lying about knowing more about the holding company than he shared, and had he not made me suspect that there was more than gentrification behind his remodeling plans. Some of what I needed to know was going to require another favor from my sister. The rest of what I wanted to know about Alex Boudreaux was going to require help from the Chief of Detectives. Chief Avery's plate was full and he wasn't going to appreciate my adding to it.

Chapter 5

Joaquin Guera, Strada Ammazarre's general manager is a stubby Cuban with a thin line of a mustache and disarming smile. He had reduced the wait staff on duty so they didn't outnumber the diners. He was standing in the bistro's open double-doors trying to coax the trickle of tourists passing by to come inside and enjoy dinner. The weeks between Thanksgiving and Christmas are a time we know the locals are too busy shopping to drive to the Quarter to give us their money. It was seven o'clock and Jason, the lone male bartender on our staff, was pouring drinks for me and a half dozen of our happy hour regulars when Tulip and Katie arrived for dinner. They had changed into jeans and light sweaters from their work clothes for a night on the town. I should have known better than to trust my sister to keep her word about leaving Katie and me alone before dessert was served. Katie's figure was accented, rather than hidden, by her choice in clothes. Her long brown hair was pulled into a simple pony tail, but she had touched up her makeup. I let myself believe Katie was making the effort on my behalf. I was trying to look casual in a pair of slacks and a button-down shirt, and dry socks.

"My sweet darlings," Joaquin crooned as he led them, arm in arm, to the Chef's Table in the kitchen. The table had no reservations for the entire week. Tulip and I normally have our meals here for privacy's sake. My scheme had been to use it to impress Katie, but Tulip's intrusion was cramping my style.

"I can take it from here," I told Joaquin and seated the ladies myself. Tony and I had only recently hired him and he was still learning how to deal with having two bosses. He is nearly my parents' age and was hired on the recommendation of our gay waiters. Joaquin Guerra left his career in Santiago's theatre world during the Mariel boatlift thirty years ago. He wanted to live in a place where he was free to live a more flamboyant life. Joaquin progressed from being a waiter struggling with his English to become a charismatic bi-lingual Maître d' who knew how to handle people. We hired him away from his previous position by offering only a little more money, but a lot more autonomy. Tony and I hate the day-to-day business of actually running our restaurant. I think we only got into the business because I like free meals and booze and Tony just wanted a place to cook.

Tony worked as a chef in some of the best kitchens in his Sicilian hometown and on the Italian mainland for many years. He had even been an embassy chef in Rome as part of his cover when he was blackmailed into working for Iraqi's intelligence service. He ran a café in Baghdad's Green Zone as part of a covert operation I was running out of the same building, until I was nearly killed and we both had to leave the country abruptly. Miss J was now schooling Tony about New Orleans locals and how to feed them properly.

Tonight's meal began with two dozen char-broiled oysters, slathered with garlic butter, and a bottle of Marquis de Perlade champagne. We stock this label for one of our favorite regulars, a retired catering manager named Ryan Kennedy. Ryan was one of the handful of regulars presently standing at the bar. He was the only one, however, trying to take our only male bartender home with him. This had been their nightly ritual for over two years, with slim hope of Ryan ever having any success now, or ever.

"Have you told Mother about your new case?" Tulip asked while Tony personally refilled her champagne glass. He handed me the bottle so I could top off Katie's glass, and my own.

"No. I'm going to have to before someone else does, though."

"Don't worry about it being me. I don't want her to even know you came by to see me about it." My sister said. "The more distance I can put between myself and what you and Bill are cooking up, the better."

Katie set her glass down and grinned at us.

"You make having dinner with your mother sound like eating with a rabid animal."

"It is." Tulip and I laughed when we gave the same answer.

"I love family dinners. We used to pack my grandparent's place on Sunday. We never ate like this, but nobody went home hungry." Katie's happy recollections were at odds with the childhood memories Tulip and I share.

Our family dinners were where Tulip learned about conflict resolution and I learned how to lower an opponent's defenses long enough to destroy them. Such was life with an old-money New Orleans socialite mother and an ambitious working-class cop father from the Midwest.

"How nice for you. Maybe you'd like to join me on Friday?" I challenged her.

"Sorry, Tulip and I are going to see Tab Benoit at the House of Blues. Maybe next time."

"Uh, huh." I turned from Katie to my sister. I caught her smirk before she could get rid of it. Her turn with Mother was just weeks away.

Tony returned with chilled plates bearing a terrine of alligator, mirliton, and crawfish dabbed with Remoulade sauce. Tony was using the bistro's seasonal slow period to experiment with items he might use on our spring menu.

"Did you learn anything helpful from Alex?" Tulip changed the topic with each course.

"I learned how to make a bucket load of money by rigging the real estate market."

"Oh, really?" Tulip was always interested in anything she might take to court.

"Your classmate is renting houses at high rents and then selling them to investors just to bump the appraisal values in a neighborhood. He's financing the sale of his overvalued houses so the appraiser sees the price of that sale when the same house gets appraised a year or so later. He said I could see about fifty grand in appreciation after just one year on a two hundred grand investment in one of his houses."

Katie held up her hand to interrupt the conversation. "You have that kind of money?"

"I don't make a big deal about it. You've seen what I drive for work." I own a pair of Cadillacs. I drive a CTS-V station wagon as my personal car. A dark red XLR convertible coupe is my day-to-day patrol car. It even has personalized plates that say COP CAR. This is also why my nick-name within NOPD is 'Cadillac.' It is not meant as a compliment.

"I find something else to like about you every day." She was making a joke about money she would be wise not to repeat around my mother. "So what is wrong with his system? How is that not legal?"

"Legal isn't necessarily ethical. All I know is he is tearing apart neighborhoods by raising the property values beyond what the people already living there can afford to maintain."

The terrine was barely appreciated before chopped salads topped with crabmeat, hearts of palm, and marinated artichoke arrived. Tony allowed us a few minutes to digest these lighter courses before he hit us with one of his favorite dishes. His next course was lamb shanks seared on a grill and then braised with fresh fennel. The meat sat on a bed of julienned carrots with minted butter and quartered red potatoes tossed with rosemary and Vidalia onion. Tony brought a plate for himself and joined us. He somehow managed to change clothes between courses and was now wearing jeans and a polo shirt. I bit my lip rather than ask Tulip if she invited the chef to join Katie and me on our date as well.

Tony served us a bottle of wine from his personal cellar. The robust 1989 Barolo Mascarello, too pricey for the bistro's wine list, proved to be a perfect match with the lamb. It was the pairing of my sister and Chef Tony that held my attention. I had put my foot down in the past about there ever being any romance between these two. Tulip was the one trying to strike the spark; Tony struggled hard to honor my prohibition. I was eventually going to lose this fight and we all knew it. I switched my attention from their furtive flirting to telling Katie my thoughts on the offers being made on the Brad Pitt houses.

"I have to believe that Alex has some knowledge of CSA Holdings. I would have let it drop if he'd admitted he ever heard of them and knew they were shopping for homes less than a mile from his latest project."

"Do you just assume everyone is lying to you?" Katie said it politely and didn't seem to be looking for a fight.

"I've learned that it saves a lot of time and disappointment."

"I thought I was the only one who does that." I liked the twinkle in her eye. "Do you think they're acting together?"

"No. That's the part that bothers me. Two different players suddenly turn up in a market nobody has cared about for years, then one says he has no idea about the other. Alex is too smart to be that guy."

"How do you know he's so smart?" Tulip asked before washing the last bite of her lamb down with a big gulp of wine.

"He went to Tulane, the same as you."

"Oh, right." This brought back her favorite smug smile. "And he did come to law school with a master's degree as I remember."

"He mentioned that. Alex is in a business with only a very small number of local players. Anyone coming in from out of town should catch their attention. CSA trying to buy the most high profile properties in the entire city should have set off some sort of alarm."

"Who else should have picked up on this besides Alex?" I was glad Katie was showing any interest in our rather boring discussion.

"The City Council and the Planning and Zoning Board have let people have their way down there since the storm. They could slow anyone down if they wanted to, but they're perfectly happy letting people like Alex rebuild the neighborhood with their own money instead of the city or state's. I would like to think the Councilwoman down there would take a local guy's side in any fight. The only people who genuinely support letting people back into the Lower Ninth Ward are the mayor, who's supposedly leaving town after the election, and residents who used to live there but can't afford to move home. They can't vote if they don't live here, so apparently nobody feels there's any reason to consider their opinion."

"You can really ruin a meal." Tulip frowned. "Why would anyone spend so much money to get rid of people they think don't even matter?"

"They must matter in a way I haven't figured out." I hate being in the dark about anything. I am prone to light my way with the fiery wreckage of suppositions and theories that didn't pan out.

Tony had a waiter clear our dishes and serve coffee before rolling a cart with the makings for bananas Foster alongside the table. The waiter sautéed ripe bananas in butter and cinnamon before deglazing the pan with dark rum. He set the bananas atop squares of vanilla bean ice cream Tony made earlier in the day and then poured the still warm sauce over both to finish destroying our dinner companions' holiday diets.

Chapter 6

I answered the phone and looked at the wind-up alarm clock on my night stand. I wondered what Katie was doing awake at six AM and why she was calling me. It takes me a while every day to remember that not everyone shares my internal clock. That hour of the morning is actually a pretty busy time of day for many other people. I am the one who patrols the streets of the French Quarter until three in the morning while they sleep safely in their beds. I usually go to sleep about five in the morning and get out of bed when these day-people are headed to lunch. I had taken last night off and crawled into bed, alone and more than a bit drunk, just after two in the morning. I assumed Katie had done the same after I put her in a cab on Frenchman Street.

"Did I wake you?"

"Just from a dream of you sleeping next to me."

"Stop. You're probably still trying to sleep off that meal from last night." I couldn't quite tell if she took my comment as an invitation. "I think I may have an angle for you to look into about your case."

"Okay."

"My ex-husband left a voice message on my phone last night. He's all excited about landing a big contract for personal protection on a real estate developer coming to town."

"Let me interrupt. Why is your ex-husband calling you with something like that?"

"It's a long story. Part of why we split up is that I didn't think his security company was ever going to amount to anything. I supported him the last three years we were married. He just wants to prove me wrong, so he calls me when he gets a big contract. He was doing something for Homeland Security a month or so ago. He was pretty smug about having to keep what he was doing a secret."

"Huh. Go on with what you were telling me." I was much wider awake now and sat up in my antique brass bed to finish the conversation. I was pretty sure I would need to get out of bed once she was finished telling me about the real estate developer.

"The developer is from Tampa, Florida. It turns out he has been quietly nudging a project through the planning offices downtown and is coming to town to make his formal presentation to the City Council."

"What sort of project?"

"I don't know, but I do know why he wants a bodyguard. The project is planned for the Lower Ninth Ward. Do you think there might be a connection?"

"Couldn't possibly be one," I chuckled. "Do you have a name?"

"Two Crows Taylor."

"No, really. What's the guy's name?"

"Write it down. Two Crows Taylor. He's part of some Indian tribe's real estate operation out of Florida. They have supposedly put up a bunch of housing along the Gulf Coast in the past few years and are working their way west. They seem to be following the beaches."

"The Ninth Ward doesn't have a beach."

"I realize that. Maybe they're going to build one. Anyway, that's all I got out of my ex. Thanks again for supper last night."

"You're more than welcome. Maybe we can do it alone some time."

"That would be very nice, Detective. Oh, one other thing."

"What's that?"

"You're going to want to tread lightly with this guy and Alex. They are putting money into projects nobody else will and the City Council won't take kindly to you running anyone off by accusing them of evicting poor people the Council doesn't give a hoot about."

"Is anything off the record with you, Prosecutor?"

"Sure," Katie assured me. "Everything I told you about my ex."

Chapter 7

I gave Tulip enough time to get to her office and start the first pot of coffee before I called her for help with Katie's tip about her ex-husband's client. The resources I had weren't going to tell me what I really wanted to know on such short notice.

"I need you to have your research geek look into a guy named Two Crows Taylor out of Tampa, Florida. He is some sort of developer and has something going in the Ninth Ward."

"Two Crows Taylor? Are you serious? Who has a name like that?" Tulip ignored my latest insult to the young man she used to scour the internet for articles and public documents she could weaponize against her opponents in court. I had to threaten bodily injury to make him stop trying to find anything about my post-Army intelligence work.

"Indians, I guess."

"What sort of project?"

"This is why I'm calling you. I figure you can work your charm on your contact at the Planning Commission. I'm afraid this Two Crows character plans to make a bigger splash in the neighborhood than Boudreaux has."

"Probably so. I'll call you with what I find. How did you find out?"

"Katie called me. She said her ex-husband just landed a job as the guy's bodyguard." I heard Tulip's brief snicker about this. "She is also upset that I questioned Alex Boudreaux without any probable cause. I think Katie's afraid that I'm going to get myself in trouble."

"I'm sure she is." My sister was openly laughing at me when she said this. "You're going to have to learn that your new girlfriend worries a lot more about things like probable cause than you do."

"She's not my new girlfriend, yet."

"And she isn't going to be if you keep telling her every boneheaded move you and Avery come up with."

I had no reason to doubt my sister's free advice. I also didn't want to start discussing my potential romances with her. She was aware I had figured out before last night that she and my business partner were getting cozy in ways she knew made me uncomfortable. She still had no idea why I tried to keep them separated. Tony knew my reasons, but he was never going to be the one to break our code of silence on our mutual history in Iraq. My telling Tulip those details was far more likely to create a wider distance between the two of us than I wanted between them.

Chapter 8

There was no mention of any real estate projects in the Ninth Ward on the agenda the City Council posted to the *Times-Picayune* newspaper's website on Tuesday. Then it inexplicably appeared on the revised agenda posted barely an hour after I called Tulip on Thursday morning. I had to believe that Tulip's inquiries about Two Crows appearance forced the Council to update its post.

The City Council's meetings have been noticeably more raucous and argumentative than the circus-like atmosphere which marked them before the storm. The Council prides itself on listening to all of its citizens. It also has a history of ignoring public opinion that runs contrary to the decisions already made in private. The Council avoids any appearance impropriety by sending things back to committees 'for review' any time a public hearing makes too much of a negative splash. Invariably, the committee in question would agree that the Council's private decision was in the community's best interest.

The Council has also perfected the science of basing

their agenda on what else is happening in town. The members know to bring up any controversial matters when the fewest people are likely to be paying attention. The session held the week after Thanksgiving is traditionally poorly attended. I should have realized that Esther and Lionel attend every meeting; Esther has a better attendance record at these meetings than most Council members. I should have also anticipated they would check the final Council agenda to check the original agenda for any revisions.

Tulip and I took seats beside the Batistes on one of the light oak benches closest to the Council's dais. The pair were dressed in their Sunday best, minus a hat for Esther. Lionel looked uncomfortable with his shirt buttoned and the clip-on tie dangling in his lap. Tulip was dressed in her usual business attire, which left me feeling very under-dressed in jeans and a polo shirt with the State Police logo.

The Council's business began with a bullet-points reading of the minutes from the last meeting and then made praising the Saints for their so-far undefeated season the first order of new business. This unexpected winning streak was significantly increasing the amount of tax dollars in the city's coffers from what fans were spending on food, booze, and souvenirs.

The Council's remaining business matters were pretty boring. They approved a dozen or so zoning changes, including commercializing four properties Alex Boudreaux owned in the Bywater neighborhood. I noticed the tone of deference the Council showed Boudreaux in comparison to that given other developers seeking even minor variances.

The Council also heard numerous complaints by new residents about street musicians playing their music too loud and of the number of patrons still smoking in their neighborhood bars. The lame-duck mayor was the one to remind them that the new smoking ban didn't cover bars or nightclubs. The gripes still received more attention than they would have before the storm, but the bands and bar owners being complained about were still not going to lose sleep over the likelihood of any immediate action. The Council members largely shared my hope that the unhappy newcomers lodging these complaints would decide to go back where they came from before the next meeting. There were other mundane matters as well. Nothing on the original agenda sparked any response from the Council observers.

That changed when the floor was opened for Council members to tout any new businesses in their districts. Delia Adams waited until the other Council members covered their topics before she spoke up.

"I wish to bring the Council a matter of great economic potential." The timing of her agenda item so late in the meeting was a calculated move; she'd waited until roughly a third of the crowd in the room at the start of the proceedings left the Council meeting. She would have been happier if no one but the members were present to hear what her guest came to say. "There are people here today with a major development proposal they have for my district which, as we all know, has not yet fully recovered from the storm. If the Council would please indulge a representative of Tribal Investments from Tampa, he would like to make a presentation ahead of the submission of their plans to the Planning Commission. I believe that once you hear what they have in mind you will understand why I am so excited. You'll also understand the scope of the work ahead of all of us to see this transformation take place."

The nearly empty gallery barely stirred when she began her introduction, but Esther and Lionel were just about the only Ninth Ward residents at the meeting. Most real estate developments, especially ones by companies from outside of New Orleans, are initially repelled like an attack upon a medieval castle's ramparts. The prevailing opinion is that only somebody with strong ties to the city, or at least to a local politician, could ever possibly have an idea worth considering. The problem with this thinking is that anyone from New Orleans with the money for a major development usually has a personal agenda that rarely benefits the city's poorest citizens.

Real estate development in Orleans Parish has always been a can of worms, but post-Katrina land development projects involved as much confusion as they did demolition and displacement. The National Trust for Historic Preservation filed suit just the day before to block construction of the new VA and LSU hospitals. The state pumped millions of FEMA block-grant dollars into rebuilding a very historic neighborhood sitting in the footprint of that project. Now the same powers that be were planning to use more of FEMA's money to demolish that very same neighborhood. The newly-elected governor was intent upon putting his name on the cornerstone of a hospital complex he openly admitted was larger than necessary rather than repair the landmark Charity Hospital which served the city for decades.

The Council President gave Councilwoman Adams' guest a warm welcome and thanked Two Crows Taylor for his interest in investing where others have avoided doing so. The politician phrased this in other terms, but even those who had no interest in the proceedings understood what he meant.

Based on its past record, there was every reason to believe the City Council was going to give this latest out-of-town developer about twenty minutes to make his best pitch before they sent the matter down to the Planning Commission's version of bureaucratic purgatory. No formal decision would likely be made for months to come, if ever. The deciding factor in what happened behind the Planning Commission's closed doors would be how many local partners wound up with a piece of the pie as either investors or as builders.

It was important to see the original idea because it would show the developer's attitude towards New Orleans and the neighborhood they were planning to change. Tulip opened a note pad to take notes, and to record which Council members raised any objections.

Two Crows Taylor was not a man who lived on any Indian reservation I knew about. He was over six feet six

41

in height and wore a tailored suit and expensive watch. His immaculately capped teeth were as white as chalk. They were set off even further by his dark skin, which favored an olive tone over red. His suit was cut to accentuate what looked to be nearly three hundred pounds of pure muscle. Elaborate tattoos peeked from beneath his crisp shirt collar and across the back of his left hand. He was not naturally bald, but his shaved head made it appear so. It increased the sense of menace he seemed to cultivate.

"Thank you for your kind introduction, Delia," he said and smiled at the Black councilwoman. Delia is a petite woman in her mid-forties. She keeps a trim figure without dieting or exercising, and she has a face that would scare the devil when she doesn't get her way. She has a reputation for trading her votes to any other council member who will back her projects in turn. "And let me thank the Council for indulging me on such short notice. We want to move ahead as soon as possible."

"Our pleasure, sir," the Mayor assured the Council's esteemed guest. Who would say no to such an obvious pile of money?

"My name is Two Crows Taylor. I proudly represent Tribal Investments. We are a real estate development company from Tampa, Florida, that is wholly owned by descendants of the Ouachita Indian tribe. The Ouachita harbored escaped slaves during the colonial and pre-Civil War years and we wish to continue the tradition of aiding our brothers of color by creating the means for more of them to return home."

I braced for some sort of reaction to this poor choice of words, but it slipped past the room without even a cough. I did see Esther's face tighten just a bit. Even Lionel glanced at her to see what her response would be. Two Crows had so little in common with the people he was claiming to be here to help that I had to pinch myself to be sure I wasn't the one dreaming. Tulip wrote an expletive and pressed her notebook into my hand to show me.

"Our architects and urban planners agree with the

majority of studies made post-Katrina regarding the resettling of the Lower Ninth Ward. Many of those studies suggested abandoning the community entirely and to focus the city's already stretched financial and manpower resources on neighborhoods showing the ability to make a full recovery. Most experts also concluded that multi-family housing would be the best solution to rebuilding this part of town. The problem with the Lower Ninth Ward is that it is a drain on the city's already strained budget. The neighborhood requires, and deserves to have, the protection of fire stations and police substations, as it had before Hurricane Katrina. Public schools and mass transportation are also necessary to rebuild the community. These services cost money, and they cost more than the city will ever receive from sales and property taxes generated by its reduced population. Advocates of rebuilding the Ninth Ward complain about feeling a diminished sense of community when they live in an area with a high percentage of rental properties. Their protests and sit-ins have driven away many post-Katrina efforts for viable redevelopment in the Lower Ninth Ward, because they will only support plans that bring back the single-family homes lost to the storm. However, the local, state, and federal programs meant to encourage people to rebuild the proud neighborhood have not produced results anyone can take much pride in. The primary catalysts for building have been private investment, such as Musicians' Village and the Make It Right Foundation. Even their efforts haven't created a secondary building boom."

"But you have the solution?" Councilwoman Adams prodded the developer. She knew how short the Council's attention span gets towards the end of its weekly session.

"Not just a solution. Tribal Investments has the financial resources and experience to see such a major development through to completion. We are prepared to work with any local housing advocates and existing organizations, as well as the city and state, to create large scale housing and retail development on land that has lain fallow since the storm. Besides slowly draining away your limited resources, the community remains financially nonviable for small businesses. Grocery stores and retail outlets cannot justify investing in serving such a small and stagnant housing market."

A young male assistant, with far clearer ethnic bone structure and coloring in his features, hastily positioned a large covered cart between the Council and Two Crows. The cloth covering was covered with silk-screened Native American designs. The assistant then returned to the bench he emerged from a moment earlier.

I noted that he was sitting with a half dozen other people in the rear of the chamber. I pegged the young man and his near-twin as go-fers, an attractive raven-haired woman as being Taylor's personal assistant, and the heavy-set older man with braided salt-and-pepper hair as either a major investor or Taylor's attorney. Their private security detail stood flanking the chamber's doorway. Alex Boudreaux was seated beside the group and was trying to engage the stoic woman in conversation. We made brief eye contact without acknowledging one another.

"Welcome to Jackson Towers," Taylor declared and deftly pulled the cloth away to reveal the large scale model of the project Councilwoman Adams was going to take credit for in her re-election campaign. The council chamber's cameraman panned to project a view of the massive model on the screen. The image momentarily hushed the crowd, then the murmuring began. The striking first impression was mostly in reaction to the scale of the project.

Twin multi-story residential towers were aligned with a slight offset. The offset would allow each tower to have unobstructed views of both the city skyline and Lake Ponchartrain. The architectural design of the rear tower served to block the lake-side tower's view of the blight on the other side of Claiborne Avenue. Both buildings were erected atop multiple floors of covered parking that would protect the structures from any future flooding.

The lower floors of each building were wider than the upper structure and formed solid bases for the towers. The residential portion of each tower looked to be at least twenty stories high, or higher. The city, much less the Lower Ninth Ward, had rarely seen construction of this type or scale in its history.

The upper floors shared a graceful bend, like a pair of parenthesis. The two structures were designed to be linked by a gigantic mall atop the parking structures. Anyone living here would have no reason to leave this sanctuary, or ever step into the Ninth Ward everyone else would still know. It was obviously going to be of no "help" for their Black brothers. It wouldn't even benefit the residents it didn't displace.

"That is amazing," one of the Councilmen said. The tone of project-envy in his voice was pitiful.

"This rear tower will have retail space and the forward tower will feature office space designed for small and start-up enterprises. We will be entering negotiations with regionally owned businesses, such as grocery and coffee-shop companies, to open outlets in the retail area. Priority will be given to minority owned businesses, and the mix of stores will reflect the needs of the community as a whole."

"Which companies have signed on to date?" the Mayor asked.

"We need to have something built before anyone is going to formally commit. I'm sure you can understand that." Taylor was pleasant in deflecting the question, but his face couldn't conceal a flash of anger in response to the interruption.

"This rear tower is intended as long-term rentals for a mixed income clientele. Your city has had considerable luck with this housing format in the rebuilding of the outdated housing HANO and FEMA replaced following Hurricane Katrina. These units will make good use of the lessons learned from those endeavors. The front tower will be developed with two and three bedroom condominiums that provide stunning views of Lake Ponchartrain. We also want to sign leases for a bank branch and a satellite medical clinic in this tower, if we can reach an agreement with one of the local hospitals. The green space between the buildings will allow room for a full schedule of performances by members of the nearby Musicians' Village and other local and regional performing acts. We may develop neighborhood festivals in the future."

I caught myself wondering what one of the condos would sell for. Their views were going to be spectacular and the level of convenience being built into the location, with grocery shopping and medical attention within walking distance, was tempting. This was going to be a game changer for the entire city, if it was ever built.

"This ambitious project certainly gives us something the city can take pride in having. We look forward to learning more about this project in the near future." Councilwoman Adams's polite interruption let her guest know it was time to wrap things up. I glanced at Tulip and saw she had nearly filled her notepad with her cryptic scribbling. She looked up at me and we both raised our eyebrows, but we said nothing aloud. Esther and Lionel were busy whispering back and forth.

"I suppose we should open the floor to questions." The Council President said this in a tone that sounded as though he hoped there weren't going to be any.

Esther wasted no time in approaching the lectern. I could see the City Council's collective defensive reaction to the determined look on her face. It was an angry look they had all come to recognize, but had no chance to warn their guest about. It was all but inevitable that Esther Batiste would object to this proposal, and Two Crows had managed to put Esther into her worst 'Angry Black Woman' mode.

"The Council recognizes Esther Batiste," the Council President sighed audibly into his microphone as Esther tapped at the microphone on the podium. It was his way of letting her know that she need not introduce herself, and that all present were aware of what she was likely to say. The Council's own security officers took a more alert stance out of habit. The change in their posture prompted the Indians' detail to pay closer attention as well.

"I find it disgraceful that this City Council sat quietly by while a plan was laid out that clearly violates every zoning law on the books. These buildings violate the height restrictions for the Lower Ninth Ward. Perhaps the Council has already told Mister Two Crows that they will approve whatever he wants?" Esther's sarcastic tone wasn't meant to hide her insinuation that the Council had endorsed the project before it was unveiled today.

"I believe you misunderstand the situation. There will be plenty of opportunities for spirited debate on what is best to do with the undeveloped acreage available in the Lower Ninth Ward." Two Crows seemed to be trying to charm Esther rather than to get into a debate with her. Delia Adams may have warned him about her before the meeting.

"That isn't undeveloped land," Esther wasn't going to be charmed and she wasn't going to wait on a different forum to argue her case against the Indians' plans for her neighborhood. She had the stage right now. "Those are blocks and blocks of family histories washed away by the walls the damned Army Corps of Engineers and Levee Board said would protect the people I grew up with. People I know still own that land and they tell me every day that they want to come home."

"Well, there will finally be a place they can again call home." Two Crows was wrong to add a smile to this. It was gasoline on an already roaring fire.

"You can't be talking about them condos because nobody I know is going to be able to afford no condo like you're talking about," Esther said with just a little more anger. Her rage was ratcheting its way upwards the longer she spoke, and the more she stared at the scale model of her worst nightmare. "Do you think it's alright to buy a man's land and then try to rent it back to him?"

"I think it may be the only way some of your former neighbors will ever be able to return home." Two Crows tried to turn the question back on Esther. He sounded as though he practiced for these confrontations. "I assure you that I am not the one who wants to buy your land. My project would not require any of the homes built by the Make It Right Foundation to be destroyed. Deslonde Street is going to lose its present view of the sunset, but you'll all have these shops and facilities at your doorstep."

Esther paused before launching another volley at Two Crows. She glanced back at Tulip and me, but I was the only other one who had caught what she heard. The Council President had recognized her only by name. Two Crows was unusually well informed about her. He knew the name of the street where she lived, and that someone else wanted to buy her home. I wondered what else the man knew about the Batistes.

Esther abruptly surrendered her place at the podium. My sister and Lionel both stood up to take her place. I was as surprised by this as anyone else in the Chamber. Tulip is a noted courtroom warrior, but in venues such as this she has more of a reputation as an observer. She would take her copious notes and then research her questions before pouncing on her opponents like some panther in high heels.

"We would prefer that you address the Council one at a time," the Council President admonished the pair. Tulip whispered something to Lionel and then handed him her notes. I could tell that the Council would have much preferred dealing with my sister than with Lionel armed with her notes, but she didn't have a dog in this fight.

"How much do you believe this project will cost to complete?" Lionel began fishing through Tulip's notes for the basic information the developer neglected to include in his flowery presentation. Two Crows used a disturbing number of qualifiers in describing what was going to happen once he was given permission to transform the Ninth Ward. Most developers like to brag about the business connections they have lined up and give a much better idea of how much money they were going to spend in a community. Two Crows was quiet on both of these subjects.

"I don't believe that is a proper question for this forum," Councilwoman Adams snarled into her microphone. "You should wait until Tribal Investments holds its public hearings to ask such direct questions."

"Well those won't matter much if the City Council has already decided what's going to happen, now will it? I'm sure Mister Two Crows knows how much money he's going to spend and should have no trouble telling us right now." Lionel was not waiting for anything, especially to make his own reservations about the project known.

"That's all right," Two Crows forced a smile and turned to address Lionel. I sensed he had not anticipated tangling with the Batistes quite so soon. "We are prepared to spend approximately sixty million dollars. Land is traditionally the largest initial expense. We are lucky that all of the land we will need is already available, and will require only minimal displacement of any current residents. This project ought not to face the hurdles your city's plan for a new hospital encountered. They built over a neighborhood which was well on its way to being restored. This community has remained largely vacant since the storm. Our hope is to be be what gives people the means and incentive to move back to the neighborhood."

Lionel was no more placated by Two Crows' silver tongue than Esther was. Neither of the Batistes saw the double towers as being any sort of neighborhood.

"That's a lot of money to spend in a community this City Council keeps saying is too small to justify providing with bus service at a buck a passenger." Lionel kept the focus on the economics and ignored Taylor's dissertation on the city's recovery efforts. He could tell smoke from fire. I could see the developer's body language and facial expression stiffen when he realized he was facing an opponent who didn't need a white attorney speaking for him to get his point across.

"Do you have a lower price tag in mind for revitalizing the Lower Ninth Ward? Your neighbors are the citizens who have carried this city on their shoulders for decades, for generations. They are the people who work for next to nothing to keep the hotel and tourist industries going. They are the men who put their backs into digging the foundations of every major office and bank building you see. Their wives struggle just to keep their families fed and clothed, and the city has always told their children not to expect anything better."

"I am glad you recognize the contribution of the neighborhood, but I can't believe you have come this far to spend money you don't expect to see returned many times over. You dress far too well for a philanthropist."

Two Crows called forth yet another smile and tried not to let the room see his frustration.

"Look at our track record on the Gulf Coast. We invest in struggling communities and their people. To date, our business model has proven to be no less lucrative for us than buying stocks and bonds has been for other types of investors. Hurricane Katrina was a tragedy, but one that provided a rare opportunity to approach problems in a different way than those that have failed in the past. There is no reason the Lower Ninth Ward has to remain the place the city warehouses its poorest people."

"True enough," Lionel shrugged and seemed prepared to concede the point. "But, how can we be sure you really have the financing necessary to complete this project?"

"I am sure we could still include you in our investor pool, if you are truly interested in helping the community." Two Crows knew he scored a direct hit on Lionel. He also managed to avoid a direct response to the question. "We can never be certain what a project of this size will cost until it's built. We will also be applying for any available local and state bond money and tax credits to defray what costs we possibly can."

Tulip finally smelled a little blood in the water.

"How much incentive financing do you have in mind?" she spoke up from her seat next to me.

"Approximately thirty million dollars initially, to carry us until we are able to secure our principal financing." The man said this as neutrally as he could. It was obvious from his response that he had not anticipated Tulip's ability to find his project's weak spots so fast.

"So, now you're saying you haven't actually lined up the financing, and you expect someone else to shoulder half your costs?" Tulip didn't need a microphone to be heard. The room had become very quiet.

"The Ouachita Indian Tribe operates casinos in northern Louisiana and eastern Oklahoma. Money is never going to be an issue for Tribal Investments," Two Crows snapped at Tulip before turning towards the Council members. "I assure you that if we come back to the Council with our hat in our hands it will be for no more than is absolutely necessary to succeed in getting such an important project off the ground."

Lionel surrendered the microphone and took his seat. Tulip was done with the verbal jousting. Now, she was going to go to work on learning everything there was to know about Two Crows and the thousands of other things the developer didn't want to discuss publicly. Tulip and Esther began conferring with one another over her notes. Two Crows and his entourage also took note of the two women they now knew to be their primary opposition. I think they had a pretty good idea of how difficult things would become if both of these women opposed their project. I also believed that the Batistes and Alex Boudreaux understood how little chance they stood of resisting the juggernaut these Indians were going to be if the Planning Commission blessed their project.

The handful of other people who stood up to speak were far less confrontational, and they all had much nicer things to say about the proposal. Everyone else in the room agreed that it was great somebody was finally doing something 'down there.' Some agreed because they genuinely wanted to see the community rebound. Many more thanked the out-of-town investor for wasting his money, and not their tax dollars, on the project. Those were the taxpayers who did not understand where the thirty million dollars for those bonds and tax credits was really going to come from.

It came as no surprise when Councilwoman Adams

made a motion to immediately endorse Two Crows' development proposal and to send Tribal Investment's plan to the Planning Commission with the Council's full support. The career bureaucrats in the zoning office understood what a unanimous, even though ceremonial, vote by the Council meant. There would be hundreds of hours of hearings, impact statements, permit reviews, and building inspections that could derail the project before completion, but none of these were going to be more than speedbumps beneath the wheels of a fast moving bus once the Planning Commission knew the Council wanted the project approved.

Then again, there was no rush on Tribal Investment's part. November is a notoriously bad time to pour concrete. Going through the polite motions of public hearings while they waited for better weather wasn't going to change the outcome the Council had obviously already made their collective mind up about. Nobody running for re-election wanted to go on record as saying the Lower Ninth Ward didn't deserve to be rebuilt. Today's vote would be enough to establish that the Council was now on its way to accomplish what none of the city's urban planners and FEMA's housing experts had been able to do; to repopulate the neighborhood. It looked like any support for rebuilding plans based on a close-knit neighborhood full of single-family homes was about to dry up. The Lower Ninth Ward would be getting more multi-family construction than anyone ever imagined, or previously feared.

Lionel on the shoulder to let him know Tulip and I were leaving the meeting. We witnessed the fireworks show and didn't want to stay for the closing display of ass kissing by the Council.

He whispered to Esther and they followed us into the high-ceilinged hallway outside of the Council Chamber. We stood together directly across the hall from the doors to watch Two Crows and his entourage leave. I wanted to know if anyone else approached them as they departed.

"Those people scare me," Esther admitted. "I wonder

what else that man knows about me and my family."

"He seemed to know an awful lot about people he had never met," I agreed. "Is that why you gave up the microphone?"

Esther just nodded. She seemed more than a little ashamed for not having stood up to the towering Indian, but I could see why he gave her serious pause. I have made more than a few tactical retreats in my time.

"Do you really think this will ever get built?" I turned to my sister as though she had some special insight. Real estate is much more within her professional area of expertise than mine.

"It would certainly be something if they did. You can't tell me they haven't thought about how they are going to finance this. I'm not surprised, though, that the Council gave the project a yes vote. It's an election year and they're celebrating as though the thing is already built and they can divide chunks of the credit for having done something in the no-man's land they helped create."

The doors to the Chamber opened and Taylor's group followed the two muscular white men walking ahead of them. The security detail scanned the path ahead for any threats and focused on my sister and me. These guys were ex-military, not rent-a-cops.

"Now we know what sort of real estate developer hires professional bodyguards." Tulip pointed to the men flanking Two Crows' group.

"That's what those guys are?" Esther asked as she watched the phalanx head silently towards the elevators. A couple of local reporters tried to slow them for a comment but were stiff-armed rather than merely rebuffed. The carefully worded presentation was over, and Taylor wasn't going to say a word beyond his scripted performance.

"Katie said her ex-husband was providing security for Taylor."

"Neither of those two are Ray. Even so, stay the hell away. And look who's traveling with them." Tulip needn't have bothered to warn me after I sized up the security detail.

Alex Boudreaux followed the big Indian as far as the elevator doors. Boudreaux was animated in whatever he was saying to Taylor, but Taylor was not paying any attention. A set of elevator doors opened and the security team made sure the Indians were the only ones on that elevator. Boudreaux was left standing to wait for the next elevator in mid-sentence. His acute embarrassment was obvious in the way he looked to see if anyone noticed his being shut out by the developer.

"Well, at least those two aren't working together." I noted with a sigh of relief.

"It doesn't matter. Ain't neither one of them going to help anyone but themselves." She and Lionel discussed their opinions in private as they headed for the elevator.

Chapter 9

I made it through the rest of the day without any more unexpected developments in the Batistes' situation. Tulip and I spent the afternoon trying to find any public records or news reports that linked the three developers' ideas on transforming the Batistes' neighborhood together, in any combination. Anyone other than the two of us might have found the time spent to be boring and fruitless. However, my sister is a corporate watchdog and citizens' advocate who does this sort of research for a living. I was trained by intelligence professionals to have the patience to piece small bits of information together like a jigsaw puzzle to form larger pictures. I once used a single captured cellphone to dismantle a network of insurgents planning to kill American troops in southern Iraq.

Spotting Boudreaux and the Indians together at the elevator gave me body language and facial expressions to work with. The woman and Two Crows were obviously ignoring whatever Boudreaux was pestering them about. It struck me that there was something very familiar in the way they stood beside one another. Strangers, even rude ones, will stand apart and pause long enough to assess each other's potential future value before dismissing one another. The barest of acquaintances will stand toe-to-toe because they know their use to one another and can skip straight to ignoring the other party in public. Tribal Investments obviously researched any potential adversaries. It was possible they decided Boudreaux posed no threat and had nothing to offer. I still felt that these carpetbaggers already knew one another.

None of the three developers agreed upon the best way to gentrify the neighborhood. Boudreaux preferred flipping existing single family residences; he just wanted to sell them at a higher price. Tribal Investments was firmly behind the idea of mass housing on a scale no one ever imagined. It was unclear what CSA intended to do with the houses they were trying to buy. Tearing them down seemed like a waste, but they were paying too much to rent or flip them at a profit.

Boudreaux was destroying the Batiste's neighborhood by preventing those who had evacuated from being able to afford to move home. Tribal's plan was going to change the character of that entire end of town. CSA Holdings' plans threatened to destroy the community by buying it out from under the residents. Of the three, I found CSA convincing life-long residents to abandon their neighborhood to be the cruelest form of gentrification.

Tulip was initially unable to link either Boudreaux or Tribal Investments to CSA Holdings. Tribal Investments had never partnered with other investors in their real estate developments to date. Tulip did manage to pull some useful information out of the incorporation papers for Boudreaux's operation and for Tribal Investments. CSA Holdings proved to be a shell corporation with a letter drop address, as I suspected from the beginning.

Boudreaux owned his entire company. His parents held no financial or managerial interest in it. Tulip discovered he borrowed his seed money from a credit union in Biloxi. I was a bit surprised that no banks in New Orleans wanted to finance the city's rebuilding. Tulip hypothesized that it may have had something to do with the number of banks that changed hands about the time Boudreaux arrived in New Orleans. A lot of venerable local banks wound up for sale when the real estate market took double hits from their investments in bad real estate loans and from good loans made on the now devastated local housing stock after Katrina. People who couldn't get enough money from their insurance companies to repair their home often chose to leave town and abandon the mortgages these banks held.

Tribal Investments was sitting on an impressive amount of developed and vacant real estate in Florida and Mississippi and kept substantial cash reserves. It was nothing close to what they would need to spend on the Jackson Towers project, but Tribal's cash flow was in the millions each quarter, so they could easily service a substantial debt if they had to borrow money to build their towers. Two Crows Taylor was the President of the company, which had only two other listed board members. There was someone named Ronald Badger Watson and a woman named Bristol Taylor. I looked both names up on the internet and was not entirely surprised to find that Ronald Badger Watson was the older gentleman we had seen at the Council meeting, and that the black haired beauty was Bristol Taylor. It took a little additional research to confirm that Bristol was married to Two Crows. Tulip wondered why a corporation the size of Tribal Investments would have so few officers. Publicly traded companies far smaller than Tribal Investments usually had many more levels of management listed in their required annual reports. Tulip downloaded Tribal Investments' financial disclosure statements and the latest annual report from Florida's Secretary of State's website. She said it would give her something to read while I entertained our mother.

Chapter 10

The trio behind Tribal Investments made an appearance at Strada Ammazarre while I was waiting for my mother to arrive. I was standing in my usual happy-hour place, at the street end of the bar. I intercepted them as they came through the open doorway. Bristol led the way, giving me the impression that she was the driving force in most things these three did together. I would have been disappointed in their research if they failed to connect Tulip to me, and me to the bistro. I made a special point to introduce them to Chief Avery and to Chef Tony. I also bought their first round of drinks. The chef distracted them while I told the bartender to set the Indians' drink glasses aside for me when they came back to him. I would have to find a good excuse for Chief Avery to run their fingerprints through NCIC's database. Looking for a criminal record for any of these three in the nation-wide system was going to draw attention, and my boss was under enough scrutiny from the FBI. I doubted he would want to defend fingerprinting any investors willing to rebuild the city's worst neighborhood without cause.

My mother was right on time for dinner, as usual. I

wasn't surprised to see that she brought Roger Kline. He is the animal behaviorist who came into our lives thanks to the dog mauling case I made such a mess of a couple of months earlier. My sister made temporary arrangements for Roger and the canine suspect to live in the boathouse at our parent's house near Lake Catherine while he and I tested theories about what triggered the dog to attack its owner. The investigation lasted long enough that a friendship developed between Roger and our mother. Supposedly, Roger still lived in the boathouse, but their friendship appeared to have become more intimate. I give my seventy-year old mother's love life far less attention than she does that of her children.

I was taken aback by the presence of the second man in her party. Gavin Hendricks was my late father's literary agent. Gavin's dark hair and beard had grown even more silvery than the last time I saw him. He was now trying to hide his receding hairline by combing his hair forward. His sport coat and glasses made him look like an English teacher at a liberal arts college.

"What's Gavin doing in town?" I whispered to my mother.

"He brought me some news about your father's publisher. They plan to drop his books from their catalog next year."

"I can understand that. I don't agree with it, but sooner or later dad's stories were going to be forgotten by people who buy books."

"Gavin has some ideas, though." The tone of her voice left me wondering how much my mother cared that my father's literary presence was about to vanish, as he had.

Joaquin dutifully fussed over her outfit as he led us to our table. It was just enough to make her feel special. That man is good at his job.

"Your mother probably just told you about your father's publisher. I will try to find the list another home, but it's hard when an author has stopped writing new books." Hendricks seemed considerably more upset than my mother, and not just because of any lost commission. I knew he and my father were close friends.

"I think we all knew the day would come." There was no surprise in this news. It was just business.

"I was hoping you would pick up where he left off, Cooter." He seemed to be trying to make this become my idea. Now I understood the real reason my mother invited him to join us.

"There's not much I can write about," I demurred. "My work before I got here is classified and my new boss counts on my discretion in what he asks me to handle."

"Isn't your Chief on the hot seat right now? I read in this morning's paper that that the FBI has opened an investigation into the police-involved shootings during Katrina. They made it sound like NOPD's detectives deliberately covered up the shootings."

"Is that what you bothered Felix about? Do you really want to be in my brother's debt just to help Bill Avery? You have no idea the sort of things Felix will expect you to do for him." My mother interrupted Gavin to make her point, but she didn't seem to care about the larger picture. She was being a little too quick to abandon someone I thought to be a close family friend.

"I'll take my chances." I did not want her to know just how worried I was about repaying my uncle's favor, so I returned our attention to Gavin's question. "Avery is going to get roughed up a bit, but I think Felix can at least save his job. Do we want to order from the menus or shall we let Tony surprise us?"

I saw no reason to provide Gavin with any additional information. He was quick to realize that further discussion about my boss was going to bring about open warfare with my mother, but he still wanted answers.

"Hopefully the FBI will question some other things as well. The state's official death toll claimed only two people died from gunshot wounds, but these police shootings alone would account for more than that. In fact, the official death toll claims more people died from leaking gas lines than gunshots. Does that even sound possible?" Gavin persisted.

I only answered Gavin's initial question about the FBI and Chief Avery to divert the table conversation from my debt to Uncle Felix. I wasn't about to get into a conversation with Gavin about the shootings. I had plenty to say, but not to someone so far removed from both law enforcement and New Orleans. I was suddenly right back where I started, so I turned my attention to my mother's other companion in hopes of being able to change topics one more time.

"So, Roger, how's Roux?" Roux was the name Roger and my mother came up with for the vindicated pit-bull. The dog viciously killed a man, but I faked having it put down once Roger and I determined it was trained to attack at the sound of a dog whistle. Besides that, the victim was a very bad man that few people missed.

Roger saw my dilemma with Gavin and my mother and tried his best to help me change the conversation.

"Everything is just fine. I think your mother might even want to get a companion dog for Roux."

"Imagine that." Tulip and I were denied any house pets as kids. It also meant Roger was sticking around.

"Maybe something small," my mother said with an uncharacteristic blush.

I told my guests to set their menus aside and I instructed Gina, my mother's favorite waitress, to have Tony send us four courses of his choosing. Gina wrote down everyone's cocktail order and headed to the kitchen. Tony knows my mother's finicky tastes and we have three different menus he can serve and feel safe asking if she enjoyed her meal. Free meal or not, she is not one to withhold the slightest criticism.

"Alright, I get it," Hendricks finally sighed. "No shop talk."

"I'll tell you what, though. I think I know someone with a story you might be interested in. Meet me here about nine tomorrow morning."

The police-involved shootings were going to receive more than their share of attention in the flurry of coverage about Hurricane Katrina's five-year anniversary. I hoped Hendricks' publishing connections would be interested in Lionel Batistes' first-hand account about the Convention Center debacle. Far more people died in the Dome and Convention Center from systemic neglect than the number of police-involved deaths the FBI was poking its nose into, but those deaths apparently didn't sell as many newspapers. I was sure I knew the identity of the person who intentionally leaked the story of the FBI's investigation to the media. Unfortunately, Chief Avery had ordered me to avoid the FBI's local Special Agent in Charge after I cleared Roux in the mauling. SAC Conroy was still convinced I'd murdered an FBI agent linked to the case, so it made sense to do as Avery instructed.

Gina returned with our drinks. I decided the best way to defuse the tension between Hendricks and myself was to have him do all the talking.

"How long did you know my father?"

"I met your dad when he first made detective. I was writing for *Newsweek* at the time and did a few ride-alongs with him. He was a great storyteller even then. He had some crazy story about everyone we met or that he arrested. I had no problem peddling his books when he finally started writing about crime in New Orleans."

"He could tell a story," I agreed. My father had a story for every occasion and for every audience. He would tell stories about himself that nobody else would have dared share. The irony is that he raised a son who can only repeat those same stories, because he can't tell any about himself.

"Your mother says you recently discovered what happened to your father after the storm."

"That's right, but I thought it was something we agreed not to discuss outside of the family." I turned a stern face towards my mother.

"No, no. She just said you told her he died." Hendricks was very quick to defend her. "So, I guess you haven't been back to Missouri."

"What does that have to do with anything?"

"I was just wondering if you had let your relatives there know what happened," Hendricks hastily explained, and picked up his Sazerac.

"I don't even know who to call to be honest. A friend of his retired there, and I told him. I asked him to spread the word." I was referring to Katie's father. We had yet to inform him that we were dating. I had not done so, anyway. I'm sure he would have called me if Katie told him and he had any objections.

Gina brought a bottle of champagne with our appetizers. We pounced on the two pasta bowls filled with a combination of steamed mussels, clams, and shrimp bathed in a sauce of white wine, butter, diced tomatoes and a lot of garlic and basil. There were also two plates of fried calamari with Tony's house-made marinara sauce. This course was followed by the crab salad I had already enjoyed with Tulip and Katie.

"What does Bill have you working on?" My mother was obviously trying to keep the conversation going because she never asks me this question. She hated hearing police stories after my parents formally separated and my father left her alone in the Lakefront house.

"There is suddenly a lot of real estate activity in the Lower Ninth Ward. A holding company from Mobile wants to buy the houses the Make It Right people built. A group out of Florida is planning to build condos on the lake side of Claiborne, and gentrification has finally reached the Holy Cross neighborhood."

"How is any of that a crime?" My mother's dismissive reaction struck me as being reflexive. She is always quick to defend business interests over the interests of the city's actual residents. She was also signaling me that the topic lacked sufficient entertainment value as dinner conversation.

"It doesn't fit my definition of a crime, either. It's just curious that so many separate entities are suddenly interested in that part of town. Tulip and I are trying to find some sort of connection between them."

"Would a connection even matter?" Hendricks's

question surprised me. He had sounded so righteous about how people were treated after the storm that his acceptance of their current treatment disappointed me.

"Not really." I conceded. "I'm mostly interested to see if the guy flipping houses just a few blocks away from there is involved with either or both of the others. I think he's lying about not having any idea about what's going on. It doesn't matter in the end, but it has me wondering why there's so much interest."

"What do the locals think about it?" Hendricks wondered.

"The people I want you to meet tomorrow live there and they are leading the resistance. They're convinced this is another attempt to clear them out. Their neighbors are also pretty touchy about anyone trying to kick them out of the houses they rebuilt after Katrina."

"The city didn't make it very easy," Roger finally joined the conversation, but my mother wasn't happy that his comment didn't match her own opinion.

"They never should have let anyone move into those low lying areas. They will all just flood again." She was obviously disappointed that the city had not asked her advice.

"Every neighborhood could flood again," I pointed out for the umpteenth time in our ongoing debate on the matter. "This persistent 'smaller footprint' argument is really just a way of saying the city should not invite anyone making less than forty grand a year to move back. New Orleans cannot sustain its tourist or food service industries if it pays much more than minimum wage. We need people willing to take low paying jobs to keep those things going, but they deserve a place they can afford to live for doing so. It was an unfair system that seemed to work just fine before the storm."

"If you say so." This is her code phrase to tell me it is time to change the subject because she won't change her mind.

Gina timed her return perfectly and used the momentary silence at the table to deliver plates of my mother's favorite pasta dish. Tony sucked up to my mother when he created the first menus and named it Polpetta Camille after her. The plates were swirled with creamy fettuccine alfredo and topped with a pair of tender silver dollar-sized Italian meatballs that were nestled in a pool of marinara. The color contrast is beautiful but it's mixing the two sauces together that makes the dish so divine.

We made it through the rest of the meal with no further conflict. Gina knew exactly when to tell me I was needed in the kitchen so I could make a polite escape from the table. The timing prevented my mother from starting any queries about my dating Katie Reilly. I hoped to have better answers by the time she would get another chance to bring it up in two months' time.

I reconfirmed the next day's meeting with Hendricks and went to the bar to get the glasses Jason set aside for me. He bagged and labeled each one as well. I then walked briskly towards the kitchen, as though on a mission, but barely stepped through the double doors before I stopped. I instructed Joaquin to tip Gina generously for being our referee. I then turned and pushed the button on the elevator behind me. The elevator serves as a service elevator to the second floor dining rooms, but also accesses the twin loft-style apartments on the third floor where the chef and I live. I was headed to bed and my dinner guests could see themselves out the door.

Chapter 11

Gavin arrived early the next morning. I offered him breakfast but he had already filled himself with pastries and coffee from room service at Le Pavillon Hotel. It's his favorite hotel because they serve their guests free cocoa and peanut butter and jelly sandwiches in the lobby at bedtime.

The week-long wet weather finally gave way to disturbingly cold weather overnight. WWL-TV's morning weather report included footage of snowflakes falling on the Northshore. This unfortunate change in the weather meant Strada Ammazarre's staff would feed fewer tourists over the weekend. That meant Tony and I were going to have find a way to replace the money our servers could ill afford to lose so close to Christmas.

I led Gavin around the block to the garage on Decatur Street where Tony and I store our vehicles. I was tempted to drive the CTS-V wagon I had recently purchased, but decided against exposing the expensive car to the locals' proven inability to drive on even one flake of snow. I unlocked the XLR coupe and opened the passenger door for Gavin. He did not initially move to sit down. The

Cadillac XLR hard-top convertible looks too flashy to be a police car, but its COP CAR license plates give miscreants fair warning that it is one.

"This is your patrol car?" Gavin asked as he ran a hand down one long dark red fender.

"I don't transport a lot of prisoners."

"Get in many high speed chases?"

I shook my head. "Not enough, but I usually get the girl."

I consciously strive for an image as some playboy rich guy playing cops and robbers among my peers. My position within the department and my relationship with their Chief was always going to create resentment. My decision to stand apart annoys most NOPD officers to the point that they pretend I don't even exist. Being invisible to them makes it easier to tackle the assignments their boss hands me. It is not the image I need with the public. I tell any citizen who asks that I bought the coupe at the auction of a drug dealer's belongings. Most of them see that as good karma. Criminals I encounter take this explanation as a cautionary tale that the cops can take away anything they buy with their own ill-gotten gains.

I pulled out of the garage and turned right onto Esplanade from Chartres, and then left on Elysian Fields. I took a right at the traffic light onto St. Claude. Hendricks visited New Orleans often enough to know the lunacy of cardinal directions in a city built on a curve. I was headed almost due east, while driving parallel to the south-bound Mississippi River.

"So who are we headed to meet?" Hendricks had not bothered to clarify this until we were already on our way.

"Our sous chef stays by the Lower Ninth Ward with her nephew and sister. Lionel is writing a book about the Convention Center after the storm. They were there and have the entire experience pretty well documented."

"That was a mess. I remember the news reports at the time. Those were inhuman conditions. How can we get food and water half way around the globe after a tsunami but not to New Orleans?"

"Yet nobody has written an account of it in the last five years. We have heard about everyone else's less traumatic experiences, but nothing from any of the fifty thousand people who waited nearly a week for help. You should also avoid saying the word evacuation to these two. Evacuation is what happens before a storm. They felt they were deported. There was even less effort put forth to bring any of the people finally pulled from the Dome or Convention Center home than there was to get them out of town."

"I am well aware of how sensitive the locals are about how things were handled here. Hurricane Betsy followed pretty much the same scenario. It ripped up the coastline when President Johnson had plenty of other irons in the fire, including a far less popular war. Do you know how long it took Johnson to come to New Orleans though?" Hendricks asked. I had never given it a moment's thought.

"No."

"Five hours. He got a call from Senator Long and was here in five hours. Johnson stayed and personally directed the relief effort until he felt people were going to have what they needed to get their lives back. He even went out in a boat and brought people to safety. But all anybody remembers Johnson for is escalating a war he didn't want any part of."

"Maybe you should find someone to publish a book about that. I would read it." I never paid much attention to my parents' stories about surviving Hurricane Betsy in 1965, three years before my birth. I only knew too many people died in 2004 because they thought Betsy prepared them to survive Katrina.

"People wrote plenty of books trying to bash the slow response by FEMA and the city and state, but I noticed nobody published books that blamed the President personally. The accepted version of what happened was that FEMA let him down and the locals were incompetent."

"And now?" I was surprised how worked up my

father's agent had become on the topic.

"Now everybody knows the truth, but nobody cares. I am sure nobody learned a damn thing to use next time. Too many things are going wrong for the current President to scream about how the last guy did the job. What interest there is in your city's recovery right now is only because of the five-year anniversary and the police shootings. A lot of people are still trying to find a way to make everything bad that happened here the city's own fault."

"But next year will be the anniversary of something else, right?" I glanced at Hendricks and he just shrugged with a sad look on his face. "Then why are you even going to talk with the Batistes?"

"I agree that they deserve to be heard. I may even be able to find someone who wants to give them that chance. Plus, I haven't been in this part of town for a couple of years. It looks a lot nicer, I must say."

"There's a lot of gentrification going on right along here. Plenty of new places to eat and more clothing stores selling designer clothes instead of used furniture. The city is even talking about finally putting at least one street car line back in service through here. People moving to New Orleans from other places have no idea about the city's good or bad neighborhoods. They think the houses along here are close to the CBD and the Quarter and buy their way into being urban pioneers. So far, they've mixed in with their neighbors alright, but sooner or later the house flippers are going to start squeezing the old residents out and then we'll see what happens."

"I've never known that to be pretty," Hendricks sighed. "And I have never known anyone to stop the inevitable. NOPD will have its work cut out for it when the class wars begin to happen."

"Good thing they have a great rapport with everyone down here." My passenger looked at me and couldn't tell if I was serious or joking, but he knew my statement was wrong in more ways than it was right.

We were well beyond the rebuilding process along St.

Claude Avenue by the time we got to the bridge over the Industrial Canal. Storefronts were becoming increasingly vacant, and the houses in greater need of repair. I had come this way because it showed the apparent loss of interest in putting money into the community's recovery as one moved away from the neighborhoods being gentrified. The entire city suffered equally in the storm, with forced departures and uncertain futures, but the recovery efforts were being handled anything but equitably.

I pointed out the lingering piece of graffiti on a collapsed house that bore testament to the neighborhood's tenacity. Spray painted letters spelled *CANT STOP THE FUNK* just above the flood water line. I don't know if this referenced the city's strong cultural traditions or the pervasive odor of half a million dead refrigerators that hung over New Orleans for months after the storm. I also chose this route so I could drive past the string of shotgun houses built by Habitat for Humanity for musicians whose homes were destroyed by Katrina. I wanted Hendricks to see Musician's Village before we crossed Claiborne and he was confronted with the starkly modern designs of the Make It Right houses, which looked like misplaced beach houses.

These new homes lined only a half dozen blocks of two streets, one of which backed up to the Industrial Canal's rebuilt concrete flood wall. An almost even mix of still vacant and rebuilt original homes dotted the remaining roughly one hundred and fifty blocks, which were packed shoulder-to-shoulder with homes before the storm. A major demolition operation by the city over the last year removed the last hope of ever returning for dozens of families. Now there were dozens of blocks after blocks with nothing but tall grass hiding the concrete steps and a few brick piers marking where homes once stood. Gavin gave me a look as he surveyed the area; one that was as shaken as it was saddened.

Chapter 12

I knocked on the door and waited as Esther noisily took down the chain lock on the front door. I introduced Gavin to the Batistes and waited around long enough to see that they were going to be able to get along. Lionel wasted no time in pulling material out of his stacks of reports and waving at the white boards to draw the agent into the story he needed to tell. I realized Hendricks was now directly under Uncle Felix on the list of people to whom I would owe a favor. I lecture Chief Avery about Merton's Law of Unintended Consequences' usually unpleasant results even as I constantly place myself at its mercy. Merton's Law doesn't catch up with me very often, but it is always a life-changing experience when it does. My career in intelligence didn't end because I was wounded in a Baghdad ambush. It ended because I chose to trust the wrong guy.

The consequences of leaving Hendricks with the Batistes came four hours later, when he called to invite me to join them. What I found on my arrival was Tulip and two of her friends engaged in animated conversation with Hendricks, Lionel, and Esther. One of Tulip's companions was an attorney with an office in Tulip's building. The other was Jason Bradley, an investigative journalist who did a lot of political muck-raking articles for a local weekly magazine called the *Gambit*.

The attorney was not a problem for me. The reporter was someone I need to avoid. My first year as a State Police detective was marred by my difficulties with differentiating between the devastated New Orleans of 2005, which was still occupied by military troops and had a curfew, and the life I left behind in Baghdad. While this confusion initially mitigated my PTSD, any such comparison would have been a disastrous thing for a member of the State Police, or my family, to say out loud. Chief Avery has wisely banned me from any contact with the media.

"You didn't tell me there was a party," I said to Hendricks. He was sitting at the kitchen table with Lionel, but was obviously the ring master of the circus I found in the Batiste's living room.

"You're going to love his idea!" Tulip nearly shouted in my ear when she saw me and gave me a hug. I was used to seeing her this way drunk, but I saw no alcohol in the room.

"Which is?" I asked Hendricks after I plopped into one of the open seats at the table.

"I can't sell the book they have right now," he admitted. This did not seem to have put any sort of damper on the festivities, and it hardly explained the presence of the trio who arrived in my absence. "But, I can sell one about how the experience drove a young man to run for office!"

"Excuse me?"

"Lionel is going to challenge Delia Adams for her seat on the City Council," Hendricks said and grinned. "I can sell the heck out of that story."

"I can't imagine he'll win," I pointed out.

"He still has time to file. Right now she is running for

her fourth term. I'd say it's time for a change," Tulip told me.

"She ran unopposed for the last two terms. There's some lawyer from Florida named Donald Ursin running against her this time, but people like her." I had no idea how many voters even knew Lionel Batiste, much less liked or hated him.

"No matter," Hendricks waved off my objections. "The story isn't about his running for the position. I just need be able to sell how he made his bad experience into some sort of transformative moment. He goes from just being a college student taking care of his sick mother to a politicized community activist out to bring back his neighborhood."

"How are you going to make that into a convincing story?" Things were making more sense, just not very good sense.

"Bradley has it covered." Tulip said and pointed to the reporter. He was in a serious conversation with Lionel. Lionel was actually listening to the white reporter. "We can get Lionel on the ballot if we sign him up on Monday and Bradley will be able to get their interview published in the next week's edition of Gambit."

"Did anyone else ever watch the Robert Redford movie *The Candidate*?" I was looking for ways to make them rethink their plan. I was loathe to admit that the idea actually seemed like a harmless means of creating a happy ending to a tragic story that wasn't going to get published without a better ending than a bus ride to Houston. I just didn't think they had taken the time to consider all of the possible outcomes of a neophyte like Lionel running for office against an entrenched opponent like Councilwoman Adams.

"As I recall, Robert Redford won the race in the end," Hendricks pointed out. He was correct. Also, the candidate's last words in the movie were "What now?" I was having that moment right then. "How bad could it be if someone as passionate about their neighborhood as Lionel was actually given a chance to make a difference?"

"Idealists don't have great political track records," I reminded him. The agent was certainly old enough to have seen the passions of enough politicians smashed by the realities of bureaucracy and special interests to know what I was saying. "Besides, who's going to run his campaign?"

"Charlie." Hendricks said and pointed to the third new person in the room. I knew the attorney for his pro bono work on liberal causes and on a few projects, like offering to defend Guantanamo detainees, where I would always hope he failed.

"Charlie is a white guy. How is that supposed to work in Lionel's favor in this neighborhood?"

"Esther will technically run the campaign. Charlie will raise money to make yard signs and such. Like I said, I don't need Lionel to win I just need him to run to be able to sell the book."

"Well, I wish you all well with this exercise," I said and stood up. "I leave this circus in all of your very capable hands. "

I was glad Hendricks was able to figure out a way for Esther and Lionel's story to reach an audience beyond their living room. I really was. There was simply no place for a state police detective in what amounted to a publicity stunt, particularly one that involved my own sister and our father's literary agent. My professional talents were of little use to this group unless their next idea was to topple the City Council. Planning things like that are how I fill my time on stake outs. It's a professional bad habit.

I left the house and headed back to the bistro to make a simple plan for the weekend. I could finally have that dinner for two with Katie while my sister was distracted. I would work a shift on Saturday night and sleep late on Sunday, rising in time to watch the Saints game with the usual bunch of rowdy patrons at the bistro's bar. I could wait until Monday to tell Avery that none of what was happening in the Ninth Ward was illegal and I was ready to move on. The Chief of Detectives was going to have to find out about City Council Candidate Lionel Batiste from somebody other than me.

Chapter 13

Lionel Batiste's challenge to Delia Adams was lost in the media coverage of the state's Lieutenant Governor tossing his hat into the ring for the city's mayoral race. Mitch Landrieu's father left huge mayoral shoes for his son to try to fill, but most people wanted to support him and felt he was up to the challenge. The idea that the city would have not only a competent mayor, but one with a sister in the United States Senate, boosted the city's morale overnight. The only people being left outside the tent were the ones campaigning for the job they had to accept was no longer available.

This is not to say that Lionel's announcement did not go entirely unnoticed. Chief Avery called me to say Councilwoman Adams wanted to see me in her office at nine o'clock on Monday morning. I dressed in a blue Brooks Brothers suit and hung my gold shield on a black alligator skin belt. I left my sidearm at home. I wasn't going to get it past the security at her door, anyway, and felt pretty good about being able to take her down in hand to hand combat.

"What is your role in Lionel Batiste's running for my

seat?" Delia demanded once we were alone in her office.

She waved the rolled up morning paper at my face as though she was about to punish a disobedient puppy. I sat down without her offering to allow me to do so and waited until she let out enough hot air that she could descend into her own desk chair before I responded.

"Nothing direct." It was an honest answer to the specific question.

"And indirectly?"

"I introduced Lionel and Esther to my father's agent. Lionel is writing a book about the Convention Center and I thought an agent might give some advice on finding a publisher if he ever finishes the book."

"Let's hope he never does." Delia grumbled and continued glaring at me. "That whole chapter just needs to be put behind us."

This was not the time or place to have that argument. I was, though, very surprised and disappointed that she was among those with such an opinion.

"How did that turn into Lionel running for my seat on the City Council?" she pressed.

"My father's agent told Lionel there would be a better chance of selling the story if he ran for office. Hendricks wants to make the experience into some sort of transformational event in Lionel's life."

"I thought running against the white kid from Florida was bad. Now I'm also going to have to run against someone challenging me just to sell their version of what happened at the Convention Center after Katrina?" The Councilwoman seemed less relieved than I thought she would be. She should have been relived that she could focus on the post-Katrina interloper whose platform seemed to echo a lot of Alex Boudreaux's thoughts on rebuilding the district into a much more expensive place to live. The guy's polling numbers were pretty bad, but the race was just beginning.

"From where I stand you're running unopposed. Don Ursin just moved here. He doesn't stand a chance and Lionel doesn't even want the job."

"You don't really understand this, do you?" Delia began softening her facial features and adapting an annoyingly patronizing tone. "Any opposition is a bad thing in a race. It doesn't matter that I win in the end. What matters is that there is the appearance that I am not satisfying everyone in my district until then."

"Do you really think you're making everyone happy?" Surely she was not that delusional.

"Of course not, but as long as I can talk my opponents out of actually challenging me for my seat I appear to represent the interests of my entire district. Running unopposed gives me the power to say that I represent an entire voting block with needs and concerns that the rest of the Council must reckon with. If I start having people like Lionel take shots at me then I lose that image. It's not good for anybody if the Council believes they can ignore me until my replacement arrives because they think they can control them."

"I see your point, but I have a hard time believing that anyone sees your council seat as being remotely challenged by Lionel Batiste. Lionel doesn't even think so."

"There was a time that was true. Since the storm my district has seen more change than any other district in the city. It was almost all Black and all poor before Katrina. Now we're getting a lot of white people from other places moving in and they want entirely different things than the people they replaced. I am walking a tighter and tighter rope than ever, by trying to serve both sets of voters. What do you think is going to happen to the Ninth Ward if someone like Donald Ursin gets my seat?"

"If you're so worried about that happening then why aren't you more vocal about it? You could do more to block things like those towers going in, or even just slow down flippers like Alex Boudreaux. And what about people like the ones trying to buy up the houses the Make It Right people built?"

"CSA made everyone a decent offer on those houses. Nobody is being forced to move, but this is the best chance for any of those homeowners that are willing to move to find a neighborhood where they feel more at home."

"You don't find it strange that the Lower Ninth Ward has been ignored for five years and now three different sets of developers have their eye on the neighborhood? I'd think that you'd be campaigning on your involvement in getting things going if you had a hand in any of that." I was sure she did.

"I have to keep the residents who are already there the happiest. You don't get it. Gentrification is going to happen no matter what. The best I can do is to try to find ways to make the new work with the old. There will be a day when the new swallows up the old and somebody needs to be there to save people when that happens."

"Like they saved them at the Convention Center?" I couldn't help but swing her own opinions on that back at her. "Didn't those people deserve a better job of being saved?"

"Get out of my office, Detective!" Delia screamed and pointed to her door. It opened a moment later when her security officer stepped in to make sure she was alright. I did not run from Delia's office, but I certainly felt like I was running for cover.

I came away from the meeting with far more than Delia intended or realized. The Councilwoman obviously wanted me to discourage Lionel's political stunt. She was probably right that it was going to smudge her image as a popular and unopposed Black political leader. She was the single most influential minority politician in Orleans Parish, and that translated into a very considerable position of power in the state capitol as well. She had always been able to wrangle money and resources for her district largely by making fewer waves about the conditions there than she easily might—and should – have made.

Delia was less admired than she was feared. Her political strength was that she knew how to be both a spear for the poor and a shield for the affluent. Delia kept mass transit running and got some schools rebuilt to satisfy the repatriated storm refugees. She also managed to make the adjoining mixed and white neighborhoods feel confident that the bad elements in her district were under control, or at least contained. Anyone who eventually replaced her was going to have start from scratch and there were powerful forces that would want to keep them from ever achieving her level of influence.

My career in the military and intelligence agencies had been subject to the desires and ambitions of people with the same tenuous hold on their careers and positions as Councilwoman Adams. I was well aware of the sort of short-sighted and self-serving decision making this fosters. I don't miss that part of the job in the least. I came away from our meeting with a clearer understanding of Delia Adams' political career, and her vulnerabilities.

Her first mistake was thinking she could use me to interfere in the election process. The very idea of telling Lionel to drop out of the race was illegal. I wasn't going to create problems for myself by trying to stop him.

The second thing our meeting revealed was that Delia Adams was busy playing both sides of a very tall fence. She needed to keep voters who shared the Batistes loyalty to their neighborhood mollified, while Alex Boudreaux gradually leveraged them out of their homes. She also needed to be sure the new, white residents liked her no less than the original families they displaced.

I found it interesting that Delia used nothing but the letters CSA to refer to the holding company from Mobile. I should not have been surprised this, but I was. My inner voice had been whispering to me that one or more of the principals in each of the attempts to rebuild the Lower Ninth Ward had to have contacted her at some point. Her advice, and blessing, would be necessary for any of these parties to succeed.

In my experience her use of the initials was the sort of verbal shorthand someone uses when they refer to something with the same mouthful of syllables over and over. Delia had been talking about CSA with someone often enough that she had begun to subconsciously shorten their name.

Councilwoman Adams was keeping a very full bed, politically speaking.

Chapter 14

Unannounced visitors dropped by Tulip's office later the same afternoon. Ray Reilly, Katie's ex-husband, preceded Badger Watson into her inner office. Tulip never keeps a busy appointment calendar. Nevertheless, she was aggravated that Ray and the elder member of Tribal Investments did not contact her before showing up and expecting an audience. Tulip was also not impressed with the way the Indian took a seat without an invitation. She wasn't the sort of person someone could physically intimidate into giving a pass on such a display of entitlement. Ray would have done his client a great service had he taken a moment to warn Watson about my sister before the attorney made her into an instant enemy.

"Do you have a few minutes to talk?" Watson asked, in the tone of voice used by self-important people when what they really mean is, "Drop everything and give me your undivided attention."

Tulip responded to both the intrusion and Watson's manner with the clipped retort "I'll make a few minutes."

It let her uninvited guests know she would give them their requested few minutes, but the clock was ticking and her interest was already waning. There would be no time for the men to settle into their chairs before Tulip showed them the door, unless one of them came up with a very good purpose or argument. She will always make time for spirited arguments.

"Perhaps we should start with an explanation of your role in the company. I take it that Two Crows is your front man and Bristol is an attorney. What role does that leave for you?"

"I do our negotiating," Badger said. His Cheshire cat grin was part of an obviously practiced routine.

"The charm just rolls off you."

Watson realized his initial approach style was not going to get him on Tulip's good side. "I fear we may have started off on the wrong foot at the City Council meeting. I want you to know we are very serious about building something that will help the neighborhood as well as the city. It's our mission."

"Where did this mission come from?" Tulip wondered. "By the look of things, I'm going to find it hard to believe any rags to riches story."

"Nobody is born rich on the Ouachita reservation. I can assure you of that." Badger's tone sounded like practiced offense.

"Then perhaps that isn't where you were born," Tulip doubled down on her aggressive attitude. Watson's eyes widened a fraction, and he took a short breath before choosing his next tactic meant to win her over.

"I see no reason for us to exchange insults, Miss Holland. I simply came here to suggest allowing things to develop a bit further before you make up your mind about what Tribal Investments wants to do for New Orleans."

"Mister Watson, I make my living as a corporate attorney. That makes me all too familiar with criminal intent. I have no proof that your company is planning to break the hearts of this fine city with some elaborate scam or a money pit of a project other than the size and scope of the project your partner presented. It is out of scale in size and cost in the Ninth Ward. That makes me nervous. Do you know what I do when I get nervous?"

"No, what do you do?" Watson was now sitting with his back nearly vertical and the tension in his legs seemed coiled to leap across her desk.

"I start to dig. I pull records. I make phone calls. I research things until I know more about what is going on than the person who crossed me. I will certainly reserve any final judgment on your project until I know everything, but Ray here can attest to my tenacity once I get started."

Whatever Badger Watson intended to accomplish by approaching my sister with an argumentative and imperious manner was failing miserably. Watson may have grasped by this point that he had may have done damage to whatever peace existed between them. It was definitely too late to start over.

"I should have assumed you would know Mister Reilly." Badger flashed a furious scowl towards the man who brought him here.

"Not particularly well. It's just that my brother is sleeping with his ex-wife. She is a prosecutor in the State Attorney's office."

The sexual tidbit was patently untrue, but this is how Tulip likes to play rough with others. She had no reason to humiliate Ray Reilly or to provoke the poor guy's client. She just wanted to see the reaction on each of their faces. Ray was especially unhappy with the image that came to mind, but Badger just flashed a razor thin smile and stood up.

"Well I hope you only find good things about us," Watson said with the last of his composure.

"You should hear the stories they tell about Mother Teresa now that she's dead." The Indian was caught off guard by what he thought was Tulip's entirely unrelated comment. "Nobody who tries to be the sort of public servant you want the world to see can accomplish that much good without also being as mean as an alligator. I am sure you've crushed a few hopes and stepped on some other men's toes by now. I'll reserve my decision on what to do next until I have spoken to those parties as well. Is there anything else?"

"No, I think we're through here." Watson started towards the door. "You're likely to hear what lengths we are prepared to go to fulfill our plans. My tribal name is Badger, Miss Holland. Do you know what they say about the badger?"

"They're supposed to be the meanest animal in the forest. Supposedly even bears give them space, but do I look like a bear to you, Mister Watson?"

"My point is that you certainly will not like me if I don't get my way. And, yes, my partners and I can be as nasty as you think we are. I am simply amazed that you are ready to fight someone you know is more determined to get what they want than you are to stop them."

"You have no idea how determined your visit has made me." Tulip smiled and saw the men through the office's outer door. She counted to ten and then locked the door and went to her desk to be sure her digital recorder caught the entire conversation, and that her handgun was within easy reach.

Badgers may very well be the meanest animal in the great outdoors. That's only because Tulip Holland hates hiking. Tribal Investments had concerned Tulip from the moment she got a look at Two Crows Taylor and heard his presentation. She mitigates her fear of any opponent by finding the chinks in their armor and grabbing their soft underbelly. She takes them apart piece by piece until they are her size and they have to look her in the eye and admit they seriously underestimated their diminutive opponent.

Chapter 15

My sister told me about her encounter with Badger over drinks at the bistro after work. I shared my own experience of refusing Councilwoman Adams' order to make Lionel drop his campaign for her office. The Councilwoman used Chief Avery as her messenger a second time; this time to express her displeasure with my refusal to do her bidding. Avery wasn't happy about his new role.

"What happened between you two anyway?" Avery demanded to know. He was on his second beer before he could calm down enough to listen to my side of the argument, or that I didn't think I'd even had a feud with the Councilwoman. I remember when I verbally or physically spar with someone while sober.

"I have no idea, other than letting Delia know I was not going to tell Lionel he couldn't run for office against her. I didn't bother citing the exact laws she wanted me to break."

"She claims you have been harassing Alex Boudreaux as well. I gather he may be one of the biggest contributors to her campaign."

"I went by and asked him if he knew anything about the company that's trying to buy the Batiste's place."

"What else? I know you didn't ask just one question."

"He offered to explain his operation. Alex has figured out a legal way to nearly double his money. He even offered to cut me in for just fifty grand. I said I'd think about it."

"Well stay away from him, and from anything else that's going to get the Councilwoman upset until after the election. She's threatening to call the Troop Commander and have you reassigned."

"She's really going to be unhappy when she finds out that will never happen."

Avery wasn't amused about being reminded of my permanent posting to his command and set his beer on the bar. "Just behave yourself. Strike that. Both of you behave yourselves."

"We are," Tulip insisted. "It's everybody else that's going nuts. My brother had a member of the City Council ask him to intimidate an opponent. I was threatened in my own office by a huge Indian just for questioning his motives in spending millions of dollars in a slum."

"You two got yourselves into this only because you teamed up with the Batistes."

"You're going to need a food taster if Miss J hears you say things like that," I warned my boss. This he finally found amusing. I knew better than to ask the next question, but I wasn't going to know the answer if I left the topic alone. "Is my uncle helping you at all?"

"All he has said is that we need to change the story. I have no idea what that even means," Avery lamented.

"It means he plans to put NOPD's investigation into a more flattering context. He'll get newspaper and magazine articles written about how chaotic it was after the storm, how you were short-handed when the investigation was made, and that the city just wanted to move forward. A handful of stories like could make your actions look entirely different." I had seen Felix's handiwork in the past. My uncle's theory is that you have to change the facts to change a story, and that there are always plenty of extra facts lying around when people start to make up stories.

Chapter 15

I was back to my normal routine by the next afternoon. The Batistes were not going to sell their house and my sister was the only one still playing games with Lionel and the Councilwoman. I drove my usual patrol circuit the night before; rotating between different addresses on my list to watch for people with arrest warrants. Suspects and fugitives that skip town invariably sneak home between Thanksgiving and Christmas.

I was in bed just after sunrise and awake again about one o'clock. I was swimming laps at the New Orleans Athletic Club about three in the afternoon when my iPhone started collecting text messages. I found them once I returned to the locker room to get dressed. On a normal day I would have headed from the pool to NOPD's pistol range for the second session of my twice weekly target practice.

The messages put an end to that schedule. The first three were from my sister. Each message was shorter and seemed more frantic than the last. Every message was a variation of asking me to hurry to the Batiste's house. The first message was sent an hour before I read it. The last message was twenty minutes old, and the rudest of the three.

I was already en route when Chief Avery's single text came in.

@ BATISTES/COME CLEAN UP YOUR MESS

Not one of the four messages prepared me for what I was about to run into.

I noticed a half dozen police cars parked in front of the Batistes' house as I crossed the Claiborne Bridge. More units blocked the cross streets. I turned my Cadillac coupe to the left at the foot of the bridge and found a place to park.

Three patrol cars marked the perimeter of the crime scene. Two marked the Batistes' property line and the third blocked the nearest side street. Yellow crime scene tape stretched from each car's antenna. Vehicles belonging to the first responding officers, including a canine unit, blocked the neighbors' driveways. Chief Avery was parked behind my sister's Porsche Cayenne in front of the Batiste's home. She must have arrived before NOPD. That made sense based on the order of the text messages.

NOPD detectives were working the crime scene with the canine officer. Uniformed officers were walking the block trying to take witness statements. Esther and Lionel's neighbors watched the commotion from the comfort of white plastic chairs set on the decks of their homes. Some of them were using their smartphones to film a running commentary of the scene below them.

I spotted detectives next to the open trunk of the Batistes' 1991 Ford Crown Victoria sedan. The trunk was pocked with impact dents from multiple shotgun blasts. It was strange that none of the impacts had penetrated more than the rust and old white paint.

"Nice grouping." I shared my opinion of the marksmanship with a senior burglary detective. He was idly watching a crime lab technician collect shot from the sedan. "The shooter must have been standing in the driveway when they opened fire. What size shot did they use, anyway?"

"Number seven. We recovered these at the end of the driveway." He handed me an evidence bag containing eight spent Federal shotgun shells. The stamping on the shell and around the primer confirmed what he said. "This doesn't make the least bit of sense."

I noticed the canine officer and his dog were working their way around the Batiste's storage shed.

"What's with the canine unit?"

"Someone called in a tip that there were drugs in the car."

"Before or after the car got shot up?"

"I don't know. The first detectives on the scene asked for a canine unit when they got here." I felt my jaw tighten. There is a considerable difference between a bona fide tip and a detective making a racially motivated presumption.

"Did you check the car?" I asked the canine officer.

"That's why we came."

"Did you find anything? Anything at all?"

"The dog caught a scent in the trunk, but the detectives didn't find anything when they searched it." He wasn't interested in discussing the matter with me. He may have been wary because I am a state police detective, but I wasn't interested in taking over any investigation into this incident.

"I'd say you can leave now, unless you think the dog's going to tell us to dig up the driveway." I suggested. He gave me a surly look before he led the German Shepard back to their vehicle.

I continued to study the impact points on the rear of the heavy sedan. The shotgun pellets struck both sets of tail lights as well as directly above the trunk lock. The rear window had held in place after taking a direct shot blast. I gave the shooters credit for hitting exactly where they aimed, but number seven shot would not have killed anyone standing beside the car.

I asked the detective where Chief Avery was. He

pointed to the stairway leading to the second floor. My boss was standing on the deck when I cleared the last step. I felt he might have been waiting there ever since he summoned me.

"Man, they wanted that car dead," I tried to joke about the situation.

Avery wasn't amused. "This has to be related to whatever you and your sister have cooked up with the Batistes. You need to find out what's going on and settle the matter once and for all. Am I clear?"

"Crystal clear. I can tell you right now that Lionel or Esther aren't running a drug cartel out of the back of a fifteen year old retired taxi cab."

Avery didn't smile, but he also didn't smack me over my attitude. "You're getting this case because it stinks so much. My kids could do a better job of framing somebody. I'm going to pull my people out of here. Do whatever it is you do to figure this out, but try to keep the surprises to a minimum this time."

Chief Avery opened the Batiste's front door without knocking. Lionel and Tulip were seated at the dining room table with two NOPD detectives. Esther was pacing the kitchen floor. She looked more upset by the investigation into the shooting than by the damage to her car. Tulip was making life difficult for the detectives Lionel was trying to silently stare down.

"That is the fifth time you have implied there are drugs involved in the attack on my clients." Tulip was directing her indignation at the pudgy white detective in his late forties. He clearly wanted to bring the subject up again. I recognized him as Detective Steve Kramer. His new partner was a local kid named Troy Frontenac. I helped the pair locate a suspect in a drug case a year ago. They did solid work and I felt Avery was creating unnecessary friction between the three of us by handing me what should have been their case.

"I trust my source a lot more than I trust your clients," Kramer declared.

"I have no idea who your source is, but my clients have

no history of drug use or sales. Lionel Batiste has even agreed to a urinalysis to prove he is clean. They complied with your search warrant for their vehicle. It was based solely on your claim about an anonymous tip that there was crystal meth in the trunk of the car. You found no such drugs. I won't recommend that my clients voluntarily allow you to search their home using this same weak pretense."

"We can get a warrant to search this place." Kramer chose to maintain a combative attitude.

"No, you can't. Not with the evidence at hand. Your alleged informant said the drugs were in the trunk of the car. They weren't. You don't get to keep guessing. When you leave here today, I am going to look up your service record. Should I find you have harassed any of the Batistes just once in the past, I will use that incident to have you barred from having anything further to do with this case."

"Do you really think you can do that?"

"She can." Avery's comment ended the interview. "You're done here. I'm handing this over to the State Police."

The detectives looked at one another and then glared at me instead of their boss. They closed their notebooks and stood up in silence, knowing better than to say another word. Even really good NOPD detectives have been shut down by their bear-sized boss at least once in their career, but very few have kept a career with NOPD after being pulled from a second case.

"Actually, can you stick around a bit? I need to know what you've found out so far." I wanted to hear their verbal report, with all of its inflections and pauses rather than read the same information in their carefully written report. I sat down next to Tulip and whispered to her before I started asking my own questions. "I got your texts when I was at the gym. How did you get here so fast?"

"I was already here. I called Bill when they started to search the car for meth and asked him to call you. The detectives want to blame the attack on Lionel. Apparently, NOPD won't let a young Black man be both a victim and innocent in this part of town."

I was unclear why Lionel was being grilled as a suspect at all. Surely nobody believed he had shot up his own car. He was also the only Black male his age in the neighborhood that I was sure had nothing to do with drugs.

"It's why I want Cooter on this. Maybe he can help us figure out what's going on." Avery wasn't going to let himself be baited by Tulip's comments.

"Oh, I get it now. You asked me here because you would rather I take the heat over this than your guys."

"True 'dat." Avery just chuckled at my epiphany and walked out the door. The narcotics detectives took comfort in knowing they were being replaced for public relations reasons instead of Avery's lack of confidence in their abilities.

I took a pad and pen from the shoulder pack I carry with me as a mobile office.

"Alrighty then. Somebody tell me what happened."

"Two Black Knights shot up our car. The police came a couple of minutes later. These two detectives showed up with a search warrant right after that. They said they got a tip that there were drugs in the trunk of our car and they think there's going to be a drug war between the Knights and me." Lionel was able to explain the incident with surprising succinctness. There was a fury in his voice, but he only gave me undisputed facts. The journalism courses at UNO were doing him some good.

"You're going to start a gang war. Really?" I knew better than to laugh by the expression on Esther and Tulip's faces. "Did anyone actually see the gunmen?"

Esther fielded this question. "Not none of us. I was at the table with Miss Tulip. She come by with a contract from that Mister Hendricks for Lionel to sign. She was gonna explain it to us before he signed it. Lionel had just brung in a pizza and some beers from Walmart when we heard them motorbikes and the gunshots."

"How do you know the shooters were members of the Black Knights if you didn't see them?" I directed this to Lionel because he was the one who claimed the gang was behind the shooting.

"Our neighbors were out front of their house and they saw them. They saw the Knight's patch on the riders."

"Have you had serious arguments with anyone in the Knights, or anyone else, recently?"

"Not with no bikers. You know about me protesting against Alex Boudreaux," Lionel thought aloud.

"Were you able to get a useful description of the shooters?" I asked the detectives.

"Just that there were two of them and they were wearing colors that match the Black Knights," Detective Frontenac spoke up.

"You know the Knights better than I do, but I didn't know they were in the meth trade." I said. The Black Knights are the best organized, and most violent, criminal gang in a part of the city full of gangs. The Black Knights don't do anything half-way. They aren't the sort to shoot an empty car with birdshot. They would empty AK-47s into an occupied school bus just to make their point. "Did anyone actually see the shooters well enough to identify them?"

"Nobody claims to have seen their faces. It would be suicide to say they could identify them," Frontenac need not have reminded me of this. The gang is notorious for eliminating witnesses and informants.

"I don't buy it." I openly laughed at what I was being expected to believe occurred. "The Black Knights have never shot anybody with birdshot, and they don't shoot up cars to make their point. You bring chalk to draw an outline instead of paramedics when the Black Knights are involved in a shooting." My opinion was meant to discredit not just the theory, but the logic the detectives used to come up with it. "Does anyone in this room really believe a college student and his rickety mother are cutting into the drug trade of the city's most violent bikers?"

Saying the scenario aloud gave everyone a reason to

laugh. Then I ruined the moment. "But, something must be going on or we wouldn't be here. I don't believe your story about the tip being any good. I do believe two riders on motorcycles absolutely did shoot up the car. Detective Kramer, you claim you received a tip. How did the tip come in?"

"I got a call on my cell phone," Detective Frontenac said. "The caller gave me a lot of detail about how Lionel is dealing meth. We had no trouble getting a search warrant for his car based on what I was told."

"The caller has given you solid tips in the past?"

"They have always been right about anything happening down here."

"Why did you only get a warrant for the car? Why not the house, too?"

"I assumed we could expand the search because anything we found in the car would have given us probable cause to search the house."

"So, you aren't entirely stupid." I didn't really mean to be quite so rude. It was conversations like this which had cost me my relationship with NOPD's detectives. "How long between the tip about the drugs and when the call came in about the car getting shot up?"

"Probably about three hours." Detective Kramer's expression showed he knew what my argument was going to be.

"So maybe the shooting was a back-up plan to give you that probable cause. Or maybe your caller thought you had ignored their tip." The two NOPD detectives glanced at one another and then turned to me to nod their heads.

"I can buy that. We had trouble finding a judge because they had all gone home for the day," Kramer conceded. It dawned on me why the detectives were so intent on finding the drug stash. They suspected that they were being used to embarrass the Batistes. Finding the meth was the only thing that was going to keep them from looking manipulated. "That would have been plenty of time for these two to have moved or sold the meth."

"Are you really willing to testify that the Black Knights messed up the paint job on a car to scare a sick old woman and her son out of dealing meth?"

"I was. I don't think I am now." I'd watched the expressions on Detective Frontenac's face change as he listened to his dubious conclusions repeated aloud. "It was the only story that seemed to fit everything together."

"It's curious that there was such an immediate police response to this particular shooting. Three guys were shot in a drive-by related to an actual drug deal a week ago and it took almost an hour to get one patrol car to the scene. I would hate to think that this has anything to do with Lionel's running for City Council. He's attracting the wrong sort of attention if that's the case."

"Do you need us for anything else, Detective?" Kramer demanded as he stood up. "We've told you what we know. I agree with you that something is wrong about all of this. I just don't want to waste any more of our day turning over stones in the State's investigation. We have cases of our own to deal with."

"Just send me a copy of your report. Thanks." I tried to be nice as the NOPD detectives walked out the same door their boss used when he washed his own hands of the mess.

"What next?" Tulip asked when the four of us were finally alone to consider where the case left the Batistes.

"I'd say your work is done. I just have a couple of other questions for Lionel, but you don't need to hang around for that."

"Are you trying to deny my client his right to an attorney?" Tulip wasn't joking with me.

"I'd like to leave here without this family needing a defense attorney." I said this in absolute sincerity, and with a very small plea for some privacy.

"Just don't forget who that will be. I will eat you for breakfast in court big brother." Tulip gathered her notes and the contract from Hendricks into her own briefcase and headed for the door as well. She left the Batistes with one last cautionary word of advice. "Remember, you don't have to answer any questions if you don't want to do so."

I waited until Tulip left before I peeked out the front door. I saw Chief Avery and the narcotics detectives were in a heated discussion beside the stairwell to the deck. Avery and Tulip had a brief exchange before she left. I turned back to the Batistes and explained why I needed everyone else to leave; including Tulip.

"I did intelligence work for twenty years before I became a detective. I've had to reach tougher conclusions than the one I made after walking into this room. There was too much work put into making sure NOPD believed there were drugs in the trunk of your car for them to come up empty handed."

"There ain't no drugs!" Esther insisted.

"You're probably usually a better liar than you are right now, Esther. It pains me to even call you one." I didn't want to start an argument.

"Do you really think Lionel or me be dealing crystal meth?" Esther was disappointed that I apparently did.

"No, but I will still need you to give me the meth."

"Does them detectives' story make any sense?"

"No." Kramer's flimsy scenario had little to do with my certainty about what actually happened. "I think someone planted the drugs while Lionel was making groceries. I'm guessing you found them when you unloaded the car and called Tulip. She used the contract as an excuse for being here when the cops arrived."

Esther tried staring me down one more time before she walked into her bedroom. Lionel's silence and body language reflected his justified frustration and anger about his family's situation.

Esther set a plastic Walmart shopping bag down in front of me. I peeled back the thin gray plastic to expose two gallon-sized Ziploc bags full of bright blue pills. I had done enough work with the narcotics detectives to know each bag held a kilo. The two bags had a wholesale price of about fifty thousand dollars.

It was impossible for the Batistes to sell anywhere near

this amount of meth and not be known by NOPD or the DEA. What concerned me was that they posed enough of a threat to someone that they were willing to spend this much money to ruin the Batiste's reputation whether the drug charges stood or not.

"That's quite a drug stash you've got there."

Lionel pounded both of his fists on the table. "You said you know they aren't ours."

"And I still say so. Do you trust me?"

"Your sister says we can, so I will." This was Esther's decision and not her son's.

"Trusting me completely is very important right now." I pulled one of the two bags out of the bag and left the second half of the drugs and the Walmart bag on the table.

"You ain't turning in all the dope?"

"Just how much meth do you want Lionel arrested for having?" I waved the bag in my hand above the second bag. "I think this should be enough to get him twenty years in Angola."

"How come you're gonna arrest Lionel? You said you know the drugs ain't got nothing to do with us."

"You may not believe this, but arresting Lionel is the only way I have to keep the two of you safe. You aren't healthy enough to sit in a jail cell and he is. My problem is figuring out how to arrest Lionel and then make sure that whatever was supposed to happen next doesn't."

"Meaning?" Lionel was finally joining the conversation. This was good. It meant he finally understood I was actually trying to help him.

"Someone is intent on getting you in a jail cell today. The plan may have been for both of you to be arrested, but I'm not going to drag you into this," I assured Esther. "For all we know the plan is to put a blade in your guts in Central Lockup. I can't see any way out of this that isn't meant to end badly."

"What if you don't arrest anybody at all?" Esther suggested.

"Whoever set this up will keep trying until they succeed at whatever they have in mind. They could wind up shooting you at a traffic light. The only way I can keep your family safe is to let them think their plan worked."

"My life ain't worth Lionel going to Angola prison." Esther was nearly in tears. Lionel was visibly on the verge of attacking me.

"I promise that Lionel will not go to prison. There is a whole process between his being arrested and even seeing a jury. Doing this will make whoever is behind this relax and buy me the time to find them. Hell, it may even help your chances in the election if we do this right."

"What are you going to do with the other bag of meth?" Lionel asked. He was trying to avoid suggesting that I was keeping it for myself, but that was the only conclusion he could draw with his generally negative view of cops.

"You know those scenes in movies where the bad guy throws a hand grenade and the hero throws it back right before it explodes? This is that hand grenade."

"Huh?" Lionel was understandably baffled. He understood the example I gave, but not how it applied to this situation.

"What do you think is going to happen when you show up in court with only half the drugs? Whoever planned all of this is going to begin to ask themselves what became of the other half. Did the guys who planted them keep some? Did I keep some? Did you manage to hide them? Hopefully this will start a small fire in their operation and I can follow the smoke. I have to admit, right now I have too many ideas about who to question about where these drugs came from. Once I find the person behind all of this, I can return the favor. You saw how fast NOPD's detectives were to assume the worst about two poor folk from the Ninth Ward. Imagine what happens when somebody rich and powerful can be taken down in the same way."

"Your plan is to frame somebody else for framing us?"

"Oh, I would never frame anybody. That's illegal. I'm just going to return this meth to its rightful owner. How some other cop interprets their possession of the drugs is beyond my control." I flashed my most evil grin and Lionel finally laughed at something I said.

"So, how're you going to keep me alive in Central Lockup?" I was relieved that Lionel was beginning to go along with my plan.

"By keeping you out of the place as best I can. I'll put you in Saint Bernard's jail overnight and transfer you to Orleans Parish before your arraignment. I think the most likely plan is to have someone show up and look like your new friend."

"Why's that?"

"It's a tactic I have used." I didn't elaborate. "It is human nature to protect yourself from any enemies. We never see the damage a friend can do until it's too late. You'll be vulnerable and they can use your trust to get past your defenses. I don't think they want to hurt either of you. They just want to get you out of their way."

"What makes you say that?"

"You'd already be dead. They shot your car when you weren't in it. They didn't even cause much damage to the car."

What I was proposing was dangerous to Lionel's health, both of their well-being, and my career. Turning the drugs over to NOPD and saying this was a bad frame job would place the Batistes in an even more dangerous position. Then again, Avery's direct orders were to do whatever I thought necessary to solve this mystery.

"What are you going to tell your boss?" Esther was still doing most of the talking for the pair.

"Absolutely nothing. Also, none of us should discuss the amount of drugs you found with anyone else."

"Are you sure you can keep Lionel out of prison?"

"I think I might know a prosecutor who will help me with that." I wasn't going to tell them anymore than that. My relationship with Katie Reilly was still complicated enough that even I didn't completely understand it.

Chapter 17

I stepped outside to check if Chief Avery was still parked behind Tulip. His SUV remained parked where I spotted it earlier, but Tulip had already taken off. I went down the stairs and found Chief Avery standing beside the forensic technician taking photographs of the damaged Ford.

"You're not going to like this." I warned him.

"Probably not. You and Tulip managed to convince Kramer and Frontenac that this whole thing was just an attempt to make the Batistes look bad. Now you're going to tell me what's really going on, aren't you?" I know my boss was hoping I was ready to confirm what the two experienced detectives had already told him. He also knows me well enough to understand that was never going to happen.

"I think the only way we can find out what this all about is to go through with making an arrest. Esther just handed over the drugs Lionel found in the trunk of their car. It's a couple of pounds of meth."

"You're kidding." My boss blinked hard and wobbled a bit. "Do you really think someone tried to frame him?"

"Here is what we can be certain of. The only things

different in the Batistes' life between now and a month ago is that someone wants to buy their house, Esther made a huge stink about an elaborate development proposal at the City Council meeting, Lionel agreed to run against Delia Adams to get his book published, and someone just shot up their car. I believe I can prove the drugs were planted in this car while Lionel was at Walmart. Knowing who did that is the only way to figure out who went to this much work to try to silence the Batistes."

"You're prepared to declare this was a frame job? We might be able to drop the whole thing if you do."

"No." I held up my hand to keep him from interrupting me, or taking a serious swing at my head. "We need to go ahead and act like Lionel is actually dealing dope while I look for whoever framed him."

"And Lionel is willing to go to jail for something he didn't do?"

"I convinced him it was the only way to keep whoever did this from trying something else. Sooner or later they would be using real bullets and somebody would get hurt or killed."

"You're probably right about that," Avery concurred. "This is one of those unintended consequences you're always talking about, huh?"

"It's going to be for somebody. I just hope it isn't me. Lionel is going to prison if I can't prove he was framed."

"Did you mention that possibility to him?"

"I was holding off on mentioning it for a while."

Avery finally had his good laugh at my expense. I had begun to dig myself a deep hole when one wasn't necessary, and he seemed resigned to the idea that my simple case was now going to get messier than he ever feared. Turning the drugs in and closing the case as a failed attempt to embarrass the Batistes was the easy way out of this, but neither Avery nor I were prepared to sign the Batistes' death warrant.

Chapter 18

Placing Lionel in St. Bernard parish's jail for sixteen hours possibly saved his life. I was still hopeful that it derailed any plans for further violence against him. Someone may have only wanted to discredit him or Esther with a televised perp-walk. It remained equally plausible that same someone paid for another prisoner to shove a fork in Lionel's throat.

I handcuffed Lionel while he was being processed into my custody at the St. Bernard Parish detention center the next morning. One of the deputies raised an eyebrow at how loose the cuffs were. The officer who escorted me to my vehicle was left in a bit of a daze when he watched me buckle my prisoner into the back seat of a Cadillac station wagon and drive away.

I retrieved Lionel from the jail before breakfast was served in his holding cell. He said he had refused to eat what was offered for a supper meal the night before. I offered to buy him breakfast and apologized that it might be the last decent food he had for a while. I pulled into the parking lot of a Waffle House a few blocks from the jail and removed the cuffs, but reminded him we would have to deliver him at Central Lockup secured.

We sat at a quiet corner table, where I tried to reinforce Lionel's faith in my plan as he gobbled down a plateful of pork chops and eggs with sides of raisin toast and hash browns smothered in onions and white gravy.

"I'm going to review the surveillance tapes at Walmart. They should prove the drugs were planted in the car while you were inside. The bikers who shot up your mom's Crown Vic probably called 911 to give NOPD an excuse to search the vehicle without a search warrant."

"You can get the charges dropped after you do that, right?" This was the only detail he cared about.

"We will. Eventually." Lionel frowned at this response. "Look, the only way to find out who wants you framed is to have that person execute whatever plan they have in mind. I can promise you'll never stand trial. I will say you were part of a special investigation and this arrest won't show up on your record. Do you still trust me?"

"Not really, but I have to now."

"Just consider the story of the African tickbird." I'd heard the parable from a soldier in Africa years ago. "One day the tickbird is pecking for food under a shady bush and an elephant takes a huge dump on it. The elephant gives the bird his apologies but the bird is so mad he screams until the elephant leaves. The screaming attracts a leopard. The leopard helps the bird out of the dung pile and shows him to a puddle where he can wash himself off. The tickbird cleans its' feathers and thanks the leopard for his kindness. The leopard eats the now clean tickbird."

"That's a really messed up story."

"The point of the story is that you need to remember that everybody who dumps on you is not necessarily your enemy, and everybody who offers a helping hand is not your friend. I want you to think of me as being that elephant. We're still looking for your leopard."

"And which of those is Mister Gavin? He's the one that got me into this trouble." Lionel had a valid point. This is not how either of our mornings would have been spent had the wily agent not thrown Lionel's hat into the political arena.

"Neither, really. Gavin was trying to do you a favor and, believe it or not, he may have. You will get tons of media attention, it will be pretty bad at first, but it should be very sympathetic when you beat this." I wasn't just trying to buck him up. I had given him the scenarios I saw and being framed *could* be a good thing for his candidacy. "Here's what you need to do while you have this time on your hands. First, get anyone from the neighborhood to give you some protection in case I am right about whoever did this wanting you killed in jail. Second, make a list of everyone you can get to run your campaign when you get out. Having my sister and her white-boy buddies aren't good optics. If you really want to win this thing then you need to do it on your own. I'll take care of your being framed, but first we need to get you to court."

Chapter 19

I had two reasons to visit the State Attorney's office after I booked Lionel into Central Lockup for his arraignment. The primary reason was to see if I could find a way to manipulate Lionel Batiste's prosecution. I needed him to be charged before a judge who would forgive my subterfuge when the truth came out. The only judge I knew for sure that might fit this bill was Judge Cyrus Rogers.

The other reason was to say good morning to Katie. I had not seen her since Sunday. We had enjoyed sharing pizza and beer on the sofa at her house a lot more than watching the Saints go down in flames to the New England Patriots. Our team already owned a place in the playoffs, but it was still aggravating to see the coaching decisions made to protect key players. Saints fans would have to endure at least a few more disappointing games before the division championship game. Militarily, I knew the objective was to win the war so these final battles were inconsequential. It still hurt.

"Good morning," I whispered into Katie's ear after sneaking up behind her. She ignored my presence until she finished discussing strategy on a case with one of the junior prosecutors.

Katie then turned around and frowned at my empty hands. "You didn't bring coffee? You really aren't very good at this whole boyfriend thing, are you?"

She shared her disappointment loudly enough for her peers to have a good laugh at my expense. I am lousy at most things that don't come with a field manual or instructions. I can assemble thirty different small arms wearing a blindfold, but coffee and flowers throw me.

"I can get some," I lamely offered. She shook her head and moved to her own desk. She silently freshened the cup of coffee on her desk from a Thermos she brought with her from home.

"Too little, too late. You'll learn. What brings you by this early in the morning, anyway?"

"I brought Lionel Batiste in for arraignment. I parked him in St. Bernard's jail overnight to avoid any publicity."

"Well there should be plenty of it today. It's not often we get to prosecute anyone who has disappointed this many people. He had a lot of people counting on him to kick Delia Adams out of office."

This was not the time or place to tell Katie that I was allowing Lionel to be framed. I knew she was going to react unkindly when she learned I was concealing the truth. I just wanted her to be able to say that she honestly had no idea what was happening in the event the subterfuge blew up in my face.

"I want to steer his case to Judge Rogers' courtroom."

"Are you looking to have Batiste drawn and quartered? I thought he was a family friend. You want Jackson if you're hoping for any sort of plea deal or probation. I am going to prosecute the case so I can suggest either judge. It's your call."

"I need Batiste in front of Rogers. He'll also need a public defender." This wasn't the time or place to start an argument about her recusal based on our relationship. I was just hoping that her taking the case wasn't a sign that things had changed between us.

"Isn't Tulip defending him?" Katie took a seat on the front of her desk and extended her long legs at an angle towards me. This made her skirt ride up her thigh a bit. I had to look.

"She just sat with him during his questioning. Lionel hasn't got anywhere near enough money to hire my sister to go to trial, and you would just beat her up over the whole family friendship thing." These were credible excuses for Tulip's recusal, but I couldn't tell if Katie was buying them or not.

"Of course I would, but he's screwed without a good lawyer." Katie frowned at me as she pulled her long brown hair off her shoulders and began twisting it into a braid as part of her game face. She is so naturally beautiful that the most she can muster when she wants to look either determined or angry is a look of maternal disapproval. Fury and indignation can't be sculpted out of her soft Irish features. It is her tone of voice that quiets any room and breaks the will of witnesses she cross examines. She is usually the prosecutor assigned to handle grand juries to sway things as her bosses see fit.

"It would be nice if it looked that way."

"What do you have up your sleeve, Detective Holland?"

"Nothing I can discuss today. I only admit that I need Lionel to look as vulnerable as possible this morning."

"I can do that." Katie said and stared me in the eye. "And then you can buy me supper this evening and tell me what you're doing. Invite your boss if you want. I'm sure the Chief has a hand in this as well. Batiste is your guy in the Lower Ninth, and you two can't afford to lose a good informant to something this stupid."

"I assure you that Lionel is nobody's snitch. What made you think he was an informant?

"I was guessing, but you would have admitted to it just now. Besides, it's my job to know the pieces in every puzzle. Everyone owes someone a favor or needs them for something else."

"Who do you owe favors?"

"Certainly not you!" She kissed me on the cheek as she

walked by me with her stack of case files. "Just remember to bring coffee next time and you might get to be someone I need for something else."

"Well, that's an incentive!"

I followed Katie into the hallway and made my own way to Judge Rogers' courtroom. His name is Judge Rogers or Your Honor, never Cyrus or Cy, and it is wise to never forget that. I found a seat in the back of the courtroom as the seats slowly filled with the families and attorneys of the defendants whom the judge would be looking down upon this morning. Judge Rogers' demeanor is always entertaining, especially when a defendant has the poor judgment to disrupt the flow of the judge's proceedings.

Judge Rogers has a schedule in his head and he holds everyone else to it. It was Wednesday, and at twelve twenty that afternoon he would be seated at Mandina's Restaurant. He would satisfy his mid-day appetite with a green pepper stuffed with shrimp and ground meat, baked macaroni, and lima beans. At two thirty he would have no problem satisfying his sense of justice by sending a defendant freshly convicted of armed robbery to Angola for the next thirty years.

Lionel was the fifth defendant on the judge's morning docket. The longest arraignment had taken twenty minutes, the shortest took ten minutes. Judge Rogers paused as he read the folder his clerk handed him. He seemed almost flustered to find the prisoner standing in shackles before him was Lionel Batiste.

"I must say, Lionel, I am surprised to see you here this morning. It saddens me that you have moved from City Council candidate to dope dealer all in the same week."

"I'm sorry as well, Your Honor."

Tulip stood beside him, for now, and Lionel used the judge's distraction with reading the arraignment file to look around. This courtroom was built when high ceilings, tall windows, lacquered wood, and imposing judge's stands were still being used to remind everyone justice is serious business.

Detectives Kramer and Frontenac were here to get vindication, but neither Chief Avery nor Esther were present. It took considerable arguing to convince Esther to stay home to give the impression that her baby boy was alone in the world. I doubt anyone who knows the Batistes believed Esther would ever turn her back on her son. I scanned the gallery for anyone else taking note of Lionel's case.

"Will Miss Holland here be representing you?" Judge Rogers inquired.

"I will be stepping down after the arraignment. Lionel will be applying for a court appointed attorney after this hearing, your Honor," Tulip spoke up.

"I'm actually sorry to hear that." The judge frowned. "And what plea do you wish to enter Mister Batiste?"

"Not guilty, your honor."

"For your sake, Lionel, I hope that is how it turns out." Judge Rogers broke his own tradition of appearing objective in saying so. "Considering the severity of the charges and evidence in hand, I am going to place your bond at one hundred thousand dollars. All cash."

"Your honor, there is no way Mister Batiste can raise that kind of money. The defendant is no flight risk and has limited funds at his disposal." Tulip went through the motions of objecting. Judge Rogers had his reasons and wouldn't change his mind on something so mundane as the amount of a defendant's bail. I didn't want the judge to give him a bail amount that Esther might raise anyway.

"I agree that Mister Batiste is no flight risk, but he must have money stashed away if he can afford to buy a kilo of crystal meth. Besides, I don't think the defendant has anything to tend to before his trial. Do you even have a job, Lionel?"

Tulip didn't take the bait and Lionel just hung his head rather than mention his college courses.

"Defendant is remanded to the custody of the sheriff. Bailiff arrange for him to meet with the Public Defender's Office this afternoon."

Fifteen minutes, start to finish. Lionel was officially

dangling like a worm on a hook and all any of us could do was to wait and see who took the bait.

Chapter 20

I left the courtroom and headed to Chief Avery's office. My boss was in a good mood because the drug I had him turn over to the crime lab was high quality crystal methamphetamine. Avery had been worried the quality might be so low that there was some possibility Lionel cooked it himself.

Avery rummaged around on his desk to find the search warrant necessary to retrieve copies of the video surveillance footage from the Walmart in Chalmette. Proving someone planted the narcotics in the trunk of the Crown Victoria was the only way to get Lionel out of the legal mess where I had just left him. I tucked the search warrant into an inside pocket of the blazer I had worn to court.

"Oh, one other thing, Chief." I tried to sound as casual as possible as I reached into my satchel bag. I pulled out the drink glasses that had been gathering dust on my coffee table. "Can I get you to run some prints for me?"

"Whose do you think they are?"

"The principals from Tribal Investments."

"And what crime do you suspect them of committing?

I can't justify running their prints without a good reason."

"Let's say I want to eliminate their prints from consideration in finding who put the drugs in Lionel's trunk."

"I can do that without running the prints." Avery was taking an unusually hard stance on procedure.

"I can ask the State Police, if you'd rather." This is my over-used ploy of getting his cooperation. Having the State Police do any lab work or background checks for me alerts them to the cases he assigns me.

"Just give me the damn glasses and get out of here."

It was approaching lunchtime when I left Avery's office and headed towards the State Police headquarters in Baton Rouge. I stopped for a fried oyster po-boy with bacon and Havarti cheese at Ye Olde College Inn on Carrollton Avenue before I headed out of town. I felt a little pang of guilt when I considered what Lionel Batiste was going to be offered for lunch.

I had to drive all the way to the capitol to meet with my State Police captain because the only thing he hates more than me is being in New Orleans. Being out of sight allows Captain Hammond to imagine that I don't exist and he doesn't care about the things Avery has me do to free up NOPD's own detectives. He is, though, insistent upon knowing about anything I do that resembles serious police work.

Captain Kenneth Hammond has been with the State Police since college. He is many years my senior, but remains a six foot tall mass of muscle and considers it his duty to set an example for those in his command. Hammond is on the State Police marksmanship team and runs ten miles a day. He wears a pressed uniform to work despite holding a position which would allow him to wear a suit.

I knocked on his door before poking my head inside. "Good afternoon, Captain Hammond," I said and opened the door when he didn't wave me away.

"Cooter," he ushered me into the office and locked the door behind me. He looked me up and down with his usual frown. "I know Chief Avery doesn't make you wear a uniform, but dammit is every day Casual Friday in New Orleans?"

I changed clothes after court. My shiny gold badge now hung on the belt holding up my denim jeans. I wore a short sleeved blue polo-shirt with the State Police logo under a light jacket. I carried my Glock 20 handgun and two spare 15 round magazines in a nylon shoulder holster. The ten millimeter pistol is not considered an authorized sidearm in either department I answer to. The list of such rules that Chief Avery allows me to ignore is just one of Captain Hammond's many issues with my New Orleans posting. Patrolling in my personal Cadillacs bothers him the most.

"I wanted to check in with you about a case Chief Avery has assigned me. NOPD detectives received a dubious tip about methamphetamine in the trunk of Esther Batiste's car. I think whoever called in the tip got impatient, because two guys wearing biker colors from the Black Knights shot up the Ford's trunk before the narcotics detectives could serve the warrant just to be sure somebody searched it. Chief Avery and I are convinced it was all a set-up to frame Lionel Batiste. He's running for City Council and he and his mother are always agitating about a number of things. I can't single out anyone they may have pissed off who'd spend so much money to get rid of them."

"So, are you telling me that you're investigating this as a frame-up?' Hammond asked me to confirm. I just nodded. "What steps have you taken so far?"

"I had Lionel Batiste arraigned on drug distribution charges this morning."

"Case closed. So glad you dropped by," my boss chortled. "No, really, what's your play going to be?"

"I need to smoke out whoever planned this. The only way to see what they intend to do is to let them think they can still pull it off. My plan is to figure out where the finish line is and meet my mystery man there. Chief Avery and I are presently trying to find the original source of the narcotics planted at the scene. I need our lab to look at them."

"Why bring the dope from a case in the Ninth Ward all the way here? NOPD has a lab. How much dope did they find on Batiste?"

Hammond's eyes widened when I set the evidence bag on his desk. It made me wonder what his reaction would be to the actual amount of drugs used against the Batistes. "I see what you mean about somebody spending a lot of money to do this."

Captain Hammond picked up the evidence bag. I had placed each of the bags of meth into separate evidence bags before labeling both bags with the same information. I then logged only one bag into NOPD's evidence locker. I was continuing my dangerous ruse by having Hammond sign a chain of custody form for this duplicate bag.

"I need to see if you can match this meth to other batches seized by the Drug Task Force."

"Sure, we can do that for you. I'll let you know what the lab finds. It should be sometime tomorrow, unless they were cooked in some new lab. That's not very likely."

"One other thing. What do we have on file about the Black Knights? I know them more by reputation than anything concrete." I was pushing my luck asking for help with both the drug analysis and intelligence on the bike gang. Hammond considers me to be more of an NOPD appendage to his command than the other way around.

"Not much." Hammond said and grinned as the silence grew.

"What will it cost to find out what you do know?"

"I'll show you what we know if you tell me anything else you learn." He typed something on his computer and his office printer began churning out a surprisingly short report a moment later.

"We really don't have much more than the basics on the gang. Nobody has ever snitched on them and their members don't leave the gang alive." Hammond explained. "I will tell you this much. They are violent just for the sake of it. They like to be bloody, but they have a way of being sloppy and inept about it."

"I've seen the inept thing first hand. Batiste's car was

shot up using bird shot."

"Huh, that's not their usual style." The shooting story would be getting spread far and wide as soon as I left the office.

At least the report contained their chain of command and their club house address. It was all I really needed. It was doubtful that I could prove the Black Knights were the ones who attacked the Batistes. It was a waste of time to press charges anyway. The damage inflicted was such that the most I could hope for out of a prosecutor, even Katie, was vandalism to the car and a firearms charge. Restitution would have been less than an average biker's weekend bar tab.

"Thanks, Captain. I'll get back to you after I talk to them."

"And I'll call you when I hear something from the lab. I doubt either of us will be of much help to the other, though." I started out of the office but Hammond had one last piece of advice. "Oh, and don't get shot by those idiot bikers. It would be embarrassing for all of us."

What he was really asking was for me to not be the one shooting any bikers. I laughed because it was silly of him to expect me to make either promise.

I had pushed my luck getting Captain Hammond involved in my case. I decided to push it a little further and arranged a meeting with Uncle Felix. Meeting him in Baton Rouge was a bad idea, if only because it was the one place it was riskiest to be seen together.

I called his office and they took a message. He called me back almost immediately, lecturing me on keeping my distance before telling me to meet him in a parking lot in the shade of Tiger Stadium. It was a short conversation we chose to have through our open car windows. He only took the meeting to give me the bad news in person.

"Your boss is in bigger trouble than you two know. The local FBI had no interest in opening their investigation. I imagine they have things of their own to hide." I wasn't about to tell him how right he was. "Someone above them wants to distract NOPD with the threat of a consent decree agreement while something else is going on. I don't know what that is or what I can do for your boss if he is just a cog and not actually a gear in what's happening."

"So, we're even?" It didn't sound like he was going to be able to do what I had asked of him.

"Heavens no," he laughed and rolled up his window. Avery remained in peril and the debt to my family's devil remained unpaid. This was exactly what my mother had tried to warn me about.

Chapter 21

I exited the interstate at Paris Avenue on my return to New Orleans. I drove towards the lake and slowed down as I passed a strip mall built out of cinder blocks at the very end of a commercial stretch of Downman Road. Having outlaw bikers as tenants had a negative impact on the mall's occupancy rates. The bikers were high on my list of people to interview, but I wasn't prepared to confront them just yet. It was possible the Knights were trying to lure the police onto their home turf. It was an obvious trap if that was the case, but I believed the Knights' merely intended to intimidate the Batistes. I could teach the bikers about intimidation if that's what it took to clear Lionel.

I drove past the clubhouse again after turning around to head to Chalmette. The Walmart nearest the Batiste's house is on Judge Perez Drive. The Batistes' loss of their Crown Victoria was going to have serious consequences. The Walmart is the closest grocery store to their house, but it's still a ten minute drive away. Every grocery store in Orleans Parish would be even farther away. Public transportation in either direction remained minimal and especially unhelpful when traveling with things like frozen food or to Esther's dialysis appointments.

The Walmart wasn't busy when I arrived. It was mid-afternoon in the middle of the week. I had the front end manager page the store manager; a fifty year old guy named Doug. I showed him my badge by way of introduction and the search warrant to show I was there on business. He was duly impressed by both and hustled the whole way to the security office. He handed me off to a young woman named Trudy and scurried away.

"Trudy, I need to see your parking lot footage from about ten until one yesterday afternoon."

"Alrighty." She went to a rack of digital recordings and picked out the ones she thought would cover what I needed. She cued up the first one. "Each camera covers a specific area. You could be here a while unless you know where to look."

"You seem like pleasant company," I applied what charm I have. She didn't know I was prepared to stay until I had what I needed, even if it meant she collected overtime. "Why don't we try the widest angles first and then narrow it down?"

"That's why I loaded this disc first," Trudy smiled and hit the play button.

The color image was grainy and marginally focused. Lionel arrived in the parking lot at eleven fifteen and parked as close to the entrance as he could get. Trudy set the machine to make a copy of the footage from the time Lionel parked until he entered the building alone.

The second camera's clarity was such that I could even read license plate numbers, but it wasn't so good that I could read any bumper stickers. I realized I was incredibly spoiled by the quality of drone and satellite imagery available in my previous line of work.

I expected to see bikers approach the vehicle and plant the drugs, but it was as an older model Chevy pickup truck with a weathered green and white bed topper that stopped behind the Crown Vic. The truck also had chrome rims and a moderate lift kit.

The truck blocked my view of the open trunk. The passenger who jumped out of the truck was very obviously a white male. Barely ten seconds passed between the time he popped the trunk and he closed it. Both of the men wore ball caps and sunglasses that kept me from getting usable images of either face.

It was possible that one of them made the call to Detective Frontenac's cell phone. I needed to account for who called the Black Knights as well, since they didn't plant the drugs. It was going to be very interesting if the same person had made both calls.

"What was he doing?" Trudy wondered. She busied herself with duplicating the footage when I didn't answer the question. I was frustrated that I could show the trunk of the Ford was opened in Lionel's absence, but not why.

"Can you find an angle to show what he was putting in the trunk? That one just shows he opened the trunk and fiddled around a bit."

"Maybe this will be better." She cued up a camera that showed the sedan's trunk from a profile angle. The angle was enough of an improvement to show a gray sack moving from under the lanky man's t-shirt to the trunk of the car. The angle also captured the lack of a license plate on the truck. This told me the perpetrators anticipated being observed. The ball caps made the perpetrators look like a hundred thousand other rednecks in that Walmart. Nobody was going to remember ever seeing them. I clung to a hope that the illegible bumper stickers might provide a clue. At least they would make it possible to pick the truck out in a parking lot if I ever saw it again.

Walking to his car, Lionel's body language gave no indication that he expected a drug drop, nor did he examine the trunk's interior; he just put the groceries in the trunk and drove away. Unfortunately, you can't determine knowledge or intent from a video tape.

I could have asked a crime lab to apply some sort of

enhancement software to the discs. I wasn't going to bother because nothing on the tapes proved that the shopping trip to Walmart was not an elaborate means of taking delivery of the meth. I would need to leverage the footage into an admission by the men in that truck that they had indeed planted the drugs. There is no software for accomplishing that.

Chapter 22

Katie called me about our date just as I was heading to my apartment from the parking garage around the corner from Strada Ammazarre. She informed me that a date at any place I own wouldn't be sufficiently romantic. I would need to spend money for her to think of dinner as a real date. She had a point so I promised to make a reservation.

Katie's recent divorce left her with a two-story house on Nashville Avenue that was built sometime in the late 1930s. Owning a large house made more sense when she was married and planned to have children. There were plenty of restaurants in her neighborhood that fit the monetary requirements for a romantic dinner date. Finding a good one that would be able to seat the two of us before ten o'clock even on a weeknight with such short notice was no small challenge. Clancy's and Norby's were both close enough to walk to, but neither could fit us in. I wound up using being a Jesuit alumni, of sorts, to get a reservation at Restaurant Etienne for eight thirty.

Etienne is the hard work of the Belin brothers,

who are the sons of an immigrant cook from France. The brothers and their chef attended the same private high school I attended before I was packed off to military school. I know the older brother from alumni events I still get invited to because I can afford to make donations to the school. Etienne's atmosphere and dress code are upscale casual, but I was going to wear at least a nice sport coat for the date anyway. Katie arrived in a barely knee length skirt and cowl-necked sweater, with her hair loose across her dark leather jacket. She was wearing calf boots that left a flash of tanned skin between where they stopped and the skirt began. She turned more heads than just mine as she approached the bistro's bar.

We had cocktails while waiting to be seated. The hostess led us to a two-top by one of the plate glass windows facing Laurel Street. I privately wondered who we bumped from such a prime table. Katie and I made small talk that avoided either of our jobs and watched twilight descend on the neighborhood as we dined on grilled octopus and a robust duck confit salad followed by Gulf fish in a citrus almondine sauce for her, and a hanger steak for me.

We were nearly through a second bottle of Beaujolais noveau when Pierre Belin stopped by the table. Both of the Belin brothers are too handsome and successful for most guys on a first or second date to compete with. Pierre spoke with Katie in French while I sipped my wine and contemplated both the idea of dessert and the silver BMW sedan parked across Webster Street. I first noticed the car when it pulled to the curb just after I sat at the bar. No one had exited the vehicle since then. I said nothing to Katie about the BMW, just as I did not acknowledge hearing her say nice things about me to Pierre. She was flustered when Pierre and I also exchanged greetings in French before he moved on with his rounds.

"So, you speak French," Katie blushed.

"I used to learn the local language anywhere I was posted. It was important to know what was being said around me."

"What languages can you speak?"

"French, Spanish, Arabic, Kurdish, Dari, Russian, German, and a smattering of Korean. I have picked up quite a bit of Italian from Tony as well." I saw no reason to tell her the number of hours I spend each year maintaining my language skills.

"You're quite the Renaissance man." Katie tried to joke her way off of the topic.

"Dessert?" I asked to help change the subject.

"I was thinking more along the lines of some ice cream once all of this has settled." She caught my quick glance out the window and turned her head to see if she could find what had caught my attention. "Am I boring you?"

"I'd never tell you if you were. No, that sedan caught my eye."

"Which sedan?"

"The one across Webster. The BMW, on the left, behind the Mustang. They've been there as long as we've been here, but nobody has gotten in or out of the car."

"And your conclusion is what?"

"I haven't reached one. I don't think it's your husband. That's a silver Seven-series sedan and your ex-husband owns a black Five-series. They are watching somebody, though. I'd say that whoever they work for has a small operation or they would have been relieved at least once by now."

"I suppose it could be Ray. He bragged that he had been hired to help some private contractor a couple of months ago. He said they had a bunch of former military guys like you used to be working for them." I was interested to hear more of what her ex-husband believed he knew about me, but this was neither the time nor place to talk about her ex-husband or my past. My attention remained on the sedan until Katie placed her hand over mine and I looked at her. "You're not much fun when you're working, has anyone ever told you that?"

"I've never had a really fun job." I couldn't fully explain that, but there were things she needed to know. "Actually my problem is what the doctors call hyper-vigilance. It's a form of PTSD."

"You're sister warned me that you're a hot mess."

"Oh, I'm a lot better than I used to be. I couldn't stand to be around people. Owning a restaurant did a lot to get me past that. I used to assume every car that cut me off was part of an ambush and that every parked car was about to explode. Now I just tend to focus a little too hard on what's going on around me to be sure I don't get surprised again."

"Considering what you do for a living that may actually be a good thing." She said this with a smile, but I could tell she was deeply concerned.

"Probably so. I'll also confess that what I did before I got here did not prepare me for a job with so much oversight or expectations to adhere to procedures."

"Neither of which Chief Avery seems to hold you to anyway. I checked up on you when I realized I was going to have to question you about Lionel's arrest. You've been a detective for four years, but have never testified in court. The credit for your work tends to get handed off to NOPD. Even that dog case you brought me a couple of months ago wound up pleading out, just like you said it would. Are you Avery's secret weapon or are you just trying to be some sort of super hero?"

"Hardly the latter." We both had to laugh at either of those terms being an accurate description of my relationship with Chief Avery or my motivation.

"Well you're going to face a rough day in court when Lionel Batiste goes on trial. You picked a hard-ass for a judge and Lionel won't let his public defender take a plea deal. He could get off with less than five years in Angola. It will be more like twenty years if he goes to trial."

"I hope to have him cleared before his trial starts." It

was the truth, but Katie's reaction indicated how seldom she heard this from an arresting officer.

"I knew you were you were up to something." Katie set her wine glass down and leaned across the table on her forearms to hear my full explanation. "Spill the beans."

"Somebody planted the dope in the car. They staged a drive-by shooting and then called 911 to be sure the drugs were found. Even Chief Avery agrees that it was a setup, and I will testify to it being one if Lionel does end up in court."

"Then why did you arrest him?" I could tell that Katie wanted to know the answer to this question from the minute I showed up in her office that morning.

"Because somebody went to a lot of work to get him arrested. They would have kept trying to bring him down if this didn't work. They probably would have shot someone eventually. Lionel agreed to be dangled as bait while I find out who the drugs really belong to."

"Why would anyone even bother with Lionel Batiste?" Katie was still working on the basics.

"I think it has to do with his running for the City Council. Nobody has made a run at him yet for battling against gentrification or for trying to write his book about the Convention Center, but days after he put his name in the hat to run for office someone planted meth in his car."

"Who do you suspect?"

"Everyone. That's the problem." I poured the last of the red wine into her glass and tried to let the topic drop.

"So, Lionel's arrest is really just a smoke screen."

"Pretty much. It's really more of a fishing expedition if you are looking for the right metaphor."

"Judge Rogers will not be pleased."

"I've had worse enemies." She already knew that.

"Well you'll have made a few new ones after this, trust me." Katie didn't sound like she would be one.

"And what about us? Are you mad that I'm using

your office to set a trap for somebody?"

"No. I don't know how long I can keep your secret though." Katie's expression did not show any sort of consternation or conflict about what she should do.

"This won't work if you blow the whistle. Lionel will be back in the crosshairs and I won't be any closer to finding out who set him up."

"I'll give you a week before I take it to my boss. How's that?" Katie and I both sensed the pleasantness of the evening slipping away.

"I'll figure out a way to make it up to you if you can do that."

"Fine. Keep in mind that his was supposed to be your way of making up for the last dumb things you did." I was beginning to realize she used such comments and her easy smile to vent without picking fights. I was just glad to see she was at least making an effort to salvage what she could of the evening.

"How about a nice weekend getaway?"

"Alone, or will you be joining me?"

"Well, if you're giving me a choice..." I started, and took her hand. She did not pull her hand away. She actually leaned forward to whisper to me with her wine glass hiding her face from the restaurant staff.

"You're getting better at this dating thing, just so you know."

"I'm still surprised you ever agreed to go out with me."

"Why? I've known you since I was your sister's babysitter. I always liked you." Katie was genuinely surprised at my own reaction to our dating.

"Well a lot has happened since then." We'd need a few days to go over everything on the list of those things in both of our lives.

"I know that. Your own sister calls you NOPD's kinder, gentler machine-gun hand. The things she used to tell me about you when you first came home are why I never reached out to you then." Now it was my turn to look surprised, and more than a little disappointed.

"But, I want to believe the nice guy I grew up with is still running the show inside that dark mind of yours."

"This is probably a conversation for a much different time." The servers were quietly doing their closing side-work and trying not to stare at us, or to send an envoy to let us know it was time to go. I paid the considerable bill and tip in cash and added a bit more to the tip for the time we had the place to ourselves.

Katie had walked to the restaurant so there was no question of whose car to take to get dessert at Creole Creamery on Prytania. She obviously planned on there being only one car and already knew where we would have dessert. The ploy put her within easy walking distance of her home if the date went sour. It gave me a reason to drive her to her door if things went well. This was far more thought than I had given the date. I believed I had done well just getting the reservation. She was right about my dating skills needing improvement.

I maneuvered her to the curb side as we strolled to where my car was parked. I hoped she didn't realize I did this so I might push her behind one of the parked cars while I pulled my handgun if need be.

Katie may well have understood exactly what I was doing. She glanced at the BMW down the street before she took a seat on the passenger side of the Cadillac XLR coupe. I pulled away from the curb and then made a U-turn in the intersection and headed towards Prytania Street. We grinned at one another when we realized we were both watching the rear view mirrors to see if the sedan gave pursuit.

Chapter 23

Lionel took my advice and surrounded himself with everyone he knew from the Lower Ninth Ward. The neighborhood contributes disproportionately to the day-to-day population of Central Lockup so there were plenty of his neighbors to keep him company. They all claimed to believe his story of being framed. Then again, not one of them committed their crime, either, as far as they were concerned. Most of the other defendants would soon be back on the street after making plea deals to lesser charges. None of them wanted to be the one to tell Lionel that he was headed to Angola no matter what deals he might make.

Lionel was lying on his bunk Monday morning when one of the Sheriff's deputies said someone wanted to see him. Lionel had no idea who it might be. I refused to give Esther a ride to see her son and was secretly grateful their car wasn't running. There was no reason to believe I cracked the case and he was being released. The only person left was the public defender assigned to his case. That attorney began their first meeting by advocating plea deals with a chance for probation or diversion to a drug court. He rejected the idea and walked out of the meeting. It was doubtful the novice attorney devised a new strategy so soon.

The deputy led Lionel to a table in the visitors' room where a meticulously groomed white man was already smiling at him. The man's perfectly combed hair and bespoke suit looked very familiar. Not familiar in the sense that Lionel knew who the man was, just what sort of older white man wears expensive clothes to do business with poor young Black men. Lionel couldn't contain a grin when he caught himself imagining the unexpected visitor as a hungry leopard.

His unexpected visitor proved to be a high-priced attorney Lionel knew he could not afford and certainly had not called. Lionel was sure I would have let him know if I arranged an attorney on his behalf. Something would have gone quite wrong with my plan if that were the case.

"Lionel Batiste?" The attorney handed Lionel his business card. Lionel nodded to confirm his own name.

"Your name is Bear Brovartey? What kind of name is that?" Lionel was impressed by the card.

"It's my nickname from my college football days." The attorney kept smiling at Lionel. Lionel had been fake-smiled at enough times to know that this was supposed to make him trust the man. It didn't. "I was retained to offer you my services by a party who wishes to remain anonymous. They have taken notice of your efforts to repopulate your neighborhood and would hate to see your chances in the upcoming election hurt by the fabrication of charges against you."

Lionel noted to himself how much the attorney seemed to know and how many words he used to express it.

"So, someone else believes I was framed?" Lionel's defenses were beginning to tighten rather than relax. The kind of people rich enough to pay for an expensive lawyer to defend him were rich enough to pay somebody to frame him in the first place.

"They don't even care, Lionel. They just want to give you a chance to get out of here and to have a fighting chance in court. Are you ready to go home today?"

"You're going to put up a hundred grand to get me out of jail? Today?"

"Your bail is being posted as we speak." The attorney motioned for Lionel to take a seat at the table. Lionel stood beside the table during their introductions, but he took a seat as Brovartey pulled a stack of papers from his briefcase and set them on the table. Lionel did not touch the papers or the pen on top of them. "This is my standard contract, Lionel. I assure you that someone else has already guaranteed payment of my fees, but you still have to formally hire me as your attorney."

"I just need to sign these papers and I can go home?"

"Lionel, you can go home whether you sign these papers or not. Signing this contract merely guarantees you the finest legal representation possible and the very best chance for a positive outcome in court. I have a great track record defending clients such as yourself."

"What sort of client am I?" Lionel thought to ask.

"One being railroaded by a legal system designed to crush poor Black men."

"You're the great defender of the poor Black man?" Lionel didn't want to laugh in the man's face, but he could have.

Lionel's trust issues extend well beyond the police. His late father was no role model and he was old enough to have been involved in the arguments and negotiations with the insurance companies and the Road Home grant trustees after Katrina. He trusted me only because his mother and aunt told him he should. All the same, he'll never fully believe me when I say I am on his side about anything. The only people he knows he can really trust, whether it be to have his back or to stab him in the back, are his own family and the kids he grew up with in the only neighborhood he's ever known.

"I'd certainly like to defend you," the attorney pressured Lionel. His tone lost a bit of its cheerful friendliness. The frost in the man's eyes over having his intentions questioned confirmed everything Lionel believed about his supposed white knight. "We can start preparing your defense as soon as you sign on the dotted line."

Lionel picked up the papers and signed them without even reading them. He didn't figure there was the option of any haggling over the terms being offered. Lionel also knew he needed a different lawyer to explain this lawyer's contract.

"As I understand it, you are charged with possession with intent to distribute two kilos of crystal methamphetamine. Have you ever been charged with possession or distribution in the past?"

"I have been, but it was for possession of less than a gram of marijuana when I was still a juvenile. I never dealt drugs, and I've been clean ever since my dad whupped my butt for the joint." Lionel had the presence of mind not to correct the attorney.

"You are a college student and a housing advocate, is that right?" Brovartey had no notes in front him, just the legal pad he was using to record Lionel's responses. Lionel felt Brovartey knew more about him than any stranger should know.

"Well, I have been trying to get people to move back to the Lower Ninth Ward."

"And you own one of those houses Brad Pitt built? You live in one of the most expensive homes in that part of town, did you know that?" Lionel didn't know that. He also didn't know how Brovartey knew his name was on the title to the house.

"I never really thought about that. We gave the folks at Make It Right all our insurance money and I helped with building the house. I don't know how much it cost to actually build the house."

"Almost four hundred thousand dollars. They could have built a lot of shotgun houses down there for that kind of money," Brovartey said in a faintly dismissive tone. "I guess you are trying to get others to make the same deal as you struck?"

"I got no control over that," Lionel insisted. He never felt guilty about having a roof over his head. His new home is built on the same plot of land that his grandfather built the house where Lionel grew up. This was the house water from the collapsed flood wall surged through during Katrina, killing most of Lionel's family. The attorney was beginning to make him feel bad for having accepted Make It Right's offer. "I just want for the people I grew up around to come back, and for things to be like they was before the storm."

"You know that's not going to happen." The lawyer laughed at him. Lionel no longer cared for the attorney's help, and even less for the attorney himself.

"You need to fix one thing in your stuff. I am only charged with possession of one kilo of meth, not two." Lionel said this just to see Brovartey's reaction. The disclosure sent a flash of anger across the man's face.

"What happened to the remainder?" the attorney blurted out.

"What remainder? There was only one bag in the car. I was framed, like you said, but they only hid one plastic bag with a kilo of meth in my car. Check it out."

"I guess I'll need to. I was sure you had been arrested with two kilos."

"Maybe that's what somebody told you." Lionel secretly enjoyed the mixture of frustration, anger, and confusion on the attorney's face.

"I don't usually get my facts wrong." Brovartey was not very good at covering for his being misinformed at moments like this. He paid his paralegals and investigators to be sure he had the most accurate and current information in these interviews. He expected his other minions to do what he told them to do as well.

The attorney shook Lionel's hand and gave him a copy of their contract. Lionel ignored the paperwork for the moment. He did, though, carefully study the business card again. David 'Bear' Brovartey worked for a law firm with offices in Lake Charles and Baton Rouge in Louisiana, and Jackson and Pass Christian in Mississippi. They did not have a branch in New Orleans and Brovartey had not said which office was his own. The card gave only a toll free number to contact the firm, but no street addresses for the location of any of its offices. Lionel cracked a grin as he carried the papers back to his cell. He had just petted a real live leopard. He had Brovartey's business card to prove it.

Chapter 24

I brought barbecue from The Joint when I visited Lionel and Esther mid-day on Tuesday. Esther certainly didn't need to be eating the heavily sugared and spiced meat, but I needed to bring something in the way of a peace offering. She was far happier to see the sauce slathered ribs and brisket than she was to see the cop who put her son in jail for five days.

"What do you want to do with Lionel now?" were the first words out of Esther's mouth when she opened the door.

"I just wanted to make sure he is alright and made it home in one piece."

"He did all that by his own self. No thanks to you on none of it."

"Chill out," Lionel shouted from his work space in their living room. He was busy reorganizing his notes about the debacle at the Convention Center into possible chapters. Lionel was buried so deeply in the details that he lacked the emotional distance to ever complete his book, even if Hendricks delivered on finding a publisher. Lionel's incomplete journalism degree was not going to be of much help in crafting a coherent story from all of this.

"How's the book coming along?" I asked him without sharing these opinions.

"It don't matter much right now. Mr. Hendricks said he can't even try to push it so long as the drug charges are still on me. I told him you're gonna prove I was framed, but he said he was still gonna have to wait 'til you did before he could sell my book. Besides, it turns out getting it off that wall and onto paper is harder than I ever thought it would be."

"I'll talk to Hendricks myself." This was a wrinkle I never considered when I arrested Lionel for what I still thought to be his own good.

"Tell him 'bout the new offers." Esther prodded Lionel. I wonder if either of them noticed the reversal in their roles since my first visit.

"Everybody else on the block has a new offer for their house. They are up to three hundred thousand dollars. We didn't get any new offer. And there's this thing, too."

He handed me a flyer somebody paid to have professionally designed and printed. The flyer encouraged Lionel's neighbors to kick him out of the neighborhood because of his alleged drug dealing. Whoever was plastering the walls and telephone poles with these wasn't waiting for a court to find Lionel guilty before passing their own judgment. The name of the group behind it was Neighbors for a Good Neighborhood. The storefront minister whose name was also on the flyer was well known in the neighborhood, but Esther swore none of their neighbors ever heard of this community organization.

Making up fake groups to channel public opinion about a position or person is one of the oldest dirty tricks in politics. Using a popular local figure to front it was as well. I had taken part in just such campaigns while trying to disrupt or influence foreign elections, back when I worked in the shadows. "I'll look into it.

Have any of your neighbors said anything to either of you about Lionel's arrest?"

"They ain't saying nothing thing good about you," Esther assured me, pointedly. "Everybody around here knows he's a good boy and didn't do nothing."

"Oh, you're gonna love this." Lionel told me as he rummaged around on the heavy oak table. He handed me Brovartey's business card and contract. The business card was printed with a three color design and raised letters. Daniel "Bear" Brovartey was employed by a firm simply called Caplan, Smith, and Anderson. I suspected he was one of a great many gears in a legal machine designed to grind its opponents down. I glanced at the densely worded contract and agreed with Lionel that Tulip was going to have to decipher it.

"I thought your plan was crazy until I met that lawyer guy. You're right that somebody must have a reason to be going after me." Lionel admitted.

"Tulip can make sense out of this for us. It's going to cost me a fortune in favors by the time we get you set straight again."

"Don't forget what you're going to owe me."

"You mean clearing your name isn't enough? My, but you're an ungrateful sort."

"You arrested me and you didn't have to."

"Look what we got because I did." I waved the lawyer's contract to illustrate my point. I was counting on finding a connection between Brovartey's law firm and Tribal Investments because they were the two parties I trusted the least. Linking either of them to the Black Knights would be the challenge. Lionel's wall taunted me with a reminder that there are often unseen things between points A and B, and that even the alphabet has its secrets.

"That's what you got. I have a court date in three weeks."

Chapter 25

It was finally time to pay a visit to the Black Knights. The outlaw bikers should have expected to be questioned about the shooting from the minute word hit the streets that they were suspects, but I still only had thin circumstantial evidence it was the Knights who shot up Esther Batiste's already battered Ford sedan. It was going to be interesting to hear the bikers' explanation for the flimsy evidence against them. The use of birdshot was unprecedented in the bloody history of the Black Knights. They had a preference for automatic and semi-automatic rifles, and never once fired a warning shot or waved a gun they didn't plan to use. There were also only a couple of times they hadn't handled their dirty deeds as a pack.

I borrowed a State Police patrol car for my visit. I wanted to look as official as possible, and to let the state's car take the brunt of any abuse the bikers decided to dole out. Two prospects were detailing a row of Ducati motorcycles when I parked in front of their club house. One of them immediately scooted inside to sound the alarm. Hopefully one of the members would instruct him about things like probable cause and illegal searches so he would look less panicked in the future. I nodded at the other prospect, who made a point of ignoring me, and entered the club house uninvited.

The bar's doors and windows were heavily tinted and it took a dangerous moment for my eyes to adjust to the gloom. I was a perfect target silhouetted by the blast of sunlight flooding the room through the open door. A well-stocked bar dominated the center of a low-ceilinged room whose drooping acoustic tiles were stained by water leaks and nicotine. Heavy wooden tables and chairs filled the space between me and the bar. There was a kitchen to my right and three billiards tables on the other side of the bar. Heavy double doors behind the pool tables led to the club's inner sanctum. More than half of the guys in the place looked like they spent the night there and were waiting until their hangovers stabilized enough to get astride one of the bikes out front. I headed to the bar rather than approach the office doors directly.

"I need to speak to the Grand Poohbah."

I was wearing a windbreaker jacket with the State Police emblem on the breast, but extended my shiny gold badge towards the less than friendly bartender. He was another of the Knights' prospects. The biker looked at the badge and then at me without any sort of change in the expression he had shown towards the dirty sink water he was staring into when I arrived.

"You got a warrant?"

"Nope. Do I need a warrant just to talk to the boss?"

"Maybe." My negative answer to his question prompted him to pick up a phone and punch in the number to reach whoever it was that fit the description of Poohbah.

The dossier Commander Hammond gave me listed a guy by the name of James Hancock as the current chapter President. The only thing more impressive than 'Jimmy' Hancock's arrest record was his nearly perfect acquittal record. He was thirty six years old with a string of misdemeanor and traffic convictions. His extensive indictments for witness tampering and obstruction of justice suggested some reasons for the absence of any felony convictions. I didn't ask to see Hancock by name just to see who came through the office doors first.

Jimmy coming first meant the bikers felt there was absolutely nothing to fear about my being here. I doubt the leader of the Black Knights would show any sign of concern no matter who kicked in his door. I was going to assume something worried them about my presence if anyone low on the totem pole came first. There would be a whole lot to hide if they sent someone to simply bounce me to the curb.

The reaction I created was a mixed bag. The doors opened and a guy matching the mug shot of Dennis Earlman motioned for me to come forward. I could see Jimmy sitting at the table behind him. Earlman had done time for assault and armed robbery before joining the Black Knights. This timing coincided with his continued accumulation of felony arrests, all without convictions. Whatever other expenses the Black Knights had, they invested wisely in legal counsel.

"What brings you by this morning, Detective?" Jimmy asked with practiced casualness. He made this sound sociable.

"I'm doing a bit of community outreach. I figure the community ought to be willing to help one of its own." I remained standing to the left of the desk rather than sit with my back to the doors as Jimmy motioned for me to do. "Someone is trying to make NOPD think the Knights shot up a car. You guys have a reputation to uphold and vandalism isn't your style."

"Well, I sure do appreciate you being worried about our good name. You're right, just scaring people ain't our style." Jimmy even laughed. "Besides that, none of us ever want to get Esther Batiste mad at us neither."

"That's what I told NOPD. The Knights have a reputation to keep and nothing about that shooting made you look good. Any idea where somebody might have come up with a couple of sets of your colors?"

"Would you believe me if I told you two of our prospects disappeared in Biloxi two weeks ago?"

"Wouldn't it appear to be a little too convenient if everything were somehow connected?"

"I think they just might be." Jimmy continued playing coy and I went on letting him do so. It wasn't like he was going to admit to any of his membership jaywalking, much less what I came here about. "Maybe somebody used those colors and bikes to make it look like we did that thing they say we did."

"Oh, so you aren't prepared to defend your turf?"

"I think we both know that isn't what happened." Jimmy wasn't amused by any suggestion of weakness.

"Do we?" I needed to prod him in hopes he would let something slip about either situation.

"There would be a whole different story to tell if we did that shooting. Do we look like the kind of businessmen who protect our interests with pea shooters?" Jimmy said this and grinned, as though he was proud of himself for having walked some imaginary line between confession and obstruction. Jimmy was also still trying to figure out why I was really sitting here.

"You don't look like either one." My response confused him. My smart mouth didn't help clarify things. "You're neither businessmen nor users of pea shooters."

This comment took much of the mirth out of the room. I saw the immediate change in Jimmy's demeanor. I would be lucky to ask one or two more questions before Jimmy cut the interview short.

"Tell me the story about your missing prospects." I probed in a different direction.

This story was obviously going to be their explanation for how they were implicated in the Batiste shooting. I hoped showing interest in the disappearance of the prospects might convince Jimmy to let me stay a while longer.

"The club went to Biloxi the week before last. We were staying at a hotel on the beach and I sent the prospects on a beer run. They never came back and we haven't heard from them. They haven't been seen at home or at work, either."

"That would have been a week or so before you supposedly shot up the Batiste's car, right?" The timetable of their excuse wasn't very helpful to my investigation, at least not to my theories. This timetable put a hole in my idea that challenging Councilwoman Adams prompted the shooting. "So, you've reported them missing, right?"

"No. I still hope they might show up. We've got guys over there every day looking for them."

"Let me suggest you get their girlfriends or families to file missing person reports. Today. Your story will shine a bit brighter if it looks like *you* believe it. Two of your guys disappear and your reaction is to treat them like lost toys? That getting out won't help your recruiting drive much."

"Thanks for the free advice. Anything else?" Jimmy was done.

"Give me a call if your prospects ever turn up."

I thanked them for their time and lovely conversation and made my own way to the door. Neither man said another word while I was in the room, but I am sure they had a lot to discuss when those doors closed behind me.

Chapter 26

Avery and Tulip were waiting for me when I returned to the bistro just before nine that morning. He had not let dining with my sister deter him from his usual breakfast portions. Tulip was trying to explain my rationale for having arrested Miss J's nephew to the distraught sous chef. I knew the arrest was going to upset her, but I hoped she would come to me directly with her concerns. She left the table after exchanging the briefest of polite greetings with me. She seemed afraid she might say something that would get her fired, even though I was the one who had done the questionable thing.

"She still doesn't get it. But she trusts you." Avery reassured me as he reached into his briefcase and pulled out a manila folder. "I also need to stop doubting your instincts about people."

"How so?"

Avery handed me the folder and went back to eating breakfast. He and Tulip both watched for my reaction. She had already seen the file's contents.

"That explains a lot." I barely opened the folder

before I had a reason to smile. Avery nodded but went right on eating. There was nothing to say.

The mugshot and fingerprints belonged to a much younger Two Crows Taylor. The name on both forms was for a person named Franklin Robert Taylor from Sioux City, Iowa. Being from a place called Sioux City was the extent of Taylor's Indian heritage. His skin tone came from being the adopted son of missionaries who had brought him home from American Samoa.

Taylor's parents lost control of him well before he graduated high school. Avery had no access to Taylor's juvenile record, but it seemed to be a safe bet that it was an extensive one. His lengthy adult record began with a string of home burglaries at eighteen, which is not a crime for beginners. I read through another five years of misdemeanor thefts, and small time grifter escapades before I was able to connect a single dot with his present identity.

Taylor's only felony conviction was for punching a drunk frat boy half to death in a bar in Birmingham, Alabama. He accepted a plea bargain for seven to ten years in the Staton Correctional Facility. His cellmate was a repeat offender his fellow inmates referred to as 'Badger.' The warden's report of the incident that led to this moniker claims Robert Wilson crawled under two tables to get to his considerably larger victim before attacking the man while he ate. Badger claimed to be half-Indian so the inmates gave Franklin Taylor an appropriately Indian-sounding nickname for his crime as well. A flock of crows is called a 'murder.' Two crows is not quite a flock, and he was only convicted of attempted murder for the frat boy's beat down.

Tulip and her researcher found more about the development company and its principals than I expected. Bristol Wilson was Badger's niece, and his attorney. Her mother was a member of the Ouachita tribe. That is what allows Bristol to validly claim membership in the tribe. Her uncle and Taylor have absolutely no such validity in their claims.

Taylor and Wilson chose carpentry from the list of vocational training programs the prison offered and held construction jobs in Alabama until their probations were completed. Tulip offered to have her assistant contact Alabama's parole authorities for a list of the companies they worked for, but there didn't seem to be much reason to do so. Bristol Wilson may have understood that the only way to keep the two men on the straight and narrow was to provide a legal means to channel their aggressions and criminal talent for manipulation. There was no reason to believe either man had been rehabilitated by their prison experiences.

A boom in the luxury condo market in South Florida gave Tribal Investments its start. Badger and Two Crows arrived on the scene claiming to be minority businessmen as members of the tribe that only Bristol could legitimately claim membership in, but she vouched for both of them. Two Crows looked the part and Badger dressed the part well enough nobody dared dispute their claims.

Bristol made the most of her male companions' interpersonal skills. Two Crows could talk the chrome off a trailer hitch, and Badger had no trouble making people nervous. This tag team approach made it possible to muscle in on half a dozen rehabilitation projects in Miami Beach's Art Deco District they were able to flip at handsome profits. Bristol kept her partners in check long enough to actually build an apparently legitimate business. They leapt from renovation projects to building huge new condominiums at the peak of the boom.

"So, they started as crooks, but they're clean now?" I didn't believe it, even if this was what the public records all indicated.

"When are crooks ever clean?" Avery dismissed the very idea. "There should at least be a penalty for impersonating an Indian."

"I think I might keep looking for something a bit more serious. Didn't you say that Badger guy tried to intimidate you?" Avery asked Tulip. He was fishing for any charges we could find to bum-rush the group out of town without too much of a fuss.

"Tried, yes. Succeeded no." We both had a laugh at the Badger's very poor decision to make a run at my sister. "He just pissed me off."

"Do you think they might have set up Lionel?" Avery turned to ask me.

"They seem to like doing the dirty work themselves, and neither of them looks like they could ride a motorcycle to save their lives."

None of us liked the developers, but not being liked is even less of a crime than being a make-believe Indian. They had not yet applied for anything under programs that favored minority contractors. In fact, they claimed they were going to spend nothing but their own money on the project. I remembered they mentioned going after tax breaks and bond money, but those would be gone over by regulators and weren't easily ripped off. I had a clearer picture of who ran Tribal Investments, and it certainly wasn't either of the two men. Bristol was the brains in an operation more noteworthy for its brawn.

"While we're on the subject of bad people and bad news, I finally took a hard look at the attorney's contract Lionel signed," Tulip said. I now understood her real purpose in being here.

"And?"

"Lionel pledged the house as collateral if the mystery man paying his legal fees backs out for any reason. Lionel could get all the way through his trial, be exonerated, and still lose his home."

"Well, that's not good." Avery beat me to voicing the obvious.

"What can he do about it?"

"I couldn't understand why the lawyer wanted Lionel to sign a contract with him when someone else is paying him to defend Lionel. The contract clearly states that the attorney is working on behalf of Lionel at the request of an unnamed benefactor, but it also pledges the Batiste's home as collateral if the mystery man paying Lionel's legal fees backs out for any reason."

"I'm convinced whoever sent the lawyer also set up Lionel. I think they're dead set on getting the house out from under the Batistes. I'm satisfied that whoever is after those houses is behind Lionel's situation. They just had to find another way to win."

"I don't doubt you." Tulip had already reached the same conclusion and my boss offered no argument to the contrary. Tulip reached into her briefcase and pulled out a softcover book. "You should take a look at this thing."

"What is it?"

"Alex Boudreaux put himself through law school by holding real estate seminars. You know, those get rich quick classes they use to stage in hotel ballrooms at fifty bucks a head. I found this used on Amazon and thought you would find it interesting."

"Very little about Alex Boudreaux can be described as interesting." I was trying to make a joke, but Tulip wasn't laughing.

"You'll find this fascinating. Trust me." Tulip slid the book towards me and excused herself. I got the impression that she used delivering the book as an excuse to meet Avery without me.

"Anything going on between you two I need to know about?" I asked my boss once Tulip was gone.

"The women in your family are worried about your having involved your uncle in my problems. I can call him and tell him to let things fall as they as may," Avery offered. It was obvious he hadn't spoken with Felix. I wasn't going to be the one to tell Avery what my uncle told me.

"Felix understands that I am the one who is in his debt, not you. Has he been able to help you?"

"He's managed to change the media's focus from the police gunning people down to an overdue discussion of the stress we were under after the storm. There is no way to sweep what happened under the rug, but I just hope putting it into a different context will help." Avery's legal exposure called for a lot more than hope.

I changed the subject to give him a high-points review of my meeting with the Black Knights. Avery was livid that I met the bikers on my own and not surprised that I came away with nothing very useful. He left after warning me against doing anything else so stupid or dangerous.

I retired to the comfort of the reading chair in the den of my apartment above the bistro to read Alex's book. It was titled *Real Estate Opportunities in Post-Disaster Recovery*. The blurb on the back cover promised to explain various ways to exploit calamities to the reader's financial benefit. I poured a tall bourbon in anticipation of what was to come.

Alex initially tracked a dozen substantial rebuilding efforts which occurred in the wake of massive natural disasters, beginning with the 1811 earthquake in New Madrid, Missouri and ending with the 1994 Northridge earthquake in California. Alex put forth the theory that such massive disruptions in the housing markets offer developers a brief window of time to upend the marketplace before the demand for a quick return to the status quo slams that window closed. Using his theory, Alex developed a blueprint for financial success using a targeted response by real estate investors and developers to reshape a city's demographics by transforming the neighborhoods of temporarily displaced undesirable 'elements.' It was an extreme variation on the stock market's maxim of 'Buy low, sell high.' The difference is that his plan was to buy up already cheap real estate and make it into something he could sell at a massive profit. He went so far as to sell the idea that affected municipalities would embrace the idea of doing so. Alex believed city fathers could avoid being accused of discrimination if they created a housing market that simply held minorities at bay financially. I did not finish reading the book. Reading it pained my soul nearly as much Alex's writing style hurt my head.

Chapter 27

I wanted to see if Alex Boudreaux was prepared to defend his college-year theories this many years later. What really interested me were his continued assurances that he had no connection to Tribal Investments, even though the Indians' business plan seemed to mirror his book. I could not accept this as being a coincidence.

Tribal Investments began building their empire only a year after Alex published the book. They were now one of the world's largest builders of residential towers for the ultra-rich, with prices for their condominiums starting at over five million dollars per bedroom. I was hoping that Alex would be willing to walk me through Tribal Investment's business plan for Jackson Towers and explain how such an expensive project could ever hope to make a profit in the city's poorest neighborhood. I was also looking forward to his explanation for why foreign billionaires would buy a condominium in the Ninth Ward in order to escape poor people in their own countries.

I found Alex in one of the homes in his collection of freshly renovated houses in the Holy Cross neighborhood. He was supervising the final staging of furniture in preparation for the investor showings. The interior of each unit was decorated in tasteful but neutral colors which the furniture fabrics matched perfectly. He was a craftsman at what he did, however objectionable I found that to be.

"Can you spare me another few minutes?" I asked as I trailed him from the kitchen towards the master bedroom.

"What is it this time?"

"I need help figuring this out." I pulled his book from my satchel and was delighted by his pained expression. "I think you may have been less than honest when we spoke earlier."

"I have never lied to you, Detective."

"That doesn't mean you were completely honest. I'll give you as long as you need to tell me everything this time."

Alex made no effort to conceal his obvious distress about speaking with me. He did not feel he had done anything wrong. He may have thought I believed he had and was trying to trick him into confessing. I could tell he wanted to have a lawyer, or at least a witness, present.

"Five minutes. Ten tops." I even tossed in a smile.

"Fine. Let's go to the trailer."

The last time a suspect kept leading me to the same spot it turned out they had surveillance equipment set up to record our chats. I didn't believe this was Alex's plan. I think the trailer was just his Happy Place and he felt comfortable there. I thanked him for the cold drink he handed me and sat down in an arm chair by the dining table, leaving him the sofa to cry on and room to walk around as need be.

"Here's the rub, Alex. You've obviously been exploiting the sort of situations you laid out. You find disrupted cities and buy abandoned or damaged houses to fix up and sell at inflated prices to the carpetbaggers. I get that and can live with it because I can't stop it. Now there is a bigger player in town and they seem to be using pages right out of your play book, but you say you don't know who they are."

"I wouldn't call it a play book, and I think you are

giving me credit for doing things that were going to happen anyway. My theories were based on things that had already happened, and what worked and what didn't work in each case. I had some ideas of how things might have been handled differently to get more lucrative results."

"So, taking advantage of tax incentives and government subsidized housing programs to build large scale housing that you intend to convert to upscale housing is an idea that could have come to anyone? Especially those builders who don't have your family background in real estate and a pair of degrees in urban planning?"

"Exactly what are you accusing me of?"

"I think you and Tribal Investments have a plan to divide up this part of town and drive out the people who live here."

"They might want to do that, but I certainly don't. I would like to see the place a lot nicer looking and safer, but you probably would like that as well."

"Am I supposed to say I like it dirty and violent? Of course I don't, but I think that can be reversed without displacing anyone."

"Not unless you're paying for it." Alex stopped pacing and once again grabbed his marker. "The only people who have the money to create the neighborhood we both want to see here are moving here from other places. They have ideas of what they want in a house and will pay to have modern conveniences, landscaping, and proximity to an area that supports their lifestyle. It won't be long before you start seeing restaurants and shops popping up near these houses, because these people have the money to spend in them that the current residents do not."

"Now you're saying that the big condos and shops the Indians want to build are good for you." I didn't bother hiding my sarcasm.

"Maybe. I think this could go a couple of ways in the end." Alex ignored my tone and began drawing a map of the area on his whiteboard. It began at the River levee and moved as far towards the Lake as the outflow canal flanking Paris Road near the interstate. The side boundaries were the Industrial Canal and the parish line. Claiborne Avenue was the primary route to the parish line from New Orleans, with St. Claude Avenue, running parallel but closer to the river, playing a secondary role.

"Here's the good thing that could happen. Tribal Investments would build their towers and shopping mall above Claiborne and I'll keep flipping single family homes and doubles south of Claiborne. Shops and cafes will begin to line Claiborne and St. Claude, maybe even stretch out along Paris Avenue all the way to the interstate. I am sure they intend to push the easy access to the interstate as a selling point in terms of getting back into the city. Our combined efforts will gradually transform the Lower Ninth Ward and Holy Cross into an upscale, young, white, and single community. Doing so will create a vacuum that draws investment through the neighborhoods stretching back to the Quarter."

Alex set his marker down and looked at the map he had just drawn. He was satisfied that he had made his point. He may well have even thought he had convinced me that this was somehow a good thing for everyone.

"And the people who live here now?"

"They'll get bought out, but at prices that will give them at least a decent down payment on something over in the Treme or off Broad Street in Mid-City. It's not like the city doesn't need poor people to do its menial work."

"It's just best if they are all crammed into a smaller and smaller part of town." I finished his thought differently than he would have. "So, if that is what you call the good version then what is the bad one?"

"When I told you I had not heard of Tribal Investments I only meant I had not paid them much attention. Anybody in real estate has heard of them in the last few years because they are making so much money. I think the City Council may have given its blessing to the equivalent of a Trojan horse."

"What do you mean? What do you think they really

plan to do down here?"

Alex picked up his marker again. This time he paused at each step to be sure I was actually following the scenario he set forth.

"They'll build exactly what they say they plan on building, but they are playing a long game. They can get tax breaks for putting low income housing into the mix. They can legally pick and choose who they put in those apartments. It would be a lot of elderly tenants with few kids and none with young adults still at home. They don't want tenants that are going to set deep roots in their units. Tribal can legally evict every tenant once the tax incentives expire, if they are doing renovations. They are under no obligation to allow the displaced tenants to return once the renovation is done, but they aren't planning to do so anyway. They've always converted any long-term rentals into vacation rentals in previous developments."

"Who is going to vacation in the Ninth Ward?" I scoffed.

"You forget. We're talking years from now. The entire area will be gentrified. There will be nightclubs, good restaurants and music clubs, and plenty of shopping right outside their door. It is a fifteen minute drive to the Quarter or the Superdome and less than an hour to the beach and casinos in Biloxi." He went back to drawing and creating an entirely new map of this part of town. "Gentrification will force out most of the families. That means the city saves money by not having to build any schools. Everyone has a car so the city doesn't have to provide more than minimal public transportation. Neighborhood groups will create their own security zones and pay for security patrols so NOPD won't have to come around without an invitation. The area goes from being a drain on the city to becoming its main benefactor, with higher property taxes and all that retail sales tax money. Do you think the City Council will even hear, much less listen to, any gripes about displacement or relocation from people that actually cost them money?"

"Cynicism aside, I can see this happening. What is the scenario you find so scary in all of this?" The man made sense but I couldn't form the words to admit it.

"Tribal is going to wind up dividing this part of town in two. They will control everything above Claiborne and leave people like me to renovate the old stuff below Claiborne. What makes this part of town so attractive is the Industrial Canal. It is a moat between us and the rest of the city, particularly the rest of the Ninth Ward." He began coloring in entire swaths of the area as he continued. "They might talk the city into abandoning the aging bridge on St. Claude; then the only way over here is across the new bridge at Claiborne. Imagine leveling a city block's width along Claiborne to build shops and restaurants. Doing that gives Tribal an excuse to build a sound barrier between the businesses and the residential towers. If Tribal builds a wall to do that, they can reduce how many streets open onto Claiborne."

"And so you get your enclave." I wanted to let him know I had read at least some of his book and was following what he had drawn.

"Two Crows' claimed the towers will have their own support system during his little show at the City Council. He told them they would open grocery stores, banks, medical clinics and restaurants. It means the people living in those buildings won't need to leave the place. That means they won't be spending money in the French Quarter. They may not even spend money in the neighborhood bars and restaurants."

"And you can't have that." I had to take at least one shot.

"Tribal's plan eventually kills its own golden goose. It's already happening in Florida, but only a few people see it happening. Tribal's business model is to eventually sell its condos for twenty to forty million dollars. The Eurotrash, Russians, and Chinese they palm them off on aren't going to be attracted to the thriving neighborhood full of dining and partying because they won't even live here. Regulators are already looking at condo sales the Indians made in

Florida that look a lot like money laundering. We could end up with an absentee population, so all those shops and cafes begin to close. The Millennials I'm counting on to buy my houses don't have any loyalty to the city and will go wherever the party heads next. That will start a fire sale of houses in the area and people will wind up turning their houses into rentals just to cover the note until they can sell out and just break even or take a small loss. Thirty years from now you'll have the same slum you have now, but Tribal and I will be long gone."

"So I should just wait until I'm seventy and this will all be over?"

"You don't strike me as the patient sort, Detective."

"Just out of curiosity, do you remember seeing any of the Indians in your workshops?"

"Like I said, they didn't have to read my book. Anybody greedy enough could have figured this out on their own. It's really just a matter of feeding the market without worrying about the consequences."

"You used to advocate for the Tribal Investments model, but that's not what you have been doing. Why is that?"

"For one thing I have never had the millions of bucks to build the initial towers. The other is that I saw there is an unavoidable end of these booms. The bubble needs a constant stream of newly rich singles to sustain itself. Any economic downturn, or just the homeowners getting married and having kids so they need to be closer to schools and day care, can crash the boom. It can happen if people just get bored. Gentrification isn't a bad thing. It's the shallowness and lack of roots of those behind it that make it bad."

"And having lived in so many cities is what makes you the expert," I poked.

Alex allowed himself to grin at this particular stab. We were both smiling, but neither of us was amused.

"I know. You like to blame me for all of this gentrification. Believe me, though, I am not your real enemy."

"You're just the arms dealer." Alex didn't find this to be particularly amusing either.

I really needed to be nicer to Alex. He was taking time out from destroying the fabric of the neighborhood to explain the benefits of his doing so, and they were benefits I had definitely not seen. Alex knew the damage he would do in the long term, but he planned to be gone by the time that happened. He was, though, on my side about needing to keep Tribal Investments out of this neighborhood if possible.

"I know they say that home is where the heart is, but my having no real home doesn't make me heartless." Alex said in his defense.

"Actually, the best version of that I ever heard was from my best friend. Tony likes to say that home is a place you would kill for." He has done more than say it actually.

"I haven't heard that one."

Few people ever have. Anyone who has entered another man's city and tried to change their culture unilaterally comes to appreciate how counter-productive that approach can be.

Chapter 28

I had one more stop to make before heading to Strada Ammazarre for Happy Hour. I needed to have a word with the preacher leading the campaign against Lionel under the banner of Neighbors for a Good Neighborhood. I was curious to learn why one of Lionel's staunchest allies in the fight against gentrification was now his loudest critic.

Reverend Billy Sharpe was not who one usually thinks of when they hear the term 'activist minister'. He came to the ministry in a circuitous route. His problems began with trusting one of his cousins. The cousin was a twice-convicted heroin dealer, but Billy agreed to give him a ride when the cousin called to say his own car was in the shop. They were pulled over Uptown for the all-too common violation of 'driving while Black' and the cops found nearly two ounces of brown heroin in the car, along with the pistol Billy kept in the glove box. Billy worked in the chapel at Angola during his three years' of incarceration, eventually forming a choir and sharing the pulpit with the ordained minister. I generally tread lightly around Reverend Sharpe because my father was one of the officers who arrested him; Katie's father was his partner.

Reverend Sharpe served a sparse congregation in a three room brick church blocks from the Industrial Canal flood wall until the Lord he faithfully praises saw fit to displace him with floodwaters of Biblical proportions. His new pulpit was under the roof of a former variety store on St. Claude Avenue, but his followers had more than doubled in number since the storm. Reverend Sharpe built this new congregation with the help of the gospel music show he began hosting on WWOZ radio after the storm. Most of the station's talent was displaced by the storm and his show helped to fill dead air time. It became so popular that it is now part of their regular lineup and he is known around the globe thanks to WWOZ's presence on the internet radio dial.

I knew Sharpe more for protest marches he and the Batistes organized against real estate developers like Alex Boudreaux and rallies to encourage the efforts of the Make It Right Foundation and Musician's Village. He and Lionel were always in the forefront of those condemning the renovation-by-bulldozer mentality of the city's leadership. I couldn't imagine what prompted Reverend Sharpe to condemn such an ally.

I tracked the Reverend down to a studio at the radio station. Most people know the debt modern music owes to the early Blues and Jazz musicians. Few of them give gospel music the credit it deserves for giving those musicians a place to hone their talents in the first place. More than a few of the best known Saturday night honky-tonk musicians played hymns in some clapboard church the next morning. The Reverend's own choir enjoyed transforming songs I grew up with, like Spirit in the Sky and Peace Train into foot-stomping gospel music. It was part of what made the choir from Sharpe's church one of the top draws at the Gospel Tent during Jazz Fest every spring.

"Good afternoon, Detective," he hailed when he noticed me standing behind the young sound engineer. He knew this was not a social call.

"We need to talk about this campaign you started

against Lionel." I said through the intercom. Reverend Sharpe held up a hand and pulled off his headphones. He waved me into the sound booth with him. I made sure the session's tape was no longer running before I joined him.

"Are you ordering me to stop?" he demanded. I wasn't; I wasn't going to debate him on the matter either.

"You know better than that, Rev." I knew he would find a way to fold my doing so into his next sermon if I even hinted about making him stop. "I just want to suggest you reconsider your position."

"My position is pretty clear about not wanting a drug dealer for my Councilman, or my neighbor. What part of that do you think I should say is okay?"

"I am well aware of your past, Billy. I agree with your taking a hard line on young men dealing drugs, but maybe this one time you could preach harder on the part about innocent until proven guilty. Maybe even toss in a little judge not lest you be judged."

"Do you really think Lionel Batiste is without sin?"

"I don't think I'm without sin, Reverend, and neither are you. But stop and think about Lionel for a second. Has he ever done anything truly illegal in all the time you have known him? Do you honestly believe Lionel Batiste is capable of selling pounds of meth in your neighborhood without anyone ever having said a word against him?"

Reverend Sharpe was not prepared to defend his reaction to the news of Lionel's arrest. He understood he was too quick in passing judgment upon an ally based on the mere accusation of his spreading poison to those the preacher considered it to be his religious obligation to protect.

Reverend Sharpe is a proudly devout man and a disciple of what he believes is the word of the Lord. He is also guilty of passing the Old Testament's intolerances through the lips of Jesus to serve his own beliefs, as many evangelists do, but is among the few to admit he gets carried away and may not always be right. My only purpose in making this visit was to convince him not use his literal bully pulpit to convince his congregation that

Lionel deserved to be banished.

"I admit I may have been driven by a fear of his being the very beast I do battle against. I would feel shame if it is a man with a badge who is defending the soul of one I have called a brother and not the other way around."

"Well, Reverend, I think the devil may have been whispering in your ear. This is a pretty fancy flier for a man with such simple tastes." I showed him the flyer Esther had given me. I did not think shoving the sixty-year old man against the wall and yelling in his face was the way to find out who was actually behind the campaign.

"I believe you may be right. I might have trusted the judgment and taken the advice of someone who wanted to use me for their own plans."

"Would that happen to be Delia Adams?"

"I been knowing Miss Delia since she was a baby in her mama's arms. Her daddy's parents were part of my church before I ever stepped up to the pulpit myself. The kids moved after the storm."

"Delia has brothers and sisters?" This was news to me. I also missed that his quick response did not actually answer my question.

"Just brothers, both younger. She all but raised those boys herself. Her daddy worked for the railroad and her mama worked nights at the Roosevelt Hotel while they was all growing up."

"What are their names?"

"Christopher and Samuel."

"Do they still live in New Orleans?"

"Oh, no. Delia's the only one still living here. She bought herself a nice place over on Royal Street some years ago. They all went to college. She got that degree in public relations and the boys got degrees in business something or another. They sell real estate over on the coast now."

"Really. Do you happen to know who they work for?"

"No. I never see them no more. Delia says they got their own company though. She's real proud of them and I guess they still talk all the time."

"I guess so." I wasn't done speaking with the Reverend about Lionel, but a large part of my concentration was already heading in a new direction. "Can I talk you into holding onto these flyers for a while? I think you might find yourself on a different side of this fight real soon and we'd both hate to see you look like somebody else's fool."

"True dat, Detective."

"You gotta have faith, Reverend," I reminded him.

Chapter 29

I had almost totally forgotten about turning the second half of the crystal meth over to the State Police Crime Lab. I was driving back to my apartment, ready for a long night of trying to confirm CSA Holdings was owned by Christopher and Samuel Adams when I received a call from Commander Hammond.

"Those test results you wanted are in. I hope you can make more sense out of them than we can here. You should stop by so we can look at them together."

Commander Hammond's invitations of this sort are rarely a good thing. He knows when one of his detectives is working an angle without telling him. I was running more circles around him than angles past him, and I began to feel the grip on my badge growing looser. I couldn't imagine how I'd break the news to Lionel if I were fired and the drugs my captain held could have vindicated him.

I drove to Baton Rouge the next morning at speeds above those posted for civilians. My XLR coupe is legendary among the department's patrol officers. The most I got was a wagged finger from one of them who gave half-hearted pursuit as I roared by with my blue light flashing. Commander Hammond could yell at me for breaking the rules about speeding if he wanted, but I was anxious to find out what he had learned.

The evidence bag and report were sitting on his desk when he waved me into his office. Hammond spared me his usual comments on my attire.

"I think you already know what I am about to tell you." My boss was not usually so cagey about these things. "What I want to know is what you have found out so far."

"I just found out that the Councilwoman who Lionel Batiste is running against has two younger brothers. They may be the ones buying the houses in the Lower Ninth Ward and I believe they paid someone to plant these drugs in the Batistes' car. It is a classic campaign dirty trick meant to ruin Lionel's chances against their sister. I have no proof right now that she was directly involved in framing Lionel, but it's something I plan to pursue."

"I wish it wasn't." Hammond sighed and opened the folder. "Samples of this particular batch of crystal meth have been found in a half dozen arrests in Mississippi in the past two months. They were manufactured in Mexico and smuggled into Biloxi in a container of produce. The Drug Task Force knows who is distributing this meth over there and would love to chat with you."

"Did they tell you who that is?"

Commander Hammond's face twitched towards a smile.

"Yes. And, no, I won't tell you. Go see them for yourself and get these things out of here." I started to reach for the evidence bag and folder but Hammond put his hands over mine and looked me in the eye. "And you be damn sure what you're doing. I am not going to bail you out if you say a member of the New Orleans City Council had anything to do with this unless you can prove it. You've got yourself in another pickle and I'm glad you're Avery's mess right now and not mine."

"So glad to have your support, sir."

"Go. And keep me updated." I placed the evidence into

my satchel and headed for the door. I know he only wanted the updates so he could be the one telling stories about me instead of hearing them from the other Commanders. I probably should have told him about the speed traps I blew past, but at least those stories getting back to him weren't going to be a big surprise.

Chapter 30

Katie invited me to join her for a late lunch. She had a case that had gone to the jury and nobody expected a verdict for a few hours. She wasn't just looking for a distraction while she waited. She also wanted to use the time to discuss our spending the weekend together.

The cafeteria at the Orleans Parish Courthouse is one of the nicer places to eat in that part of town. It is run by an affable older blind Black man and his fiercely loyal kitchen crew. I especially enjoy their tuna salad. The secret ingredient is minced jalapeno. The place is just one more example of how hard it is to get a bad meal anywhere in New Orleans.

"So, you want to take me away from all of this." Katie was in a good mood despite the prospect of losing her case. Since the storm, juries preferred taking a suspect's word over that of any NOPD officer. She was in one of her pinstriped power suits, which combined the very serious cut and pinstriped cloth of a tailored blazer with a pin-striped pencil skirt. Her long, firmly toned legs could hold any male juror's attention.

"Just for a day or so. I know how much you enjoy smacking into brick walls. What's your case today?"

"Possession of stolen property. The defendant claims he had no idea the guy who loaned him a new Mustang couldn't afford one. He can't remember the name of the friend and the defendant's prints are the only prints that don't belong in the car. He's boosted half a dozen other cars in the past." Katie went back to picking at her salad.

"What I have in mind is wining and dining you to your heart's content at a nice inn in Pass Christian. I read that they've reopened the Jefferson Davis museum and we could hit a casino or two if you want."

Katie intentionally took a bite of her salad and studied my face while she delicately chewed her lunch. I waited patiently for her carefully considered response to my offer.

"That all sounds fine. Do you know what I really want you to do?"

"Let me grant your wish." I knew whatever she had in mind wasn't something I would guess.

"I want you to explain why you're putting so much time into solving a case that doesn't involve a crime. Is it something beyond Lionel Batiste being framed?"

"Esther said something that has stuck with me since the day I went to see her about the offer on her house. She said that everything that's a crime is not illegal. I believe the constant push to keep the Lower Ninth Ward from getting its footing is one of those genuinely immoral acts that is not a crime."

"I see your point."

"Do you remember when the mayor had his press conference during the last election and he told people to write New Orleans as their home on the census form no matter where they were staying? He caught a lot of crap for it, but I've started thinking a lot more about what home really is."

"How so?"

"You know the phrase about a house is not a home. Well if that is true then what, exactly, is home? Is it a physical place or an emotion or both? Tony defines it as a place you would kill for, but that's Tony." I hoped Katie didn't think my friend and I were always this melodramatic.

"Well, if I say I am going home for the day then there is a street address I have in mind. If I say I feel at home somewhere it can be any place that makes me feel comfortable and safe. I can't describe it any better. But you've felt it, right? You go somewhere and you think to yourself that you would be happy if you never left."

"I've seen a lot places like that, but I never felt I was home. I lived half my life away from here, but every time I stepped off a plane in Kenner I knew this is where I belong. New Orleans has an electrical charge to it or something, and people seem to either be drawn to that sensation or repelled by it and leave as soon as they can." I tried to explain.

"I wouldn't call that an electrical charge. You can just look out the window of any taxi from the airport and know if this is this the place for you or not. It's smelly and dirty and nothing works the way it does anywhere else. That drives most people who move here insane. But they keep coming, don't they?"

"And they keep leaving," I pointed out and joined her in laughter. Too often these people blame the city for forcing them out as well.

"That they do." Katie went back to her salad. I think we both may have felt that we were turning something we fundamentally agreed on into a topic we might begin to argue about.

"What do I win if I am sufficiently impressive this weekend?"

"Ooh, impressive. I like your use of that word." She grinned and took another bite of her lunch. "You win my heart, you big lug. Is that incentive enough?"

"It certainly is." I assured her. "But, do you know what I really think this is all about?"

"What do you think this is all about?"

"Your ex-husband has obvious psychological problems

and you're worried that I might have even worse ones, based on what my sister and I have told you about me. I can tell you that's not the case, but I know I have to convince you I am a better person than your ex-husband was."

"You *are* a detective aren't you?" She seemed a lot less beguiling. "If you're so damn smart then what am I thinking right now?"

I studied her beautiful face. Her large green eyes were staring me down, but they were bright and seemed more amused than any other emotion that came to mind. The very edges of her mouth were also turned up in a barely suppressed grin.

"That I should shut up about your ex-husband while I am ahead."

"So smart," she chuckled and gave me a peck on the cheek.

Chapter 31

I could have waited until the following week before following up with the Gulf Coast HIDT Drug Task Force about the drug analysis Captain Hammond provided me. I felt pressed for time because of the impending Christmas and New Year's holidays.

My contact at the Task Force in Biloxi was a State Police Captain named Nick Williams. He agreed to meet for lunch at my expense and told me he wanted to include a DEA agent named Bruce Jenkins. We agreed to meet at eleven o'clock at The Sycamore House in Bay St. Louis. I love their wood-fired pizza and the place only serves lunch on the weekend.

The Gulf Coast High Intensity Drug Trafficking Task Force interdicts the flow of narcotics from Texas to Florida along the I-10 corridor. They also investigate the local production of meth and marijuana cultivation. My contact with them in the past was limited to helping them execute arrest warrants against suspects with a long history of violence. It wasn't that much different than my work rounding up high level jihadists in Iraq and Afghanistan. Task Force members have understandable trust issues dealing with anyone outside of their office, but Nick said the DEA was interested in seeing the evidence against Lionel Batiste. It was the first time the Mexican meth had appeared in New Orleans East.

Their interest sounded like it was much more about something else they were working on, but I hoped it would help my own situation. I was, in fact, hoping that other details they shared about the drugs would give me something to track down that very afternoon.

The weather was unseasonably warm so I asked for a table on the pizzeria's patio. I ordered a round of beers to go with the barbecue-themed pizza I ordered just before my guests arrived. The take-out business was beginning to back up the kitchen, and I knew I was the only one at the table with an open schedule after lunch.

"Tell us about this Lionel Batiste character." Agent Jenkins went straight to business. There was no banter about each other's mamas or the month of crappy weather we were getting a day's respite from. Jenkins was younger than the Captain and me and gave the impression that he was new to both the DEA and the Gulf Coast.

"Lionel's a Black kid in his mid-twenties. He's taking journalism classes at UNO and writing a book about the Convention Center after the storm. We think he got set up by one of the groups trying to buy the houses in his neighborhood."

"What's the name of the group you suspect?"

"They call themselves CSA Holdings and they have an address in Mobile. Have either of you heard of the company?"

"Yeah." Captain Williams glanced at Jenkins. He wasn't looking for approval to tell me what he knew. They would have already decided on the extent of their cooperation before they ever sat down with me.

"They've built vacation condos along the beach. They started in Waveland back in the Nineties and have made it as far as Destin. They took a huge hit after Wilma and Katrina came through. We think they may have borrowed money from some very bad people and are now stuck in business with them." The Captain was telling me little that Tulip's researcher couldn't cull from the internet, other than their financing difficulties.

"Look, fellas, I am glad to share information with you but this has to be a two way street. I'm not asking for the names of your informants or who you're focused on right now. I just need to know how and why the meth wound up in the trunk of a kid in New Orleans, and maybe who it is that wants to buy his house out from under him."

"Fair enough," the Captain decided. "I really can't tell you why CSA would want to buy houses in New Orleans. CSA hasn't purchased existing houses in the past and they have never developed any property that far west. I assume you know that the brothers who own the company are related to one of your City Council members."

"Yes, but my sources are sure she isn't involved in the company. Who crawled into their pocket when they needed the money?"

"A guy named Ronnie Hauser. He is what is left of the Dixie Mafia. Everyone calls him Junior. His dad ran things until a few years ago and now he's trying to fill a pair of shoes about two sizes too big. Junior has his hands into everything he can reach, and Katrina hurt a lot of people that he has gone right on hurting. The other local banks were slow to lend money to businesses trying to rebuild, especially anyone without flood insurance. Junior controls Edgewater Credit Union. It's a dirty bank for dirty people and their dirty money. Junior's credit union was happy to lend money, and even happier to grab part of any company that couldn't make their payments when business was slower to start back up than everyone hoped it would be. Now he has a part in about anything you want to do here. If you want to pick your house up and move it he gets a piece from the moving company he owns, from the concrete company that will set your new pilings, and from most of the contractors and construction companies you'll need to set it up. Junior has people on the docks and he runs the working girls in the casinos. He is what you would call well diversified."

"And you think he may have a piece of CSA Holdings?"

"We're sure of it. Junior's cement and trash companies get all their work and he has controls a lot of the subcontractors they hire. He is a tapeworm that barely keeps its hosts alive." I liked the DEA agent's visual analogy.

I reached into my messenger bag and pulled out a stack of photo-captures from the Walmart store in Chalmette. I handed them to Captain Williams and the young DEA agent and waited patiently while they swapped them back and forth. "Do either of you recognize the guys in these pictures?"

"I couldn't convince a jury it's who I think it is," the Captain said. "I am sure the truck belongs to Spenser Duncan. Doesn't that look like his truck?"

"It sure does," Jenkins confirmed and then grinned. "What did he do now?"

"I'm sure these two planted the meth. I just can't prove that's what they were up to, based on these pictures. I think they may have also taken biker gang colors off a couple of Black Knight prospects that went missing in Biloxi a week or so ago. They might have used those colors to make it look like the Knights shot up the Batiste's car."

"The guy in the picture is probably his brother, Jackson. They'd do just about anything if someone paid them enough. But, they wouldn't use their own meth just to frame a Black kid in New Orleans. I am sure of that." The Captain laughed at the idea. "If you want to talk to them they have a recycling place off I-10 near the discount malls. Our organized crime detectives think they are running a chop shop, pulling parts off stolen cars and then shredding the frames and junk into scrap steel. You can find them either there or at the shooting range in Long Beach. They think they're a pair of real gunslingers."

"Are they any good?" I didn't want to find out the hard way.

"If you don't want to find out, they do their drinking at a place called Gator Slim's over in Long Beach. They live nearby but I think they spend more time there than they do at home." Agent Jenkins was finally proving to be helpful.

"We haul them in for questioning every so often. Hauser uses them as muscle, with mixed results. They occasionally get carried away and cripple people we think Hauser only meant for them to toss around." Williams added.

"They sound like real sweethearts. I guess they are my best lead at the moment unless you guys have any better ideas."

"You won't get squat outta either one of them, but that's still more than you'll get talking to Junior. He'll hide behind his lawyer's skirts like he always does."

I had a sudden thought and reached into my bag one more time.

"Would this happen to be his lawyer?" I handed the DEA agent the business card for Bear Brovartey. He broke into a wide grin and chuckled.

"How'd you get this card?"

"Lionel and I set up a sting to smoke out whoever framed him. The lawyer became my lead when he showed up, uninvited, at Central Lockup to tell Lionel he wanted to defend him against the drug charges. Brovartey paid his cash bond, too."

The agent handed the card to the Captain as he spoke. "That is no coincidence. Hauser will use the lawyer to be sure the case goes any way he decides it should. Sooner or later they'll lean your kid over a barrel and get whatever it is they're after."

"That would be the Batistes' house."

"I still don't get the whole house thing. Why in the world would the Dixie Mafia want to buy a bunch of houses someplace like that?"

"I'll have to get back to you on that." I set the pictures and business card back in my bag and tossed cash into the check presenter the waitress left with our last round of beers. "Just as soon as I can figure it out."

Captain Williams and Agent Jenkins walked me to my car. Williams and I have known one another long enough that he knows my penchant for Cadillacs. Jenkins, on the other hand couldn't help running a hand over the sheet metal of the Cadillac CTS-V wagon's hood.

"This is your car?" His hand lingered over the CTS-V badging on the grill.

"Yeah," I shrugged and shared Williams' humor at the young agent's wonder and envy. "My other car is a Cadillac, too."

"Detective Holland here is the only cop I know that can't be tempted to take a bribe. He doesn't seem to need anyone else's money," Williams informed the DEA agent. I think knowing this is part of why the captain trusts me.

I tossed the keys to Agent Jenkins and let him start the car. The dual exhaust for the two hundred and seventy horsepower engine rumbled to life and I was afraid I might need a crowbar to get the man out of the driver's seat.

I decided to scout the sports bar in Long Beach where Jenkins claimed the brothers liked to drink. Two in the afternoon was a little early for the brothers to be there. I made note of how to get to it from Beach Road and then headed towards New Orleans. I slowed as I passed each of the lower end motels on US 90 in hopes of finding where the Black Knights were basing the search for their missing prospects.

I was almost to Pass Christian when I spotted four black Ducati motorcycles parked at a former Holiday Inn. It was a convincing sign that I had found them. Only the Black Knights could afford top end Italian racing bikes but have to stay in cheap motels willing to overlook their parties and noise. I took the fact that the bikes were parked in the middle of the day to mean the search might be over. It was also possible the searchers were still here because they were too afraid to report their failure to Jimmy Hancock.

The plan forming in my head involved confronting the Duncan brothers at their favorite bar. I didn't expect to get any cooperation, much less a confession, from either of them. I only wanted them to know they were linked to the plot to bounce Lionel from his home and that meant I would be a thorn in their sides for a while. I was going to push them until one or both of them gave me a reason to have them arrested, the hope being that the prospect of jail time might get them to flip on whoever set up Lionel. They struck me as easy targets for such a plan.

The presence of the Black Knights brought a different plan in my head. This one lacked the legality and simplicity of my original plan, but offered greater odds of success and shielded my own involvement. Ideally, I could find a way to free Lionel without having to explain my actions to Judge Rogers or even have to face Katie in court.

Chapter 32

Timing is important in almost everything we do. There had to be a reason three seemingly unrelated developers set their sights on the Lower Ninth Ward at the same time. Alex was the easiest to explain. His trail of flipped houses had been leading this way for years, so he was bound to show up eventually. It was the sudden and simultaneous interest of the Adams brothers and Tribal Investments that perplexed me the most.

It was easy to verify William's assertion that this was CSA Holdings' first project in Louisiana, and it was hard to think of it being in their sister's Council district as a coincidence. I believed their being under the thumb of an old school mobster was over-riding their efforts to keep Delia out of their problems. Whatever was driving them to buy up the homes built by the Make It Right Foundation had to be worth involving both their silent-but-deadly partner and their sister.

Tribal Investments was also new to Louisiana, but they also had a trail of projects which might have logically led them to New Orleans. Not even Tulip's crack researcher was able to link the two development companies to one another. I remained certain that there was a hidden hand or driving force that was determined to use one or both development schemes to force everyone out of the Lower Ninth Ward before the upcoming election.

This was a business matter, so I dialed the only phone number I could think of that might give me a lead. The business editor at the Biloxi Sun Herald was helpful; he gave me a name and contact number at the Mississippi Business Journal. The editor said he had some background information on CSA Holdings, but that the Journal ran a profile on the brothers and their business a year or so earlier and probably had more of what I was looking for.

I climbed the phone tree at the Journal for half an hour before I got a call back from Josh Gardner, the reporter who had written the article about CSA Holdings. I located the article in the magazine's website archives and made a couple of notes. The answer did not spring off the page and I was beginning to lose hope that anyone could understand what I was trying to find.

"What can I tell you?" the writer finally asked after I tried to explain the situation.

"I need a reason for CSA to buy expensive finished construction in New Orleans. From what I have read, they don't usually buy things that are already built, and they have never had a deal in Louisiana. I need to find a reason behind at least one of those deviations from their routine."

"There is one thing that might explain it. CSA recently made a deal on some land in Biloxi's back-bay from a condo developer from Florida. The condo guys ran afoul of just about everybody. Their towers were too tall and the housing density and noise were going to mess with a bird sanctuary nearby, plus people just didn't like them."

"Did they happen to be Indians?"

"How did you know?"

"We became their next stop. Anyway, you were telling me about CSA." I fully intended to return to the Tribal

Investments angle.

"Yeah, right. CSA took over the option on the land when the Indians pulled out. They have plans approved for some sort of expensive condo village, but they need to get cracking because it's more than likely that the next election will bring in a lot of people that don't want this to happen. There are two women running for City Council right now on platforms that include killing the project. CSA hasn't moved a spade of dirt but have already begun pre-selling the units for about eight hundred grand apiece."

"Isn't that a bit pricey, even for Biloxi waterfront?"

"It's not considered waterfront unless there is a view of the Gulf. The press kit says the houses are being designed by world famous architects and have all kinds of solar and green construction. You know, all the right words to get the rich tree huggers excited. I think they may even have a website set up if you're interested. Give me a second." I held my breath and kept my muttered prayers to myself while Gardner searched for the website.

"Look up TheWetlands.com. Does that look like what you're looking for, Detective?"

Pieces of my puzzle began to fall in place as the website slowly unfolded on my screen. The artist's drawings of the bay side cottages were absolutely the same houses the brothers were trying to buy. The expensive condos were set on high piers to avoid storm surge from future hurricanes like Camille and Katrina. A marina and a large clubhouse with an Olympic-sized swimming pool were among the proposed amenities.

"I do believe you have answered my question." I owed the reporter the exclusive on this, but I wasn't ready for anyone else to know the puzzle was solved.

"I think I smell a story in this. Am I correct?"

"I'm going to have to beg you to hold off until after the holidays. I think there are a number of developments about to happen that you'll want to include."

"You call me, or I'll be calling you next month."

I made a note to be sure to be I called him rather than

having him track me down. I didn't mind giving him some details for his article, but I knew Avery wasn't going to let me be quoted in print, even in an out of state publication.

I finally had an answer for why anybody would pay so much money for twenty houses in the Lower Ninth Ward. They weren't going to leave them in the Lower Ninth Ward. The plan CSA envisioned was brilliant in its simplicity and breathtaking in its audacity. CSA was being controlled by a guy who already owned everything the brothers would need to move the Make It Right houses to new foundations a hundred miles away. I am sure Hauser would find a way to peel hundred dollar bills off of CSA's profit at every turn. The houses could be hoisted over the Industrial Canal flood-wall and placed on barges using Junior Hauser's cranes and barges. The barges would transit the Inter-Coastal Waterway to Biloxi. The lifting process would be reversed at that end. Moving pre-built houses onto concrete piers built by Hauser's subcontractors should involve much less noise and disruption of the animal refuge next door than building from scratch.

The only thing Delia's brothers were certain to wind up with was considerable negative press and Biloxi's enduring ill will over disturbing the bird sanctuary. The city and state were justifiably proud of the work they put into restoring the nesting areas after Hurricane Katrina scoured them from the beaches.

I sat and wondered what would happen when the brothers couldn't persuade the Batistes and their neighbors to sell their homes. I was sure there would be serious repercussions. My job had just become to ensure any fallout fell on Biloxi and not New Orleans.

Chapter 33

The second call I needed to make was one I had to make on the burner phone I keep in the bottom of my satchel bag. I absolutely could not have any telephone record of my calling Jimmy Hancock. I initially reached out to the leader of the Black Knights with a text message, telling him to take my call from the number he wasn't going to recognize.

"You're being awfully sneaky, Detective." I have no idea what else he thought about my call.

"I'm just part of that world that works in mysterious ways. I have a lead on what became of your prospects, if you are interested."

"I'm more interested in why you're telling me this and not out making arrests if you know so much." The man wasn't dumb.

"This is out of my jurisdiction and all I have are names. They aren't going to tell me anything before their attorney shows up and tells them to stay quiet. I also only have circumstantial evidence, but you know how damning that can be, don't you?"

"Yes, indeed." The gang leader was warming to

the conversation. He may still have suspected my motives, but he wanted to know what I'd found.

"On the other hand, they might very well spill damned near everything if you were to be the ones to question them."

"You'd give them to us?" Hancock was back on the defensive. I am sure he was not the only one listening to the call wherever he was. Those around him were probably telling him to hang up to avoid the trap I must be setting.

"Loan. I would loan them to you. I would need them back and able to appear in court on Monday. I don't think I will ever make a case against them for taking out your prospects, and it's not my case even if I could. You want answers and, like I said, I need the pair in court Monday morning for entirely different reasons."

"What do you have in mind?"

"Stay close to your phone tomorrow and I'll give you an address somewhere in Long Beach. You show up and grab whoever I point out and then let me know where to find them when you're done. Can you do this and not make me regret trusting you?"

"I can't promise they'll be in one piece if we get our hands on them."

"The best advice I ever heard was to never take both of a man's testicles. Only take one. That way you always have something left to threaten him with." Hancock's howling laughter over Chef Tony's words of wisdom made me put a hand over the phone for a moment.

"I'll keep that in mind," the biker said and hung up.

Chapter 34

Katie was standing on her front porch when I arrived to pick her up for our weekend getaway. Tony agreed to loan me his beloved Audi TT so I wouldn't be squiring Katie around in a car with cop car plates or a station wagon. I realized I miscalculated my choice of vehicles as I loaded her luggage into the sport coupe's minuscule trunk. My own clothes wound up jammed behind the driver's seat.

I took a long moment to scan the street for the silver BMW or any other car that seemed out of place within eyesight. I caught Katie looking at me and hastily got into the car.

"All clear?" she smirked.

"Seems to be. I guess your ex-husband had more pressing things to do today."

"What makes you say that?" I was glad she chose to laugh rather than take offense at my comment. She was still close enough to home to call everything off and put any romance back to square one.

"It was one of his operatives at Patois, right?"

"Is that a guess or are you fishing?"

"I suppose it's a little of both." I admitted.

"He swears he isn't having me followed, and I believe him. He is worried, though, that I don't know how much of a mess you are. I'll bet he's heard some crazy stories about you from his buddies at NOPD." Katie was well aware NOPD and I shared low opinions of one another. One of the reasons for this trip was to give her a chance to weigh the negative things she'd heard about me with what she saw in person.

"I doubt he knows just how much of a mess I really am," I didn't look at her after I said this. I just put the car into gear and headed east.

Katie laughed at my comment and we were able to change the conversation away from the men in her life, at least for now. She understood that I was as nervous about her ex-husband as she was about moving forward in a new romance with me. Both had great potential for disaster, but I felt her ex-husband posed a threat of violence to one or both of us while my utter lack of skills at dating as an adult was only a threat to me.

Military tier-one operators have a particularly hard time dating, and an even worse time being part of a family. Death or serious injury are almost guaranteed if they stay on active duty long enough. They aren't the guys you send on easy assignments against soft targets. The mentality that it takes for an operator to be safest and most effective at their job is entirely wrong for wooing pretty women over a candlelit table. The erratic schedule and long periods of being not just out of touch, but also unable to disclose their location make long distance romances unwieldy, at least it had for me. Moving into covert intelligence work only worsened the dangers and secrecy. I could sleep with women within my tight circle, and did, because we both faced the challenges with intimacy that secrecy brings. I spent two decades with a reputation as a great catch in a strictly catch-and-release pond. Now I was over forty and picking up with dating where I left off at twenty. My first attempt at serious dating ended just before I began dating Katie. It had been an ill-considered hot romance with a movie actress whose assistant I found to have killed a man.

Chief Avery and my mother and sister are much more supportive of my trying to date a local girl with a common background, but Avery is not very good at concealing his anxiety about me dating a Louisiana State Prosecutor. He is afraid I might say or do something that could bring unwanted scrutiny to one of the cases he hands me.

It is fortunate for everyone that State Attorney Katie Reilly never discusses pending cases in private and instinctively knows not to probe deeply into whatever the Chief of Detectives assigns me. Our conversation on the drive to Pass Christian remained focused on how well I did with impressing her with my plans.

"Where did you book the rooms?"

"Room." I corrected her and immediately sensed that I was in trouble. "It's at the Blue Rose in Pass."

"And where are we having dinner tonight?" I was relieved that Katie didn't pursue the 'one room' reservation. It wasn't worth an argument and she didn't bother hiding her amusement with my sexual presumptuousness.

"Reservations at eight in Bay St. Louis. Have you been to 200 North Beach?"

Katie smiled and pressed her hand over the one I had resting on the gear shift. "Yes. So at least you got something right, honey."

It was the first time she had ever used any words of endearment. I only hoped she was being sincere when she used it. This was all very new to me.

"Sorry about the room." I turned and looked at her.

"Oh, its fine. You've slept on things a lot rougher than a bedroom floor." That arrangement certainly offered a way to avoid any argument. I might still be able to book a second room, but then I would be admitting defeat before engaging in any hand-to-hand combat. Speaking of sexual foreplay as hand-to-hand combat was going to be something I needed to be sure I never said out loud.

"We have to get up early, anyway," I said to get in my own jab.

"Whatever for? I've been dreaming about a morning with no alarm clock and a nice brunch looking out at the Gulf."

"You said you wanted to see what I used to do for a living. I thought I might give you a little taste of it with a run on the beach. You'll have fun, trust me."

"That's probably what the recruiter said to trick you the first time." Katie grumbled good-naturedly. She had no idea how close to right she was.

Katie ordered a cocktail in the lounge while I set our bags in the room. She did not want to change clothes or freshen up, whatever that actually means, before we headed to dinner. I returned by the time she had finished her Bushmill's.

"Whiskey?" I was curious about her choice. She only drinks champagne at Strada Ammazarre.

"They don't carry my usual. Are we set?" She chugged the tumbler of Irish whiskey, hopped off her stool, and took my arm. "We can wrestle for the bed when we get back."

Dinner went well. The restaurant is on the completely rebuilt waterfront in Bay St. Louis. Pre-Katrina, there had been a steep sandy bluff between the bay and the shops, galleries, and cafes in the cozy artists' community's downtown. The towering storm surge pushed sand and water many blocks inland and leveled the terrain. The business district was rebuilt with a nicer view of the Gulf, but it had lost a lot of the charm that the demolished buildings gave the place. 200 North Beach was among the few original businesses that were able to reopen. It was brighter and cleaner than its previous incarnation, having lost decades of patina during its renovation, but the food and service were still impeccable. Our reservation was for a table on the balcony, but the early evening air was chilled enough that I reconsidered the plan. The hostess was able to accommodate us indoors.

We window-shopped along the empty streets near the

picturesque waterfront to let the meal settle. We walked arm in arm and Katie would reconnect any time she broke away to look at a piece of jewelry or a painting. We bar-hopped for a while before Katie suggested taking a stroll on the beach near the hotel. I wrapped my jacket across her shoulders to fend off the cool air blowing off the Gulf. I used my own chill as an excuse to wrap an arm around her waist and pull her close. It was after midnight when I finally piled the duvet and a couple of pillows at the foot of the bed and passed out.

Chapter 35

Katie and I slept until mid-morning, having mutually agreed to do away with the morning run, and headed downstairs for a brunch of mimosas and omelets. The glass-enclosed front porch overlooks the rebuilt yacht club marina and doubles as the B&B's dining room. The yacht club's old wharf came to rest in the inn's wide center hallway during Katrina's devastating storm surge. Years of effort had gone into rebuilding the Blue Rose and its business. Katie and I were impressed by the recovery efforts everywhere we looked. Twenty miles of this shoreline had been scoured clean, but Mississippi's rebound was years ahead of New Orleans' recovery from spending weeks underwater.

"What else do you have planned for today?" Katie didn't sound like she had an alternative plan waiting at the tip of her tongue. "Keep in mind that you're supposed to impress the hell out of me."

"Would you be impressed by watching me arrest the guys who framed Lionel Batiste?"

"You arresting anyone outside your jurisdiction

would be impressive."

"Let me correct that statement. I plan to have them arrested and for Lionel to be totally exonerated by Christmas."

"I'm listening." Katie sat back and took a sip of her mimosa.

"I spoke with members of the Drug Task Force and they tipped me off to two brothers working for the Dixie Mafia. I think they were loaned out to condo developers who intend to move the Make It Right houses over here. Framing Lionel was meant to isolate him from his neighbors and to break everyone's resistance to selling out." I held back only a few details.

"Someone actually plans to move twenty houses a hundred miles?" This was the only part of what I had just said that didn't make sense to her.

"It's not that hard. The houses are metal framed; it should be easy to crane them onto barges and float them over on the Inter-Coastal Waterway. Another crane could move them from the barges onto new foundations." I intentionally avoided mentioning Junior Hauser's involvement.

Katie took a moment to eat a bite of eggs. "So, who plans to turn the houses into condos?"

"The condo project is being put together by Delia Adams' brothers. They're in debt to a guy who stands to profit from the site prep, house moving, and setting the new piers. The brothers will be lucky to see a dime."

"That guy sounds a lot like Ronnie Hauser." Katie took a sip of her mimosa to give me time to respond. I was wrong to try to shield Hauser's involvement.

"That's the guy," I admitted and then shoved a bite of croissant into my mouth. Katie's expression let me know she was going to overlook my lie of omission this time, but it would be unwise to do so again.

"Is there any money to be made doing this in the first place? They are paying too much money for houses they have to move this far. I don't see how anyone makes any money." She made the same miscalculation I did.

"The current offer on the houses sitting in the Ninth Ward is for three hundred grand. Their price as vacation condos here is nearly three times that."

"Okay, *that* impresses me." Katie smiled and shook her head at the price difference. "Do you really think you can you prove the brothers framed Lionel?"

I was at the end of the easy things to tell the prosecutor. I did not want to put her in any awkward ethical or legal position.

"I believe the Duncan brothers murdered two Black Knights pledges and used their colors to frame the Black Knights for framing Lionel. These aren't the brightest thugs, but their confession to either the murders or framing Lionel could spike the real estate deal once and for all."

Katie's eyes began to get that intense gaze they have when she is in the courtroom. "How do you intend to get the brothers to confess to any of this?"

"Their confession is just the start of what needs to happen. I want to use them to take down Lionel's attorney. Brovartey approached Lionel with information that only someone directly involved in framing him could know. I can link Brovartey to the brothers if he bails them out after I get them arrested. What would a jury say if Lionel's attorney was also representing the guys who framed him?"

"I'd love to be the prosecutor who gets to find out." Katie was thrilled at the prospect of cross-examining a crooked lawyer. "So, what's your plan?"

"I just need to get the brothers to pick a fight with me. They should be watching the Saints game tonight at a place called Gator Slims."

"Sounds classy. I guess this means we won't be watching the game on that big comfy bed upstairs."

"The brothers can wait if that was your plan." I wasn't entirely kidding.

"No, no. Watching you work seems so much more... what's the word I'm looking for?" Katie tapped a long finger against her chin as she broke into a sly grin. "Impressive? Isn't that the right word?"

"You are just plain cruel." I complained in mock pain
and changed the subject.

Chapter 36

I put the top down on the Audi coupe for the drive to Beauvoir in Biloxi. Jefferson Davis' final home and its adjacent library and museum are on flat ground facing the Gulf of Mexico. Unlike the historic older homes on Scenic Drive in Pass Christian, which sit above and beyond the wide sandy beach, this antebellum home was built with almost nothing between it and the water. That was made horrifically clear when Katrina's thirty-foot tall storm surge ripped off its raised front porch and nearly forced the museum from its slab foundation. It took years and deep pockets to rebuild the structures, and a considerable number of artifacts and period furnishings that were lost can never be replaced.

"I'm surprised you are interested in all of this." Katie and I were standing in the shade on the veranda after touring the interior of the home. I had not been here since I was a teenager.

"Why's that?" Katie moved close enough that I

reached out and wrapped her in a loose embrace. She made no move to break away and we looked at one another's faces as we spoke.

"You don't strike me as a Southern sympathizer."

"You are correct. "I was just thinking about our conversation the other day, about what home means. The real punishment inflicted on Davis and Lee wasn't their imprisonment or the loss of the brilliant futures they could have had. They nearly destroyed the nation, but neither of them deserved to end their days living in what amounted to exile."

"No, they did not."

"People think I had to quit my job because I got shot. Tony believes I got thrown under a bus by the man who recruited us. The truth is that I was ready to pack it in anyway. I was tired of the lie that our being an occupying army had nothing to do with why we couldn't control the population. It was like we were the flu germ and our leaders couldn't understand why the host body seemed so upset about being sick. Frankly, I deserved to get shot by the kid who believed he was defending his own country."

"Is that what happened?" Katie's question alerted me that I shared far more than I should have, but I'd said too much to just drop the subject.

"I'm sure it's what he was indoctrinated to believe. The man we had in custody was a former military officer who helped create a situation where Coalition troops couldn't be withdrawn without the jihadists bragging they made our government run away from the fight. His brother was part of the newly elected interim government so arresting the guy was guaranteed to cause big problems between Washington and the Iraqis. I was ordered to leave him alone, but I still wanted to question him. My team was ambushed while we were transporting him to do so." I tried to explain all of this without breaking the confidentiality agreement I was bound by or revealing any operational details.

"So, your habit of making a mess out of things

because you prefer justice over the rule of law is something you've always done. I thought it was something you started doing after you got your badge."

"I prefer to think of it as a talent rather than a habit." I hugged her closer and pressed my cheek against hers while I stared out at the calm waters.

"You would." She ran a hand through my hair, but she didn't ask any more questions.

The weather was so nice that Katie and I drove the convertible further east after we left the museum. She had never eaten at The Shed in Ocean Springs so that is where I took her for barbecue. Katie made fast work of a platter of pulled pork and baked beans.

"Do you want to know why I won't sleep with you?" Katie blurted out of nowhere as she snagged one of the ribs from my plate. My mouth and hands were full so I could offer only token resistance.

"Trick question?" I mumbled around the bite of food.

"Your sister told me you were sleeping with prostitutes when you first came home." I couldn't deny the accusation without saying my sister was a liar and I couldn't fail to defend my actions without looking like I didn't care what Katie thought. She obviously thought enough about it to bring it up during an otherwise enjoyable meal.

"That's her interpretation." I made a point of making Katie see that I wanted to finish chewing my food before biting into what looked like could be a nasty fight. "I was a mess when I got here. I could barely move my left arm, my face was still scarred and swollen from the reconstructive surgery, and I had night terrors I don't want to describe. I didn't feel all that lucky to be alive. I had not been in a romantic relationship since I was about twenty years old. It didn't make sense to me to do so while I was doing what I did for a living; I was gone all of the time and likely to die on any given day. So, yeah, I chose to let my Uncle Felix pay for the companionship rather than look for it when I got here.

They were dancers from the better clubs on Bourbon Street and I offered each of them breakfast the next day."

"A pair of real gentleman," she chided me. It was a needlessly mean thing to say after I gave her an honest explanation. "Are you still paying for sex?"

"Well, I bought you lunch, but you've made it pretty clear there's no sex," I tried to joke. Her expression let me know the joke fell very flat. "I haven't in years. You know about my last great romance. It didn't work out, but it did make me realize I am ready to find someone to care about that way in the long term. I'm too old to have kids, but I would like to think I can still find someone to grow old with."

"Why bother now? It's not like you aren't as likely to get killed as you've ever been." She had a point.

"I was a better person when I was with Amanda. I think I am a better person when I am with you. I know I don't do nearly as many stupid things anyway."

"So, I'm seeing you on your best behavior?" Katie asked and laughed. "Good Lord, you must be an absolute mess on your own."

"Fine, fine. What's your next question?" I asked. She just smiled and grabbed a second rib from my plate.

"That's it." She shrugged. "I could ask you about your life before you came home, but you've already made it clear you aren't supposed to talk about that stuff. I was curious to know how many men you've killed before I thought about it. I don't think I want to know that number. You haven't shot anyone in the line of duty as a cop, so I've convinced myself that you don't have an appetite for killing."

I started to say something, but she reached forward and put a greasy finger to my lips. This was a speech she had been waiting a while to make and not a conversation in which I might share my own thoughts.

"So, here's my deal, Detective Holland. We start fresh today. Everything in either of our lives, your career and my marriage to Ray, is now called 'pre-you' and we will never ask one another about anything under that heading."

It was as good a solution to our situation as either of us could offer. She was tired of me worrying about repeating her husband's mis-steps while stumbling about making plenty of my own. She had worn herself out waiting for my PTSD to manifest itself in some terrible violent or manic episode she wouldn't know how to handle. I was relieved that she cared enough about dating me to have found a way to set aside the issues that could have laid like a minefield between us. Now I could focus on demilitarizing my way of thinking about our relationship.

I let her drive Tony's nimble convertible coupe back to Bay St. Louis. She chose a route along back roads lined with tall pine trees and ramshackle houses that burst in and out of view as we sped by. I was impressed with her driving skill, but it may have just been sheer luck that kept us alive. We gathered up the items she spotted during our stroll along the shop-lined streets in Bay St. Louis the night before and headed back to the inn. It occurred to me that I would need to buy her a Christmas present, if she was still talking to me after the weekend was over. She had yet to see just how many stupid things I could do in a short amount of time.

Chapter 37

I don't know if Tulip tipped Katie off about my affection for supper clubs from the Rat Pack era, but she scored points by suggesting one for dinner. My father proposed to my mother at one called Annie's that was lost to Katrina. Vrazel's in Gulfport was also damaged, but the restored interior and upscale menu seemed largely unchanged from my last visit before the storm.

Our meal began with cocktails and broiled Portobello mushrooms stuffed with crabmeat drizzled with lemon butter before moving to French champagne and a Caesar salad prepared at table-side. Katie suggested sharing a bottle of Pouilly Fuisse with our entrees, which forced me to abandon the filet with shitake mushrooms in a brandy reduction I had my eye on. I settled, if that's what one could call it, for broiled red snapper stuffed with shrimp and crabmeat. Katie savored each bite of the parmesan-topped casserole of eggplant, shrimp, and crabmeat she chose after narrowing her choice to it from four other seafood dishes.

I risked ruining the meal by bringing up a subject we had touched on at breakfast. Katie may have thought I was joking when I told her about wanting to have the Duncan brothers arrested. She was right that I was well outside of my jurisdiction. I also wasn't sure whether or not she would consider the antics I had planned as being 'impressive' or flatly illegal.

"Drunk yet?" I asked as I poured the last drops of the wine into her glass. I placed the bottle upside down in the ice bucket beside me.

"Is that your seduction plan? You were doing fine on the strength of your witty repertoire," Katie laughed.

"Would that work?" I asked, but only half in jest. "I want to discuss the Duncan brothers."

"The guys you want to question without any legal standing?" She wasn't nearly as drunk as I hoped she'd be.

"The very same."

"Tell me your plan and I'll tell you how it's going to get you into trouble." The grin she flashed betrayed how tipsy she was. "I still might let you drag me into it."

"The brothers will probably watch the Saints game at a place called Gator Slim's. I thought I might get one or the other of them into a fight." I needed to judge her reaction to this part of my plan before I wasted my breath explaining the rest. "They'll get arrested and maybe the local cops will let me question them before they post bail. I could offer to drop the charges if they help me."

"Helping you means admitting they are guilty of something a lot worse than punching an off-duty cop from another state," Katie pointed out. The face I made was meant to show her that I understood my plan had some flaws, but I couldn't share my real plan. "Do you remember the two things I told you I am expecting from you this weekend? I want to get to know you better, and I want you to entertain me. I think seeing you try to pull this off might be funnier than going to a circus. I'm in, if you are serious."

I waved for the check. I didn't want her to order coffee

and sober up, and the Saints game had already begun. "Would you like to change clothes before we do this?"

"Oh, no, these are perfect disguises for a place with a name like Gator Slim's. What better way to bait a pair of rednecks than to show up this overdressed? Hell, I think I can take you myself." She put her hands up in fists, but was laughing behind them. I opened the passenger door and tried to kiss her cheek. She turned her head at the last minute and we shared a nice long kiss.

I agreed with her opinion that looking 'too good' for the place could be used to incite a fight with the brothers. We were certainly overdressed for watching a football game at a run-down sports bar in Long Beach, Mississippi. Katie's dress accentuated her cleavage and her long legs. I was wearing dress slacks, with a blazer and tie. Our clothing would be perfect for creating a scenario in which the Duncan brothers might try to run off Katie's weakling boyfriend. I was a little concerned that using this disguise might make it difficult to limit my fights to the Duncan brothers.

We arrived at Gator Slim's when the game was already into the second quarter. I parked farther from the front door than necessary. A small part of my doing so was due to driving the only expensive import coupe in a parking lot full of pickup trucks, muscle cars, and used sedans. The Audi was a borrowed car, and I did not want to come back and find it had been keyed, or worse.

My primary reason was unrelated to such superficial concerns. We passed a work van from a local carpet cleaning service as we entered the lot. I glanced at the driver, but not long enough that Katie took an interest in the vehicle as well. She probably would not have recognized Dennis Earlman behind the sunglasses. I had no plan for explaining why the number two guy in the Black Knights was sitting in a stolen van if she did.

I scanned the parking lot for the truck I saw in the Walmart surveillance footage. I was relieved to find it parked closer to the Black Knights' purloined van than to the building. Breaking into the Duncan brothers' truck would be incredibly difficult to do unnoticed if their truck was parked in full view of the building's large plate glass windows. I also needed to avoid fighting the Duncan brothers where a spectator might catch the van or its occupants in any video they shot of the brawl.

The Saints were in trouble before we arrived, but anybody rooting for the Dallas Cowboys in that crowd was doing so very quietly. We were literally the only ones in the entire bar not wearing some sort of Saints jersey or hat. It looked like our home team might not win, but they could lose this game and remain atop their division. The team they were playing that night was one of the big rivalries on their schedule. The Saints had long been the laughing stock in the NFL prior to Hurricane Katrina. The team's unexpected ascendancy in the wake of the storm gave the weary locals and evacuees enough inspiration to rebuild their lives and communities. They were now appreciated as being part of the soul of the entire Gulf Coast rather than just the local football franchise.

I recognized the Duncan brothers from the mug shots Avery gave me from the NCIC database. The brothers weren't much to look at and blended into the bar's other clientele, no insult intended. Spenser stands about five feet nine. The combination of his tan skin and jet black hair and beard make him look like the Lebanese merchant I used to buy rugs from in Kuwait. Jackson is lighter haired, taller, and noticeably thinner. The one thing they had in common was a lot of muscle and a taste for poorly done tattoos.

They were wearing faded and frayed football jerseys bearing the last names of former Saints players. Being such loyal Saints meant they might be focused on the game and not easily distracted. I also noticed that they were alternating shots of tequila with their beer. These two were going to be mean drunks. The bartender was watching them as closely as I was, which I took as a sign that he had seen them drunk in here before.

A well-meaning waitress squeezed through the throng and waved us towards a small open space near the bathroom hallway. It had a marginal view of the TV screens, but a perfect view down the length of the wooden bar. She took our beer orders and looked me in the eye when she suggested I take my necktie off and 'loosen up a little.' Katie wrapped an arm around my waist, but I felt her rubbing as she did so.

"You're not wearing a gun." She sounded concerned about its absence.

"I'm on vacation. Plus, we're going to be getting even drunker than we already are."

"What if they pull one on you?" Now I understood her point.

"Then they'll automatically go to jail. The two of them going to jail is the point of our being here."

"But, they might shoot you."

"Been there and done that." She did not find this at all comforting. It definitely did not make her laugh.

I paid cash for our beers rather than run a tab. I did not want my credit card statement to provide a record of how much we drank. I scanned the ceiling and behind the bar for surveillance cameras. There were none. That made it our word against anyone else's for how things unfolded.

"So, what's your plan?" Katie was still at that point of being drunk that leaves people easily amused. Her eyes were bright and she seemed about as keyed up as the players on the TV.

"We need to let the brothers get a good beer buzz going. I have to distract them long enough to start a fight, but that might be tough now that the game is on. I say we make our move at half time."

"Our move?" Katie asked, but squeezed my hand. I hoped the question was meant to confirm she was included in my plan and not a sign that she'd figured out she was here as my alibi.

Chapter 38

The looming prospect of the Saints losing to their arch-rivals in Dallas cast a pall over of the bar's patrons. A Saints drive late in the second quarter glued everyone's attention to the TV screens. I saw this as my best opportunity to return the meth to its rightful owners.

"I'll be right back, okay?" I had to shout this into Katie's ear over the crowd roar when Drew Brees connected on a short pass. She just nodded and kept her eyes on the game.

Brovartey was certain to make the brothers' lives difficult once the meth appeared in their truck. I sprinted to the Audi and retrieved the paper bag stashed under the spare tire. I kept an eye on the bar's windows to be sure nobody was watching me. The brothers were confident enough that nobody would bother their vehicle to leave it unlocked. I cracked the passenger door just enough to be able to reach behind the seat and drop the bag of meth from the sack. I was both alarmed and pleased to find two pump-action shotguns mounted on a rack behind the seat.

I closed the door and used the paper sack to remove my fingerprints from the door handle. I carefully folded the bag and dropped it into the trash can behind the unoccupied hostess stand when I slipped back inside the bar.

One of the reasons criminals like shotguns so much is that forensic labs have a hard time matching shot recovered from a crime scene to specific shotguns. NOPD's lab might be able to match these guns to shells recovered at the scene and the firing pins to the shell primers. Since the brothers were too stupid to drop the shotguns in a bayou, I held out the hope they were also dumb enough to leave their shotguns loaded with Federal-brand shells with the right shot size.

I managed to get back inside just as Garrett Hartley kicked a thirty four yard field goal and put some Saints points on the scoreboard. Those were all the points the team could muster on the drive. Dallas matched the field goal with a longer one of their own to restore the fourteen point lead as time ran out on the first half. The Saints' heading to their locker room left a roomful of volatile drunks with nothing to do for half an hour.

"Why don't you go get us another couple of beers, honey?" I handed Katie a ten dollar bill and pointed to where the Duncan brothers were standing.

"Why don't you go?" She was still pretty drunk. I pointed to the brothers again and she finally understood what I wanted her to do.

"Well, hold my purse then." Katie then performed a quick piece of gymnastics which always leaves me a bit amazed. She removed her bra without loosening her dress and hastily slipped it into her purse. She handed me the purse before she went to the bar.

Spenser Duncan took the bait when Katie shouted over his shoulder for two Michelob Ultras. The can of Pabst in his hand was an indication of his opinion of light beers. The look he gave Katie's cleavage made his opinion of her breasts no less obvious. Katie was able to simultaneously lean her chest forward and act as though she had no idea anyone noticed her breasts were on display. She rubbed herself against Jackson's back trying to attract the bartender. She didn't need to try very hard to get his attention. She waited until Jackson Duncan also began to stare at her cleavage before she looked towards me. I saw this as being my cue.

"I was looking for you, dear." I said once I took a stand beside Katie, placing myself behind Jackson's left shoulder. This set Katie to my left, and separated the brothers. Jackson would need to turn around to face me. Spenser was six feet away to my left and blocked by both Katie and myself. I didn't really care which one decided to drag me outside, but I needed to make sure both of them made it to the parking lot before the second half kick-off.

"Who are you?" Spenser snarled. Jackson gave me a very sideways glance, but saw me as more of a nuisance than threat.

"My name is Cooter. I'm pleased to meet you." I extended my free hand towards Spenser after making an elaborate point of moving Katie's purse to my left hand.

"His parents even gave him a loser name." This was Jackson's opinion. "Get lost, Coot."

The bartender finally brought the Michelob Ultras Katie ordered. I paid him as Katie reached for the beers.

"You don't have to go yet." Spenser took a firm hold on Katie's wrist as she took ahold of the beers. I saw her wince just a bit.

"Oh, I think we should. The game is about to start again." I said and handed Katie her purse as I put my left hand flat on her right shoulder. Wrapping my arm all the way around her would have shown far more possession, but holding her this way would make it possible to push her close to the bar and use my elbow against Jackson's head or face if his heavier-set brother chose to fight.

I was orchestrating each move like I was acting out a chess match as ballet. I wanted to limit this altercation to the four of us, and I needed to steer it into the parking lot as soon as possible. The bar patrons around us would lose interest in this spectacle when half-time ended.

Katie's position between the brothers placed me in Spenser's blind spot. His chair was too close to Katie to stand up anywhere but to his left, which would add his own stool to the obstacles between us. Jackson didn't grasp that he was blocked by the patrons standing to his right and by Katie on his left. I could control both brothers by doing nothing more than moving Katie one step forward or backwards. Jackson's head and neck were easy targets for either my right elbow or left hand.

"She's not going anywhere. You're the one that needs to get out of here before I bust your face open." Jackson demanded. Spenser tightened his grip on Katie as he contorted his upper body to face me. It looked like Jackson was the brother that I'd be heading outside to fight.

"Nobody needs to get hurt. We can find somewhere else to watch the game." I was keeping a close eye on the time.

"Get out of here." Spenser ordered, as though his brother hadn't just said the exact same thing.

"Come on." I tugged on Katie while I took a step towards her. Jackson could try to shove his stool straight back and into me, but I would have an easier time using my own weight to shove him into the sharp edge of the bar top. Spenser's face and neck were now within reach as well. I could not fight both of them, so one would need to be taken out of the fight before I engaged his brother.

"Take off. She's with us." Spenser gave me their last warning.

"She came with me. She leaves with me." I sounded as pathetic as I could. It didn't come naturally.

"You're the only one leaving, pal." Jackson snarled as he stood up. He shoved Katie towards his brother and stepped into the small amount of clear space between us.

Jackson was nearly my height and weight, but he worked with his muscles all day. I stay in shape, but my exercise routine is light duty compared to ripping cars apart for eight hours a day five or six days a week. I could see why Junior Hauser liked to use the Duncan brothers to hurt people.

The brute gave me a pretty good shove. I was braced for it, but let myself take two exaggerated steps back. There were four guys standing at a tall bar table behind me and I used them as my cushion. I didn't figure they would want a piece of Jackson's fight. I certainly wasn't counting on any of them to defend me from him. I straightened my jacket while trying to act surprised and a lot more scared than I was. I wasn't wearing boots, but I could use the heel on my loafers to snap Jackson's knee backwards with one good kick.

"Maybe we should talk about this outside." This would have been a suicidal suggestion for most people. "I don't want to make a scene."

The brothers exchanged knowing looks and Jackson pointed me towards the front door. Spenser led Katie through the crowd by her arm, walking behind his brother and what the brothers saw as being her idiot date. I could tell that her confidence in my plan was evaporating.

The narrowing distance between Jackson Duncan and myself began to concern me as we approached the front door. I took two long strides as we passed the indifferent bouncer and opened the door with enough distance between Jackson and myself that he couldn't push or smack me while my back was turned.

I kept walking until we stood between the first and second row of cars. I turned to face Jackson, intent on avoiding his first punch. Jackson didn't throw that punch. He had been charged with assault enough times that he knew to make it look like he was defending himself against me. I would need to make the first move before he could pound me to his heart's content.

"Take off." Jackson waved towards some point beyond the parking lot. His other hand was curled in a fist.

"Okay." I held both hands up as though I didn't want a fight. "Come on, honey. We have to go now."

"She's fine right here, aren't you?" Spenser wasn't letting loose.

"You let her go." I struggled to make it sound like an order I couldn't enforce. My normal tone of voice in these situations doesn't sound like I'm negotiating.

I was disappointed that more of the patrons weren't following us outside. The smartest of the regulars wanted to be able to say they ignored the fight when the police and paramedics came to pick up my pieces.

Jackson left me no choice, but I pushed my fists ineffectively against his chest rather than try to punch him. He was ready to block my punch and I saw the look of surprise when I was actually able to shove his heavy frame backwards. I didn't mean to do so. He glanced around to be sure there were witnesses to my having made the first move before he threw an uppercut punch. I twisted to take the blast on my left shoulder rather than my chin. It still hurt.

I continued exchanging my intentionally weak swings and jabs for Jackson's heavier blows that would leave me bruised. I was continuously backing deeper into the parking lot. Spenser initially hung back, but eventually began dragging Katie along behind us. My tactical retreat left us standing behind the brothers' truck. The Audi was at the end of the same row.

I did everything I could to keep their attention focused towards the building, and facing away from where the Black Knights were parked. I was going to have to start defending myself if the cavalry arrived any later than I planned. I was relieved to see the Knights' van begin moving slowly across the parking lot and timed things so I could land a solid punch to Jackson's nose just as the van stopped directly behind him.

The pain of his nose being broken, probably for the first time in his entire life, made Jackson howl before he charged me. I side-stepped him and did a swing kick to the back of his knees to take his feet out from under him. Spenser let loose of Katie to join the attack now that I had bloodied his brother. I ducked beneath Spenser's first punch as I brought my left foot up to kick his solar plexus as hard as I could. The air was forced out of his body and he was momentarily incapable of taking a breath of air.

The brothers were startled by my moves, but not nearly as surprised as they were when the van's side door slid open. Four burly men in ski masks leaped out to drop black hoods over the brothers' heads and pull them inside the van. I ducked as Jimmy Hammond emptied a revolver into the brothers' truck.

Katie was equally startled by this unexpected turn of events. I grabbed her right arm and hustled her towards the front door before she had time to get a good look at the van or its occupants. The handful of eyewitnesses to the fight from inside the bar were unsure how to respond to what they just saw.

"Should we stay and give a statement to the police?" Katie asked, which indicated her own level of shock. She knew the answer to that question.

I walked over to the bar and confirmed that the bartender had called the police. He asked whether I wanted a paramedic sent as well. I told him no. I asked him for two beers, which he handed me without charge, and I handed one to Katie. It would calm her nerves and having a beer in her hand might discount anything she would tell any of the uniformed officers that interviewed her.

"Can you explain what just happened?" Katie was not shy about making insinuations. She would need to have been a lot drunker to not know I played a part in the abduction. I helped her take a seat in one of the many suddenly open booths. The parking lot was emptying ahead of the arrival of the police.

"What do you mean? I was about to get my ass beat

when a van pulled up and took the brothers away. Who knows what all they're mixed up in, or who else could be looking for those guys. They don't strike me as being very popular." I couldn't maintain eye contact while I lied to her.

"I have no idea who kidnapped those guys, but I do know that you probably had something to do with it. I won't let myself get implicated in kidnapping or murder." Her concerns explained why she chose to sit across from me in the booth. I was going to have bigger problems than just losing a girlfriend if the brothers didn't turn up alive.

"You aren't implicated in anything. Nobody is going to give a good account of the incident. There aren't any cameras, plus everybody was trying very hard not to watch what was going on out there." I began assessing the damage to my body from the fight. I was going to bruise, but at least I was not bleeding. My left jaw was particularly tender.

Katie wasn't about to be placated. "Tell me you aren't using the Knights to do your dirty work."

"I can do my own dirty work. I'm just glad you're safe and sound." This deflection worked.

"Me, too." Katie took a deep breath and then let it out slowly.

She leaned towards me and began gently touching the red spots on my face where Jackson's punches had glanced off. I winced at a couple of those touches. She moved her hand atop the one I had on the tabletop and laced our fingers together.

"I don't want you lying to me, so I'm not going to ask what your real plan in bringing me here was."

"And I don't want to lie to you, ever." I lifted her fingers to my lips and kissed them.

"I should thank you for a far better than average date. Nobody has ever let themselves get their ass whipped for me before. You can fight better than that, right, honey?"

"Yes, dear." I squeezed her hand and smiled at her. She moved to my side of the bench and lightly kissed my lips, which fortunately had not taken a direct punch.

Chapter 39

Long Beach police officers arrived within fifteen minutes of the Duncan brothers' abduction. I thought it was an impressive response time to a bar fight at a place that probably gives them a lot business. The first three patrol cars arrived almost simultaneously. Detectives and uniformed supervisors were not far behind. A Mississippi State Trooper joined the parade and blocked the entry to the parking lot. The dust had settled, but the police presence looked impressive for the TV crews.

We had a while to gather our thoughts after the patrolmen arrived, so I motioned for the bartender to leave the game on. The melee had not lasted the length of half-time, and the game was still in the third quarter when the detectives arrived. They did not tell him to turn the televisions off. I noticed we were all sneaking glances at the screen to keep up with the score.

The Long Beach patrol officers were efficient about identifying and detaining any witnesses to the altercation. They cordoned off the Duncan brothers' bullet riddled truck and isolated Katie and me from the other patrons. Katie and I were interviewed separately by the small town's detectives. I was counting on Katie telling the young detective precisely what she had seen, and not to offer any professional opinions or to speculate about what I might have pre-arranged.

Getting the cooperation of the police in a different state is usually difficult. Trying to get these guys to help me investigate a crime in New Orleans that implicated Junior Hauser would have been impossible. Now, however, they needed me to help an investigation of their own. I had a bargaining chip.

"Are you sure you don't need medical attention?" The stocky veteran detective interviewing me seemed unconvinced that I was alright. I was holding an ice pack on my jaw, and welcomed the ibuprofen tablets the bartender silently passed across the top of the bar.

"I'll survive. I managed to miss the worst of it."

"That you did. Jackson has put more than a few guys in the hospital. Do you remember what happened?" This was the concussion question. He would call for the paramedics to look me over if I seemed confused made any excuses involving blurriness or bad memory to avoid being questioned.

"My girlfriend and I came in to watch the game. We had been driving around after dinner and came here because we had already missed the kickoff." That should explain how we ended up where we obviously didn't belong. "The bigger guy saw Katie and tried to run me off. I wound up outside with the other one. He was getting the better of me when some guys jumped out of a van and grabbed them."

"How many guys jumped out of the van?"

"I wasn't counting, but I'd say four or five. They were big guys and I moved right out of there so they couldn't take me as well." I used the same voice I used to convince Jackson he could beat me in a fistfight. The truth was I could easily pick every one of the assailants out of a line up or mugshot book. I instinctively looked for something specific to remember about each one, be it an earring, tattoo, or one guy's droopy left eyelid.

"Did the occupants of the van say anything?" This was another question meant to test my awareness as much as it was to get details.

"Not to me. They said a couple of things to each other. You know, things like get 'em in the van and hurry up."

"What else can you remember about the van?"

"Someone shot at a truck behind us. It was like they were aiming right at it and not at any of us."

"That's strange." The detective made a note that the Duncan brothers' truck had been targeted. It would be enough to get a search warrant to search the truck for any clues about the abduction. I managed to avoid giving him anything useful in the search for the van, such as the markings or its maker.

"That's why I mentioned it." I tried to sound more helpful than I ever intended to be.

"Back to your arrival. Where did you have dinner?"

"Vrazel's. It's my girlfriend's favorite place over here and we had a nice dinner. We had a couple of bottles of wine and had a pleasant buzz going until those two guys ruined it."

"How long have you been with your state police, Detective?" He was a sly one. I liked his style. One of the patrolmen must have run our names and the detectives were well aware of who we were before they sat down with us.

"About four years. I thought I had seen everything until today."

He wasn't going to keep buying my shocked and awed witness act for very much longer. He only had to figure out if I was deliberately lying or was genuinely too drunk to remember what happened. I had just admitted to a probable DUI, which wasn't that risky of a move on my part. He wasn't about to arrest me for it. My admission was meant to make me seem forthcoming.

"Are you carrying a gun today?"

"No, I am not. I am off duty and way out of my jurisdiction. I make a point of not carrying my gun or badge across state lines if I am not on official business. I have to act like any other citizen."

"Is that why you let Jackson Duncan get the better of you?"

"How so?"

"You might not remember me, Detective, but I remember you. You led part of a Drug Task Force warrant service about a year ago. Our SWAT guys said you were sent here specifically because you're former Special Operations and used to kick in doors for a living. I'll bet you could have laid out both of those guys if you wanted to." He wanted me know he was still trying to decide how much I was toying with him. I would get only one polite warning about obstructing the investigation before I was in deep trouble.

"On a good day you'd be right, but I've been drinking and am not dressed for a street brawl. I got them away from the building so nobody else could jump in. I only wanted to get my girlfriend back so we could get out of here. I saw those two as nothing but a pair of drunken redneck idiots. Going through life that way should be penalty enough don't you think?"

"So, you really don't know who grabbed the Duncan brothers?"

"I've been working a case where two guys wearing Black Knights colors shot up a guy's car, but we're convinced someone wanted to frame the Knights for the shooting. It was part of a scheme to discredit one of the candidates in the City Council race."

"How did you know they were being framed?"

"The evidence didn't match their M.O. Two bikers used shotguns with skeet shot to shoot up the car of a guy someone wanted NOPD to believe was dealing meth on the Knight's turf. The real Knights would have killed the dealer, not his car."

The detective turned and gave a long hard look at the bullet riddled pickup truck in the parking lot. Sharing details about Lionel's case was meant to plant the possibility that the brothers' truck contained narcotics into the detective's head.

"Have you ever seen or had anything to do with the Duncan brothers in the past?" The detective was starting to rephrase basic questions because he either thought he had missed something or that he could circle back around to catch me changing my story.

"No, I have not. I've heard their names but I've never laid eyes on either one of them until this evening."

"Had you seen their picture? Could you identify them?" He was setting a very nice trap. It was likely I had seen a picture of them if their names had come up as suspects in my own investigation. This was not a good time to bring up the Walmart surveillance tape.

"I've seen old mugshots, but I never gave the pair any thought when I came here this weekend. I didn't expect to see them in here, but I have never been here, either. The Duncans looked like half the twits in this place, and my girlfriend and I were just a bit drunk. Like I said." This is called a non-denial denial. Of course I'd seen their picture. That is no reason to assume that I memorized their faces. My interrogator frowned and stood up.

"Stick around a while, okay Detective?"

"I'll just sit here and watch the game."

The Saints were making their way down the playing field and still had time to score a winning touchdown. The season had seen more than its share of blowout victories, but the Saints have a history of making last minute bad decisions. This year's bad decision was to lose possession of the ball to an interception. It was that kind of night.

I was about to know exactly how the Saints' coaches felt. What seemed like a brilliant plan fell apart when and angry Captain Williams arrived on the scene. I did not foresee him learning about my scuffle with the

Duncan brothers until I was safely back in Louisiana and could blow smoke over the phone. I failed to consider that a Captain in their State Police might be called to the scene because of his position with the State Police, and not his place on the Task Force.

Captain Williams looked at both of us, but he stopped to speak with Katie first. He introduced himself and asked her and the detective interviewing her a couple of questions. His eyes were focused on me through both of those conversations. He did not look in the least bit happy with their answers.

The detective that interviewed me also answered Williams' questions, and shared his notes. I watched the post-game show. I wanted to look relaxed and to appear ready to cooperate, but I probably looked cocky about having gotten away with something nobody could quite figure out. Williams ordered the bartender to turn off the televisions sets.

"Good evening, Detective Holland." We were eye level to one another, but his stance was meant to show he was the one now in control.

"You didn't have to come out this evening, Captain."

"How could I miss this much excitement? You get in a bar fight with a couple of guys I tipped you off to and then they get abducted. I never want to miss an opportunity to see a bona fide coincidence."

"I was just out to show the lady a good time."

"Using a state prosecutor as your alibi is an original idea. Do you think she knows it's why you brought her along and got her so drunk?" Captain Williams was a smart man I needed to avoid in the future.

"She's not all that drunk and you can't look at those legs and believe I only think in terms of her being an alibi. I deeply adore that woman. What you are suggesting is offensive, sir."

"Well I won't step outside with you about it." Williams now seemed more bemused than perturbed about all of this.

214

"That's probably a good thing for both of us. Is there anything else I can do or say to help the detectives?"

"You've done quite enough as it is. I take it you two are staying in the area tonight?"

"At the Blue Rose in Pass Christian."

"Nice." He was still smiling. "You might need to book another night. I don't want either of you leaving town until the Duncan brothers turn up and we really know what's going on. You won't feel so cute about this if I have to charge the two of you as accomplices to kidnapping or murder."

"No problem, Captain." He was going to leave it to me to explain to Katie why we were not clear of suspicion. She was not going to be as happy about being made to spend another night in Mississippi once she was fully sober and began looking at things clearly.

Chapter 40

The bartender at the Blue Rose was kind enough to track down some quart-sized Ziploc bags in the kitchen and fill them with ice. Katie carried a pair of beers, not light beer, and left me to juggle the ice bags all the way to our room. I stripped off my jacket and shirt and propped myself against the headboard.

"I guess all my heroes got their asses beat today. First you and then the Saints." Katie laughed as she said this and helped me adjust the ice bags. This was the first time she had seen me with my shirt off. "You're really a bit of a mess aren't you? Are those the gunshots?"

She touched the trio of silver dollar sized scars high on my left shoulder. Three rounds from an AK-47 had been fired through my body at point blank range. I was fortunate they were fired at close proximity, because the bullets never reached their terminal velocity.

"Yes. I keep thinking about getting a tattoo to cover them."

"Don't. Just use them to remember you're not really invincible."

"Oh, I don't think that at all." I didn't think this was the best time to tell her I had nearly bled-out on the way to the hospital, or that I had flat-lined twice while on the operating table. She was satisfied with my telling her that the experience taught me life is fragile and didn't leave me thinking I was unstoppable. "And those are just the scars you can see."

"Are you trying to be deep or do you have more scars?"

"I've had a knee replacement and there are some shrapnel scars on my legs."

"So you're suggesting you are most handsome with the lights out?" Katie brushed her lips across mine and began removing the ice packs. They had largely melted anyway. "I like to look at my lovers."

"Oh, am I about to be given a status upgrade?"

"Well you're in no shape to sleep on the floor tonight." She said this as she carried the ice packs to the bathroom. She stopped on her way back from the bathroom and stepped out of her dress. "And you've certainly exceeded my expectations for what makes a date impressive."

Chapter 41

It was close to sunrise when the innkeeper rang our room and said Captain Williams was downstairs and wanted to see me. He did not suggest that I bring Katie along as well. I wouldn't have invited her into the conversation and the way I was being summoned did not sound promising. I was going to be in quite a bit of trouble if the Black Knights murdered the Duncan brothers after I delivered them on a silver platter. I was lucky that in the initial investigation none of the detectives, nor the State Police, were bothered by the fact that two thorns in their side were missing. Williams' main concern when we last spoke seemed to be whether he could be connected to whatever I was up to after having led me to the brothers.

"The coffee's fresh." Captain Williams said as I joined him on the empty front porch. He pointed to the percolator.

"I'm not a coffee drinker. Caffeine is not my friend." I made a hand motion that indicated the jitters it could give my shooting hand. "What is so important it can't wait for the sun to come up?"

"I need you to come to the station with me." That did

not sound like an invitation. "We have the Duncan brothers in custody and they refuse to speak with anyone until they talk to you."

"Where did you find them?" I tried not to look anywhere near as relived as I was that the pair were still alive.

"They were at the bottom of a pair of holes someone had dug to dispose of two other bodies. Judging by the decomposition I'd say the dead guys have been in the sand a couple of weeks."

"Any idea whose bodies?"

"I have all kinds of theories right now. That's why I need you to talk to these knuckleheads and see what has them so spooked."

"Spooked?" That's not a typical reaction to being interrogated. Someone had really gotten to them.

"They are afraid of something or someone. I imagine lying atop a decomposing body for a few hours might be a real big part of their emotional problems."

"What's your thought on that weirdness?"

"I think the brothers were snatched by the Black Knights and roughed up until they showed them where they buried the bodies of the bikers' missing prospects. I think all of this ties into your case and I think you have a bigger role in this evening than you will ever admit, or than I ever want to know."

Captain Williams wasn't interested in making me lie to him any further about how Katie and I crossed paths with the Duncan brothers. We both knew it was no coincidence, and knowing that only left a conspiracy to explain why the brothers were abducted in the midst of my fight with Jackson Duncan.

I stood up and headed back upstairs. "Let me tell Katie where I'm headed and I'll be ready."

"She should come along." Captain Williams did his best to make it sound like a suggestion, but his tone made it much more of an order. I did not like what involving Katie in this might mean.

I woke her and told her my missing assailants were in

police custody and we needed to go to the station to identify them. I added that I was going to get to question them about framing Lionel Batiste. She made no comment on the early hour as she put on jeans and a light sweater. She washed her face, but was prepared to face the day wearing no make-up and a ball cap. She greeted Captain Williams with a smile and poured herself a cup of coffee in a disposable cup before we followed the Captain to his Acadia SUV.

Chapter 42

Captain Williams drove us to the State Police headquarters where Spenser and Jackson Duncan were being held. The brothers had been allowed to shower and were given jail jumpsuits for clean clothes. Neither of them were charged with a crime. The local prosecutor had seventy-two hours to decide how many, and which, felonies the brothers would face.

"Has either of them changed their mind about talking with Holland?" Williams asked the detective who greeted us. It was the same one who had interviewed me at the bar.

"No, sir. They still insist on speaking with him before will even make a statement." The detective and the state police captain looked at me as though I knew why this was. I was doing my best not to look like I did.

"What can you tell me about finding them? That may have something to do with why they only want to talk to me." I studied the two Mississippi lawmen for any sign that they had figured out my part in this and were laying a trap.

"We received a phone tip and found them zip-tied naked to the bodies of two dead Black guys in a construction area. They confessed to murdering the guys we found them zip-tied to and then Spenser said he would only talk to you. Jackson hasn't said anything since he was sedated. He was nearly catatonic when we pulled him out of the hole. We also found a kilo of meth under the seat of their truck at the bar that Spenser swears was planted there. You didn't happen to lose a kilo of meth during your fight did you?" The detective didn't find any of this to be very funny.

"My hands were kind of full. Katie can tell you she didn't see me anywhere near the truck until Jackson and I started fighting." Katie nodded her head to this but said nothing more in my defense. She also knows a qualifying statement when she hears one. Her not seeing me near the truck is not the same as me truly not being "anywhere near the truck."

"We'd like to tie them to the dope, but having Spenser's confession gives us a solid case for homicide. There's not a lot else we need to charge them with. There is the fight they had with you, but that makes you look as bad as it does them." Captain Williams looked at me when he said this.

I now understood why there was in no interest in pursuing the possibility I planted the meth in the brothers' truck. Williams finally had something to charge them with they couldn't beat in court. It would be nearly impossible for Spenser to retract his grave-side confession to murder.

"Feel free to add assaulting a police officer." I pointed to my slightly swollen jaw. "I have no problem with that."

"We're going to let that slide. I don't want you to have to come back to testify. I don't think I even want you in my state ever again after tonight." I would have appreciated a little support from Katie right then, but she shared the Captain's suspicions and let him do the talking. She may have still been envisioning the Duncan brothers strapped to weeks-old corpses in a sandy hole.

"Let's go see Spenser." I still figured he was the toughest of the pair. I could figure out how to push his kid brother's buttons by pushing Spenser's during my interview. Captain Williams led us down a hallway to the second interrogation room.

"I should sit in with you." Katie broke her stony silence as I started to open the door.

"You don't have to."

"I can convince him that we are putting together a case against him in Louisiana."

"Aren't we?" Everything I had done to this point had been to make certain Lionel was exonerated and those who framed him were brought to justice.

"Don't count on it. These two being arrested is only front page news in Mississippi. The most Louisiana might bring against them are firearms charges that require finding the guns they used and a misdemeanor vandalism charge for having shot up the Batistes' car. I don't know that we can convince a jury these bozos were smart enough to frame Lionel. We would have to wait until Mississippi tried them anyway; then they would have to serve their sentence here before they did time in Louisiana. All we need to do is to find a way to get them to confess to framing Lionel so I can use their statements to get the charges dropped."

"No, that's not all we need." I was disappointed about her position. "I still need to know who ordered them to frame Lionel. Can you make a case against that person?"

"Using these two as witnesses? Hah!"

"You are just no fun, Prosecutor."

"We'll be taping all of this. Try to stick to procedures, Detective." I didn't need the Captain's advice.

"No problem." I was beginning to dislike the Captain. He may have had plenty of suspicions about me, but I didn't appreciate his impugning my abilities while my prospective new girlfriend was within earshot. She borrowed a notepad and pen and followed me into the interrogation room.

Spenser Duncan was handcuffed to a metal table. He could take sips through a straw in the plastic cup of ice water someone had been kind enough to provide. He looked like he had been through a wringer, and he may well have been. His freshly washed hair was still a tangled mess, and I saw cuts and bruises anywhere he had exposed skin. His expression reminded me of a dog that had come to expect being beaten with a belt every time it saw its owner. He flinched as I walked behind him before I sat down.

Spenser began apologizing the moment he saw me. "I'm sorry about the bar thing. Honest, we didn't know you was a cop. We'd been drinking and I guess we let things get out of hand."

"Apology accepted, but it's not something that easy to forget." I tried to find a facial expression that best showed his brother's handiwork. "I am Detective Cooter Holland with the Louisiana State Police and this is Katherine O'Reilly. She is an Assistant Prosecutor with the Louisiana State Attorney General's Office. What's so important that you won't talk to the local cops until you talk to me?"

"I want to be tried here and not in New Orleans. I'll tell you anything you want to know about what we done over there but only if you'll agree to let them try us here." Spenser was understandably fearful about being sent to Angola. The Black Knights have connections there and assaulting a state trooper and state prosecutor would not earn him a light hand from the guards, either.

"Are you sure you don't want your attorney with you?" Katie had her pad open but had not started writing. He still had that right whether Katie decided to prosecute him or not, and she could use nothing he told us unless he waived the right to have counsel present. "Have they Mirandized you yet?"

"Yeah, but I already know my rights. I don't want to see my attorney until I have talked to you, and I don't want you to tell him what I'm telling you."

This was the first time either of us heard a suspect

ask that his attorney not be told what he divulged. There is attorney-client privilege, but there's no such thing as prosecutor-suspect privilege. I looked to Katie for guidance and she just nodded her head to tell me to proceed. It was Spenser's choice to confess.

All the same, I repeated reading Spenser his Miranda rights in Katie's presence before proceeding. "Okay, tell me what you think I should know."

"My brother and me was paid to plant two kilos of meth in that car in New Orleans."

"Which car are you talking about? There are a lot of cars in New Orleans." I couldn't put words in his mouth and Katie couldn't make assumptions.

'The white Ford. The one we shot up so the cops would search it. You arrested the kid we were supposed to get in trouble because of it." He looked at me with an expression that let me know he was too exhausted to worry about being precise in his wording.

"Lionel Batiste only had one kilo of meth in his possession when I arrested him. That was all he admitted to finding in the trunk of his car."

"NO!" Spenser was suddenly frantic and very emphatic. "Jackson put two kilos in that car. That was what we was told to do and that is what we did."

"One kilo, two kilos, what does it matter?" Katie gave me a confused glance. "I just need you to admit that you two put drugs into Lionel Batiste's car to frame him."

"Yes, we did that. That boy didn't have nothing to do with the meth. We were paid to put the meth in his car and to make it look like that bike gang wanted to start a gang war."

"And how were you supposed to do that?" I knew the answer to the question, but I wanted to help Captain Williams build a case of his own. It might get him to act nicer towards me.

"We killed two prospects from that bike gang over in New Orleans to take their motorcycles. We still had the bikes and those bikers' colors when we was told to plant the meth. So, we tried to make it look like the gang and that kid was fighting over turf. That's why them guys that took us made us show them where we buried those two bikers and then tied us up to the bodies before the cops showed up. The guy that did all the talking only promised not to kill us if we told you about planting the meth."

"I'm confused. Was the man who questioned you a member of the Black Knights or not?" Katie interrupted me before I could ask my next question. I was foolish to think she would not pursue Spenser's explanation for his sudden confession.

"They kept hoods on our heads so we couldn't see nobody, but the guy who did all the talking had some weird accent. He sure wasn't no Black biker." Spenser did not seem at all comfortable with remembering the things the mystery man did to him.

"That's a load of crap. You're just trying to make it sound like you weren't scared of a beat down by the Black Knights. One of them probably faked an accent to mess with you," I challenged him. Spenser stuck to his story and I didn't persist in trying to make him change it. I couldn't afford to argue too much and I dared not make Katie doubt the validity of his confession just because we couldn't agree on who compelled him to make it. I just needed to cloud his ability to identify his interrogator, who I already knew for certain was not a member of the Black Knights. The room fell silent for a moment while Katie considered Spenser's version of his questioning.

"They must be some real tricky bikers," Katie finally said, but it was very clear whose version of the story she believed. I wasn't looking forward to discussing the matter while driving home in a small car.

"So, you'll confess to killing the two Black Knights in Mississippi and to framing Lionel Batiste in New Orleans if you are guaranteed to only face the murder charges here?" Katie recapped. It sounded like she was offering him an even more generous deal than he asked for, but in reality it only reflected the realities she had explained to me before we entered the room.

"Yes."

"Who paid you to frame Lionel Batiste?" Katie knew this was the most important thing to know going forward. Agreeing not to charge them did not preclude her charging their employer.

Spenser fell silent. There was no reason to confess to two murders and then not divulge who paid him to commit the one crime he knew he wasn't going to be charged with. Spenser's expression made me think he just might be more afraid of who wanted Lionel framed than he was of the mystery man who forced him to confess to framing Lionel. That meant the man giving the orders was someone very powerful and well connected. They also weren't the sort of boss to forgive employee theft, which would was how they'd view the meth found in the brothers' truck.

"You're screwed." Katie said and slammed the notebook closed. "You can tell us who ordered you to do all of this and testify against them or you can take their name to the grave they're already digging for you. How many shallow graves do you want to be tossed into this week?"

"Katie here will lie and tell your attorney you gave us the name to make your deal. He might be the one to let it slip," I bluffed and started to stand up. I was hoping he was still fragile enough to break one more time.

"Don't do that. Please, don't do that," Spenser was not too proud to beg. He looked ready to cry. I decided to play a hunch.

"How long has Bear Brovartey been your attorney?" It wasn't like I was putting words in his mouth to implicate the attorney. Spenser might even name a different attorney.

"Is he here?" The way he asked this simple question gave Katie and me a reason to share a quick smile.

"Yeah, he is trying to arrange your bail. Why?" Most criminals aren't aware that the Supreme Court has ruled police officers can lie to a suspect during questioning.

"Damn him." Spenser pulled at his handcuffs.

"Talk to me, Spenser. You don't have to go anywhere. Let us help the two of you. Remember, you're the one who invited me here." I wasn't really trying to calm him down. He was giving away far too much in this agitated state to discourage him.

"Look, Brovartey is the one who hired us to plant the dope. We already killed those bikers so he suggested using their bikes and colors to make it look like there was going to be a gang war."

"The attorney handed you the meth himself?" Katie was stunned that any attorney had done something so amazingly stupid. Brovartey should have known to keep his distance by using an intermediary. I noted the attorney knew about the murders.

"Yeah. We've done stuff for him before. This wasn't supposed to be a big deal, but it got out of hand."

"Explain what you mean." Katie pressed.

"We was supposed to plant the dope so the attorney could take the guy's house and sell it to someone else he knows. But the kid up and ran for office by the time we could do the job. Now it's a big deal and everyone thinks we made a big mess out of everything." Spenser began tugging at his handcuffs again.

"You still aren't telling us anything we can use to protect you." What he was telling us was good to know. Katie was scribbling more notes in the notebook. "Why did Brovartey target Lionel Batiste?"

"I don't know. It's not like he explains why he wants us to do stuff for him. He calls, we answer, and that's that."

"I can't help you, if you don't help me." Katie was taking over the questioning, whether I was finished or not. "You just need to decide who scares you the most. Is it us or is it the attorney?"

"Brovartey will have us killed if he thinks we took the dope he's been looking for. He has been accusing us of taking it ever since he got back from New Orleans."

"You really think he would kill the two of you?" Katie scoffed. They had done what Brovartey wanted.

"Maybe not himself, but we are dead meat now that the meth turned up in our truck. He can find somebody to do the killing."

"What if your attorney had something else to worry about? Maybe you could be the ones who take him down instead." Katie spoke to him as if she was trying to make a partnership with the Duncan brothers. She needed a hammer to drive a nail in the attorney's coffin.

"I don't know how we could do that." Spenser was going to have to be taken by the hand to get where she needed him.

"You need to tell a judge what you just told us about being hired to frame Lionel Batiste. The judge handling this case is not going to be very happy about your plan, and I'm sure he will give Mister Brovartey a place and plenty of time to consider his evil ways. It should be enough to make him forget all about the two of you."

"Okay. I'll help you. But you have to get him away from here right now."

"I'll get right on that." I offered and left Katie in the room with Spenser to get the answers to the rest of her questions.

Captain Williams met me in the hallway. He was a lot more gracious host this time around.

"So, they just wanted to be sure they did their time in the same prison they've been in before." Williams was amused at the way these two criminals viewed the world. "Thanks for getting him to confess. I don't suppose you know who loosened their tongues."

"I can only prove it wasn't me." This didn't sound like the joke I meant it to be when I said it, not even to me.

"I don't even care anymore. Just promise me that the next time you want to pull one of these stunts you and the pretty lady will drive west instead of east."

"I'm not sure there's going to be a next time. She's not that much happier about the way our weekend getaway turned out than you are."

"I'll bet not." Williams was openly laughing at the situation I had put myself in.

Katie and I questioned Jackson next. He was obviously sedated, but he was still far less willing to confess to the crimes his brother confessed to for both of them. Convincing Jackson that Brovartey was about to post bail for Spenser proved to be enough to get him to provide even more details about the attorney's direct involvement in framing Lionel Batiste.

The tongue lashing I expected during the drive back to New Orleans turned into a strategy session for taking down Brovartey. Katie had a plan and I was not about to pick it apart or refuse to cooperate. She made no mention of the two brothers' assertions about being questioned by a guy who was obviously not a member of the Black Knights. She also didn't share her opinion on whether I framed the brothers with their own drugs. She either didn't believe them or she believed there was something to be gained from my having done so that she could live with it. The time we had just spent together made me favor the likelihood that she did not believe them. She wasn't an Irish girl that was going to tolerate shenanigans when it came to police misconduct. I also realized that I was going to have to begin behaving myself if I planned to keep dating the prosecutor.

Chapter 43

My focus shifted the next morning from Bear Brovartey and the Duncan brothers to Tribal Investments. It took Tulip only a few calls and emails for she and her research assistant to assemble the knives she needed to disembowel Tribal's operation. She invited Bristol and her thug companions to lunch at Strada Ammazarre under the guise of making a fresh start with them. Badger had to be relieved to be getting a second chance to bring her in line. I invited a guest of my own to join us, Josh Gardner. The first article he wrote about Tribal Investments was written using a telephone interview, so none of our guests were likely to recognize him. I told him this was my way of keeping the promise to give him another story involving Tribal Investments.

Tony and I were standing over the prep table when Tulip entered the kitchen and took a seat at the Chef's Table with Josh. The chef and I had a little business to discuss that neither of them were likely to find very interesting.

"Do we want to open another restaurant?" I thought my partner was either joking or had completely lost his mind. Neither of us were really running Strada Ammazarre as it was, so the idea of owning two such headaches was out of the question as far as I was concerned.

"What brought this up?"

"Mister David at the bank said they were foreclosing on the pizza place across the street and wanted to know if we wanted to take over the location. He said we could get the building and its contents for whatever was due on the loan." Tony liked the idea of owning another French Quarter property, particularly at such a steep discount, but I knew he was as ambivalent about running two restaurants as I was.

"I think you should say, 'Thank you,' to the nice man and run as far and as fast from that offer as you can go. I know you, and you'll take the bait." I was still laughing at his mock outrage as I walked away.

"Why is Tony working lunch today?" Tulip asked me as I took a seat at the table. She'd spotted the chef and knew Tony normally takes Mondays off because it is a slow day, especially during the holidays.

"He's covering for Miss J. She covered for him while he did a private catering gig Saturday night." I hastily introduced her to Josh to change the subject. I needed my sister to be my work-around for Avery's admonishment about speaking with the press. I owed the reporter a favor and used Tulip to settle the debt. I was not even going to be quoted as an unnamed or reliable source in the article.

"Your generosity is most unexpected." Badger Wilson said, sounding wary and unsure of exactly what he should be worried about as he sat down. Using the Chef's Table, which we never offer guests at lunch, was my way to make sure we were well away from any other occupied tables.

"It shouldn't have been." Tulip smiled ever so sweetly at the man who'd threatened her not two weeks earlier.

She pointed to Josh and said, "I hope you don't mind, I invited a friend of mine to join us. He is only in town for the day."

Bristol and Two Crows gave the reporter a disinterested glance and Badger ignored him entirely. Any friend of Tulip's wouldn't be a friend of theirs.

"I recommend everything on the menu." My role in this charade was to play the gracious host and I was already overacting. This also changed the subject.

Our guests began to relax and we placed our orders. I gave Gina, our waitress, no indication that we were providing any alcohol for free and no wine glasses were set on the table. There was going to be nothing for these three to celebrate and I didn't want to pay Tulip's dry cleaning for unnecessary wine stains on her clothes if Bristol began throwing things. None of our guests asked for appetizers and I didn't order any for the table to share. The developers seemed as anxious to get past playing nice with one another as we were. The ladies each enjoyed crab-meat salads while the men all feasted on beef or veal. Tulip and I kept the conversation light and focused on Tribal's enjoyment of New Orleans.

The developers had taken up residence at the newly remodeled Roosevelt Hotel, which once served as the local office of Governor Huey P. Long, the grand master of competent corruption. They ate at every expensive restaurant in the city, but were never seated in the front sections reserved for old-money locals and the sort of celebrities who would be recognized on sight. They also met as many of the local wheelers and dealers as possible. Councilwoman Adams opened many of these doors for them while unintentionally putting her reputation at risk.

"Delicious as this was, we're sure it wasn't the reason you invited us here today. Perhaps we should get down to business." Two Crows took point on their defense. He pushed his plate towards the center of the table and leaned forward on his brawny arms. I am sure the display of fabric being pulled tight on his jacket was for our benefit. Intimidation is best when applied subtly. Tulip would be the one teaching today's lessons.

"It's really very simple," Tulip smiled as she pulled folders from her briefcase. Two Crows and Badger exchanged glances, but did not betray any concern about what Tulip might know. They were confident their secrets were deeply buried. "We want to give you a chance to voluntarily pull up stakes and leave town."

"Why would we do that?" Bristol challenged her. "In fact, I might file a complaint with the State Police about one of their detectives interfering with a legitimate business conducting business in New Orleans. We could own this place with so little effort."

"You won't get along with the chef. Trust me." I quipped. "And I'm not interfering with any *legitimate* business. We asked you here to discuss some topics that are going to be brought up at the next Neighbors for a Good Neighborhood meeting."

"Neighbors for a Good Neighborhood? What the hell is that?" Two Crows snapped.

"It's a political action committee that sprang up right after Lionel Batiste was arrested. It seems intent upon shaming Lionel Batiste and helping Councilwoman Delia Adams' campaign." There was no proof for my conviction Councilwoman Adams controlled the PAC, but the accusation that she was its beneficiary drew a reaction from Bristol and Badger that told me their ignorance of the group was an act. "Being tied to any sort of campaign dirty work won't help your image."

"Has she been arrested?" Bristol sensed a bluff. "This doesn't sound like a crime."

"No, but she is about to resign. I'm filing a defamation lawsuit against her on Lionel Batiste's behalf later this afternoon. A trial of that sort is going to draw plenty of national attention." Tulip liked making the threat, but she doesn't file lawsuits she isn't sure she will win.

"National attention of this sort is something Tribal Investments probably isn't looking for." I tossed this in for good measure. Bristol gave me a thin smile.

"We aren't afraid of a little bad publicity." Two Crows tried a bluff of his own. The way his eyes shifted gave it away, as did the way his wife glared at him.

Tulip was ready to pounce as she opened the first of the folders before her. It contained a single page of paper documenting the tribal record for the Bristol family. Bristol's face perceptibly tightened. "Not a little. A lot. There is a problem with your claim that these men are members of the Ouachita Indian tribe. I can't find any documentation that allows either of the gentlemen at this table the right to claim they are members of *any* Indian tribe." She reached for another folder and opened it, as well. "I went so far as to contact the tribe directly and they were kind enough to send this from their own attorneys. It is a cease and desist order telling you two to knock it off. The tribal elders also faxed this letter to me and asked if I would tender it to you on their behalf. They are putting Bristol on notice that if she persists in putting you two up as members of the tribe she'll be excommunicated from the tribe. Is that the right word, excommunicate? Maybe just kick your ass out is better."

"Give me just a minute." Bristol used reading the letter to stall the conversation. "Fine. We can stop doing that. Done as of today."

"Well, if you do that, you will need to make restitution to any municipalities and states that gave Tribal Investments special status or tax breaks for being a minority owned business. You are the only partner who is actually a member of the tribe, and you only have a one third stake. Even if you take over the entire company today, all of your past applications and statements were made fraudulently."

"It sounds like we're being blackmailed." Badger grumbled. He wasn't used to being the one threatened. Right about now, he was kicking himself for not taking my sister seriously enough when she said she'd find the chinks in his armor.

"Blackmailing the likes of you is not worth losing my license over." Tulip smiled as she opened a folder containing the criminal records for Two Crows and Badger and turned it to face our now stupefied guests. Sharks could learn a thing or two about grinning from my baby sister. "I'm going to enjoy a leisurely dessert and espresso with my brother after you leave, and then I will walk over to the FBI and deliver all of these documents to them. I'd say that gives you about an hour's head start."

"And if we decide to stay and fight? We could fight this in court." Two Crows must have really not been paying very close attention. Bristol sighed audibly and shot him a glance.

"You have no defense against the sort of fraud you have been perpetuating. Do you think you're going to get any backing from the state of Louisiana or the New Orleans City Council for your grand design when this goes public? Those tax credits and bonds you said you'd need just dried up. I'll also bring people in from every place you've built your luxury condos to speak at great length about the long term effects your projects had on their communities at the next City Council meeting."

"Tribal Investments has money of our own and can borrow all the money we need to build here." Two Crows was going to go down fighting, I had to give him that.

"Well, you might not after you repay everyone you've defrauded, and I wouldn't be looking for a reason to borrow any more money from Junior Hauser if I were you. He screwed you once, why go back?" This was Tulip's last chance to draw blood.

This comment was enough to silence the trio. Looking like small animals caught in the headlights of a large truck on a very narrow road, they tried not to betray their collective surprise at Tulip's knowledge of their transactions with Junior Hauser.

"What do you mean?" Bristol asked, still trying to play it cool.

"Junior Hauser runs the Dixie Mafia and also controls Edgewater Credit Union, where you borrowed the money to build your project in Biloxi. I guess you didn't do enough due diligence on that deal by the looks on your faces." Tulip let them stew for a moment before continuing.

I began using what Josh Gardner told me about Tribal Investments' troubles. "You gave the exact same set of plans that you submitted here to the Planning Board in Biloxi over a year ago. They rejected them because the land Junior sold you to build on are protected wetlands."

"So what if we had to move a building project from one place to another? That's the real estate business." Badger was determined to burn up the last of his bravado. Bristol had begun fidgeting with the fax from the tribe as something to do. She knew they were done. Done fighting us, done building condos, and done as a business.

"Let me guess this next part. Bear Brovartey turned up and said he could find you a buyer for the land his boss loaned you the money to buy in the first place. I'll bet he also took a pretty big fee for finding the new buyers. The new buyers gave you a low-ball offer that didn't cover what you owed the credit union and your development costs."

"That's about right." Two Crows was done keeping up the façade. They had lost this fight before they ever sat down and he knew it. There was no reason to keep acting like it was the first time they had been bested in a real estate deal. "We lost three million bucks."

"Well, the guys who bought the land ran into the same problem, but they thought of a way around it. They came over here and tried to buy the houses the Make It Right Foundation built. They were going to use Hauser's barges, cranes, and house movers to ship the houses to the site and set them up as pre-fabricated condos."

"We had no piece of that deal." Bristol saw how savage the publicity could be about efforts to buy the Ninth Ward out from under its residents. She had quite enough to handle without proof of them having business links to Junior Hauser or CSA Holdings seeing the light of day.

"We never thought you did. You have until I walk into SAC Conroy's office to get out of town. Oh, one other thing you should know," Tulip said and jerked a thumb towards the reporter, who enjoyed his ringside seat at our little circus nearly as much as his veal Picatta. "This is Josh Gardner. You might remember an article he wrote about you a while back. His next story covers everything we just discussed. It will hit the newsstands on Wednesday."

"What happens if we decide to stay and fight the two of you?" Badger may have been speaking in terms other than legal or public relations fights. He was an idiot.

"You aren't fighting us. You're fighting the justice system and a public relations nightmare. You need to find a friendlier jurisdiction to be arrested in and accept that Josh's story only loses traction if you aren't in town when it hits the streets." Tulip advised him.

Our guests excused themselves. Tulip and I remained seated and watched them depart. The sand was pouring through Tribal's hourglass. Tulip wasn't going to have time for dessert and espresso. Tulip and I had argued about timing her handing this information to the FBI. We compromised on her turning everything over earlier that morning, and then lying to the trio about having enough time to escape. SAC Conroy was already waiting for them at their hotel.

"Champagne for everyone!" I shouted to the bartender and waved my arm across the expanse of the dining room as we adjourned to the bar. This is one of those magnanimous gestures you get to make as a bar or café owner. You also learn to time it to when the place is as empty as the bistro was when I gave the order.

"I saved the best for last. Just for you," Tulip gave me a little smirk as she handed me a folder of my own. It contained three things I decided I could look at later. Lunch rid me of the prospect of the condominium monstrosity being built where I would have to see it every time I looked out my living room window. My focus was already turning towards Katie's confrontation with Bear Brovartey the next day.

I glanced at the materials in the folder and didn't see any immediate significance to any of it. The top item was the state's latest Election Commission financial disclosures. I noticed Tulip had highlighted portions because she knew how easily I get bored reading such things. The second was a captioned photograph from the Pensacola News Journal from 1998. The next item was one of Bristol's earliest resumes. The last two items reinforced my concerns that Tulip's researcher would decide to search the internet's darkest corners to see what he could learn about me someday.

Chapter 44

"I should suspend you!" Chief Avery bellowed at me as he stormed through the bistro's patio doors. Expecting exactly this reaction was why I made sure to be on the bistro's unoccupied patio when he found me. "I ordered you to stay away from Delia Adams. She is ready to cut off all funding to NOPD unless you're fired today."

"Well she needs to get cracking." I said in response, which did absolutely nothing for my boss's blood pressure. "She might find it hard to do after this week."

"What are you talking about?"

"What was she talking about that got under your skin?" I wasn't about to tell him about the Josh's article in the Business Journal. It was going to have a ripple effect that was certain to rock the Councilwoman's boat that would, in turn, rock Avery's boat before he was sent to capsize my own.

"She said Tulip and you blackmailed Tribal Investments into pulling out of town. They told her they were leaving town because the two of you were going to spread lies about them to keep their project from being built. The Councilwoman also says you told them you are going to destroy her career. She is livid."

"Does livid mean she's calling her criminal attorney?"

I pulled a chair from beneath one of the round metal mesh tables and pointed to it. Avery needed to pace, but chose to sit while he calmed down. I flagged down one of the servers who had been trying not to stare at us through the glass doors while Avery vented his frustration. They brought us cold beers and I waited until my boss had cooled his throat before I launched my counter-attack.

"Chief, you know exactly what truths they didn't want exposed. You gave me the rap sheets on the two guys in that operation yourself. Tulip confirmed that only Bristol is a member of any tribe. Tulip was the one to threaten to challenge their minority business applications. They are dirty as hell and any lies I might tell would be nothing compared to the truth they've managed to hide until now."

"Then, what's this about going after the Councilwoman?" The Chief was beginning to see clearly again. Councilwoman Adams chaired the finance committee that controlled his budget. Avery reflexively jumped whenever she said a word.

"She used some fake neighborhood group to try to force Lionel and his aunts out of the house her brothers wanted to buy. It's called Neighbors for a Good Neighborhood. Remember that CSA Holdings outfit we couldn't sort out? It turns out it stands for Chris and Sam Adams. They are Delia's brothers and they're in hock to the Dixie Mafia for quite a bit of money. This whole thing about buying the houses in the Ninth Ward is a way to get their asses out of a sling in Biloxi. I may not be able to tie Delia to anything beyond the sham front group, but that's still something."

"Can you even do that?" Avery wanted to relax, but he saw too many obstacles still in the road.

"That shouldn't be a problem. The minister she put up to it isn't real happy about being used by her. I don't think I can tie her to the deal in Biloxi, but just being able to say her brothers are in bed with the Dixie Mafia should damage her campaign. The attorney that handled all of the deals between Tribal Investments and CSA Holdings is about to be arrested for trying to frame Lionel. The guys he hired murdered a pair of Black Knights prospects and used their bikes and colors in the process, so there are plenty of accessory-after-the-fact charges to go around."

"Don't tell me you'd really like Lionel Batiste on the City Council." Avery was still not ready to admit his Councilwoman nemesis deserved to be removed. I had underestimated the extent of their mutual need for the long-running feud.

"The city has all the liars and thieves it needs. The Council can probably lose one and still have a quorum. So, am I suspended?"

"Ask me again when the smoke clears. We may both be looking for new jobs." Avery took another swig of his beer and stared at the label. He was deep in thoughts I knew better than to disturb or mock.

Chapter 45

Katie requested an in-camera meeting with Judge Rogers before he convened court on Wednesday. I wore one of my nicer suits and less bemused looks for the meeting. Tulip had to be present because she was filing a motion to have Brovartey removed as counsel so she could represent Lionel in his stead. Filing this motion was hopefully going to be the extent of her representation. It was actually nothing more than the bait in Katie's trap.

"Lionel's present counsel should be here for this," Rogers objected when he looked around the room. A pretrial change of attorneys was usually a polite formality.

"Actually, it is his present counsel that is the purpose of this hearing, your Honor." Katie was stepping onto some potentially thin ice. She would not be the only one of us to face Judge Rogers' wrath if he was displeased when he learned the real reason she asked for the conference.

"Please explain that statement." He chose to take a seat rather than finish getting dressed for court. I spoke up and moved the judge's increasingly cool stare from Katie to myself. "I have provided the State Attorney's office with conclusive evidence and sworn testimony that David Brovartey framed Lionel to place himself in a position to defend him. His real intention was to take possession of the Batiste family's home. I believed Lionel Batiste was being framed when I arrested him. I went through with the arrest in order to uncover the parties behind the efforts against him."

"And now you say you have managed to do so." Rogers seemed more receptive than outraged.

"Yes, sir. Lionel informed me that Brovartey told him he knew he was charged with possession of two kilos of crystal meth when he first interviewed him. This was interesting because I only turned in one as evidence. The missing drugs were discovered in what proved to be a homicide investigation in Mississippi this past weekend." I wasn't about to provide precise details about that incident to the judge unless I was tortured. I was relieved that nobody challenged the way I was parsing my words. "The men in possession of the second bag of meth will testify that the drugs found in their possession were part of the drugs they were hired to use to frame Lionel Batiste. They are also prepared to testify that Brovartey personally provided them with those drugs to use for that purpose."

"So, what do you wish to do here this morning? I'll clear Lionel right now if that's all you need. I never wanted to believe he was guilty anyway, and frankly I was pretty sad that his case ever showed up in my courtroom. Thank you for restoring my faith in all of you." Katie and I gave one another relieved looks. I chose the right judge, after all.

"I want to have Mister Brovartey testify in open court about the circumstances behind his taking Lionel's case. I think I can get him to perjure himself."

"So you want to castrate him. I can help with that." Judge Rogers has higher expectations of those in the legal profession than is probably mentally healthy.

We left him to his court day rituals and went our

separate ways.

Katie joined the other prosecutor handling Lionel's case at the plaintiffs' table and quietly explained the broad strokes of what was about to happen. I took a seat at the back of the gallery next to SAC Michael Conroy.

"Good morning. Thanks for meeting on short notice." I didn't need to whisper because court wasn't in session, but the room was now beginning to fill and I didn't want to ruin the big surprise for everyone.

"Good morning. It seems Christmas came early this year. Your sister handed us those fake Indians yesterday and now you want to offer me some sort of compromise about Chief Avery." Conroy respects my sister's professionalism, but he has seen my own shenanigans up close and was justifiably worried that I was going to drag him into something to clear my friend and boss.

The FBI Special Agent and I have a professional relationship that bears an unfortunate resemblance to that which exists between Chief Avery and the Councilwoman. Conroy still harbored the conviction that I was involved in the death of one of his agent shortly after the disclosure that the agent was responsible for my father's death, and my tepid denials were doing nothing to heal the sore spot that remained between us this morning.

"Would you be willing to take Bill Avery off your hit list in exchange for Junior Hauser's personal attorney?" I knew he was very interested in the trade by the look on his face.

"It was never a hit list, and you know your boss helped the Superintendent to cover up the shootings. Avery signed off on every one of the internal investigation case files. I'll be honest, I think someone in Washington is using this to force a consent decree on NOPD so the FBI can be put in charge. I have no idea why they would want to do that, but this is how it has happened in the past." Conroy obviously wanted no part of running the local police department.

"Avery supervised the investigations, but he didn't do anything more than sign the detectives' reports. He's only guilty of trusting detectives he should have been able to trust. I can't believe you would rather have him than the keeper of the Dixie Mafia's secrets. Oh, well. I'd rather my girlfriend gets credit for putting him in prison anyway." I started to stand up. I was praying the entire time that Conroy would reach out to stop me and was nearly standing when he did.

"What's the attorney's name?" He had one name in mind and wasn't going to trade an easy high-profile win for someone working under the attorney he had in mind.

"Bear Brovartey." I reached in my pocket and gave him the attorney's increasingly dog-eared card.

"What do you have on him?" Conroy demanded. I could tell he was willing to bargain by the way he toyed with the card. He would be lousy at poker.

"Sit here for a while and you'll have him on a silver platter. Katie Reilly is going to put him on the witness stand under oath." I hoped I didn't oversell this deal. I stood up and moved away from SAC Conroy. I did not want Brovartey to see the two of us sitting together.

Tulip was seated a row behind the defendant's table. I took a seat beside her and felt her nudge me when we saw Brovartey's smug bravado as he arrived in court. He seemed blissfully unaware of how badly his day was going to get. I was looking forward to the fireworks that were certain to erupt when Judge Rogers approved Tulip's motion to replace him as Lionel's counsel.

Lionel's case was third on Judge Roger's docket. He was brought into court and looked around. I nodded at him as his eyes scanned the room for familiar faces. He kept swiveling his head rather than give Brovartey any sign that something was amiss. I'm sure Lionel saw nothing in the courtroom that gave him any reason to believe my promise that he would walk out of court a free man after today's hearing.

The bailiff called the courtroom to order and everyone participated in the ritual of standing up as a demonstration of respect for the Judge, who shuffled some papers about and adjusted his seat to allow time for the opposing counsels to prepare themselves as well. He finally tapped his microphone to be sure it was on and held up a piece of paper.

"I have before me a petition by the defendant to change attorneys. He has requested that Tulip Holland represent him going forward," Judge Rogers played his part with a perfectly straight face.

"I object!" It took only a moment before Bear Brovartey was on his feet and demanding to speak with his client.

"Motion denied. Mister Batiste no longer wishes to be your client." Judge Rogers was clearly taking delight in his role in exposing an unethical lawyer. His respect for the law and his eagerness to have any attorney who brought shame upon the Bar banished from the hallowed halls of justice were the reason I engaged in judge shopping in the first place. I knew he wasn't going to let this Bear keep running loose.

"I merely wish to remind Mister Batiste a few specific stipulations in our contract." Brovartey said to Lionel in an attempt to threaten his former client.

"Would that be the provision for taking his home? I think the judge here can rule that as unenforceable, can't you, Your Honor?" Tulip made her own opening attack. She rose from her seat in the gallery to stand beside Lionel. My sister was charging Lionel for one billable hour for her part in this charade. I would wind up paying her fee, eventually.

"I would like to see that contract," Judge Rogers said and extended his hand to Tulip, gesturing for the paperwork. Tulip had highlighted the most egregious portion of Brovartey's onerous contract for the judge. Rogers gave Brovartey an especially ugly frown. He then made a lengthy production of reading the entire contract before he looked up again. The scowl he shot at the attorney over the top of his reading glasses when he finished reading the contract was priceless.

"According to this, what happens next depends on Mister Brovartey. Has the party who agreed to pay for your services already decided they will no longer do so? We have barely reached the decision to change attorneys and you already have your hand in this young man's pocket for the keys to his home." Brovartey realized he was in trouble, but couldn't narrow down the precise direction he needed to face in order to defend himself. "Is the person paying for your services in the courtroom?"

It was a classic misdirection as almost the entire room craned their necks looking for Lionel's benefactor. Nobody came forward and Brovartey gave no sign of recognizing SAC Conroy, which was good for Katie.

"Your Honor, perhaps I can clear this matter up if Mister Brovartey will answer just a few questions." Katie sounded helpful.

"That's fine by me. What are your questions, counselor?" Brovartey agreed.

"Under oath." Katie began to set her trap.

"I don't believe that is necessary," the attorney complained. He was beginning to look truly nervous.

"It is, in my courtroom, sir." Rogers' glare convinced Brovartey to step into the witness box and take the oath that might potentially end his career.

"Are you prepared to tell us the name of the parties that hired you to defend Lionel Batiste?" Katie approached the stand after Brovartey was sworn in.

"That is privileged information. Besides, it's a moot point now that I have been removed."

"I can decide what is moot for myself, Mister Brovartey. There is no attorney-client privilege if there is a crime involved. You should consider that when you decide if you'll answer her questions." Rogers snarled.

"Again, I declare it is privileged information and I will not answer the question." He wouldn't admit to a crime until he knew all of the evidence against him.

"Then, let's try this question. How likely is it that you took this case on yourself? Perhaps you read about Lionel's difficulties and decided to give up your thousand dollar an hour fee to defend a total stranger on a pro bono basis." Katie was now directly in front of the witness stand

and her tone was far less friendly.

"Why would I do that?" Brovartey seemed to have trouble giving evasive answers to Katie's questions while trying to figure what she might know. He was visibly surprised when she divulged his hourly rate. This response only proved her point.

"That, sir, is what we are here to find out." He sensed he was being trapped, but he didn't yet grasp the size of the trap Katie was setting. "So, let's start over and keep in mind you are under oath. Is anyone paying you to defend Lionel Batiste?"

"I do not wish to respond to that question."

"I'm sorry, is that a yes or a no response to my question?"

"I was doing this as a favor."

"And now we are back to whom. Who asked you to take Mister Batiste on as a client?"

"I cannot say."

"Mister Brovartey, it is presently ten fifteen in the morning. Do you really want to start your day facing a contempt citation? Answer the question, sir." Judge Rogers was in no mood for Brovartey's stalling.

"Alex Boudreaux." Boudreaux's was not a name I had even considered. It certainly wasn't who Spenser Duncan led us to believe it was when we questioned him in Mississippi. I could, though, see motivations for Boudreaux doing so and believed Brovartey's answer was true.

"Why would Mister Boudreaux pay for an attorney for a man who has actively tried to interfere with his business?"

"I suggested that he do so."

"Fair enough. Have you worked for Mister Boudreaux in the past?"

"Not for, but with, yes. Alex was an intern with the credit union where I was the lead counsel while he was in law school. I had not spoken with him in years."

"Would you mind sharing your thoughts on Alex Boudreaux's motivation for agreeing to pay your fee?"

Brovartey knew his future depended on his ability to outmaneuver Katie in this courtroom. He was also a shrewd enough attorney to see how little room there was to dance with the truth in the witness stand of a hostile judge.

"He hoped that my doing so would enable him to solicit favors from Mister Batiste if he won the election."

"Mister Boudreaux would hardly be the first to try doing that. I can't understand why you thought it necessary to try to conceal this from the court," Katie was having fun. "On the other hand, what can you tell me about the arrangements to frame Lionel Batiste in the first place?"

Brovartey paused to decide how to play his hand. It was a weak one at best and he knew it. Katie would not be asking him anything about this matter if she did not already know some details, but he decided to take a chance. "Nothing. Nothing at all."

"So, your testimony for the record is that you had absolutely nothing to do with framing Lionel Batiste?" Katie spread her trap before Brovartey in plain sight. He knew by the way she phrased the question that she knew everything and could prove it. His choices now were to either confess or deny the charge in hopes she was bluffing at the risk of committing perjury. Neither course was going to go well for him.

"I had nothing to do with framing Lionel Batiste." His career was hanging by just enough thread to hang himself.

"You may step down for the moment." Katie waved him away and then approached the judge. "Your Honor, the State would like to call Spenser Duncan to the stand."

"I object!" Brovartey pounded on the railing of the empty jury box, where the bailiff was keeping a close eye on him. "This is not a trial."

"No, it's not. It is a hearing to determine the circumstances behind Lionel Batiste's arrest and your offer of legal services. I would say that your trial will be coming very soon. Produce your witness, Miss Reilly." Judge Rogers was enjoying his role in this drama. I glanced back at Conroy and saw he was on his phone. This was against the rules, but his position afforded him the privilege to ignore them.

I said silent thanks to Captain Williams for arranging to have Federal marshals escort Spenser Duncan into the courtroom. It showed that Williams grasped how much more important this testimony would seem if Spenser arrived in dramatic fashion. Spenser had none of the swagger I had seen in the bar. Today he was wearing a new suit, but no handcuffs to make him look like the criminal he was, as he made his way to the witness stand to be sworn in.

"Mister Duncan, can you identify David Brovartey in this courtroom?" Katie stepped back to let him survey the room. People were still coming in as word spread through courthouse of the drama unfolding here.

"He is sitting right there." Spenser pointed to Brovartey, who'd moved his seat to the side of the defendant's table. Tulip and Lionel pointedly ignored him.

"What part did you personally play in framing Lionel Batiste?"

"My brother and I used colors and motorcycles we took off of members from a bike gang in New Orleans and we planted two kilos of meth in the trunk of his car. We shot the trunk with shotguns and tried to make it look like there was a drug war between him and the bikers."

"Had you ever met Lionel Batiste prior to that day?"

"No. I didn't even meet him then. We snuck the drugs in the trunk of his car when he was shopping." Spenser looked at Lionel and seemed to want to apologize.

"You say you put two kilos of drugs in the trunk of his car. Only one kilo was placed in evidence. Can you explain that difference?"

"No, ma'am." Spenser was very subdued but made sure he showed Katie all the respect he had failed to display on Saturday. "My brother put all those drugs in the car."

"But didn't the police in Biloxi discover exactly one

kilo of meth in your possession this past weekend? Those drugs have since been chemically matched to the same drugs found in Mister Batiste's car. Do you have an explanation for that?"

"We must have been framed." There was a small burst of laughter from the gallery that Judge Rogers made no move to quiet.

"Maybe you are afraid that whoever paid you to plant the drugs believes you double crossed them. Have you ever shorted a buyer in a drug deal?"

"Not this time, ma'am." The room had another nice laugh at his expense.

"Who paid you to plant the drugs in Lionel Batiste's car?"

"Mister Brovartey. He gave my brother and me five thousand dollars and gave us the meth in a paper sack. He said to plant the drugs in the car and then shoot it up so the cops would look in the car and find the drugs. We was also supposed to make it look like another drug dealer did it, so we used them bikers' colors to make it look like their gang done the shooting."

"Would you please tell the court how you obtained the bikers' colors?"

"We killed them." This elicited absolutely no laughs from the gallery.

"Are you now facing charges related to that? Have you made any sort of deal for your testimony against Mister Brovartey today?" Katie was ahead of the attorney on this one as well.

"My brother and I made a plea bargain on the murders, but we didn't make any deal about testifying against Mister Brovartey. I came here because I promised you I would say I tried to frame that boy there." He pointed to Lionel.

"You could have refused to do so. Please tell the court why you agreed to admit to framing the defendant." Katie was a little nonplussed by the way Spenser's explanation made his testimony sound like it may not have been given freely.

"Because you said it was the only way we could keep Mister Brovartey from getting to us."

"Surely, the most he would do is fire you or maybe take back the money he paid you. Are you implying that he treats those who disappoint him any differently?" This was as leading of a question as I had ever heard in court, but Judge Rogers bit his tongue and Spenser was faster to answer than Brovartey was to object.

"Mister Brovartey probably would have had us killed."

"What makes you think that?" Katie asked as casually as she could. This was going much better than she ever dreamed.

"I object!" Brovartey managed to beat Spenser to the draw this time.

"Oh, I think we all want to hear what the man has to say about this," Judge Rogers waved off the objection.

"Because my brother and I killed some people for him before," Spenser said in a voice barely loud enough to be picked up by the microphone. He realized too late that he had admitted to far more than he agreed to when he came to court that morning.

"The State would like to recall Daniel Brovartey to the stand."

Brovartey returned to the stand with the posture of a man walking to the gallows. The attorney clearly understood the range of charges certain to be brought against him after Spenser's testimony. Brovartey was prepared to fight the various criminal charges, but losing his license to practice law was going to ruin him. Losing that would cost him any further value to Hauser, and Junior didn't keep dead wood on his organizational tree.

"Kindly explain to the court precisely how you came to frame Lionel Batiste and then appeared here to defend him."

"Let's not get too far ahead of ourselves, Miss Reilly. You'll want to save some of this for Mister Brovartey's own trail," Judge Rogers politely admonished Katie, but with a smile on his face.

"It was just how it worked out. I was asked to secure

the deed to the Batiste's house. I hired the Duncan brothers to plant the drugs so I could take the Batiste's home to pay my fees. Things changed when the young man decided to run for office. I needed to use Alex Boudreau retaining me to hide my own involvement in framing Lionel." Brovartey had no reason to lie, though he may have had a reason to throw Alex Boudreau clear of any suspicion in framing Lionel or murdering the bikers. Brovartey was clearly tailoring his testimony in anticipation of defending himself against the state's case. His plan seemed to be to limit the number of additional people with a reason to testify against him at trial.

"So, to be clear, you were paid to frame Lionel and then used Alex Boudreau's retaining you to shield your original client? If Alex Boudreau is not who hired you to frame Lionel Batiste, then who is?" Katie never lost sight of her real quarry. Brovartey did not come up with the idea of framing Lionel on his own. There was no point in his wasting time before answering the question. Whoever paid him to commit the crimes would expose themselves if they raised a finger in his defense.

"Delia Adams and her brothers. I was hired to help their company obtain homes in the Lower Ninth Ward that could be moved to a wetlands site in Biloxi to avoid doing new construction. It was Delia's idea to frame the Batistes so their neighbors would force them to sell." This admission was like getting two birds with one stone, as Brovartey linked Boudreax to Delia and her brothers. Making that into a conspiracy was above my pay grade, but the possibility of their being one would be enough to tarnish all of their reputations.

The air rushed out of the room nearly as fast as the spectators did; they wanted to get to the nearest phone to spread the news. I noticed a pair of well-dressed young men entered the courtroom and took seats next to Michael Conroy during the attorney's last minutes on the stand. It looked like Conroy and I were about to seal our deal.

"I still don't understand why they would want to frame Lionel Batiste. He's just a college student taking care of his aunt."

"At first they wanted me to find a way to discredit him and his aunt to their neighbors, because they were encouraging their neighbors not to sell their homes. Then, Delia was afraid the Batiste boy might make her look bad after he decided to run for office. She didn't think he would win, but he might get enough votes that people would think she didn't represent all of her district. That's why they changed the plan to frame Lionel on the drug charges." Brovartey's testimony was a repeat of Delia's tirade almost word for word.

"Your Honor, the State is satisfied that Lionel Batiste is innocent of all charges brought against him and moves to dismiss those charges." Katie gave me a quick wink, but avoided openly smiling.

"Agreed and so ordered. Lionel Batiste, you are free to go and good luck with your campaign." Judge Rogers actually stood and extended a hand to the still confused but relieved former defendant. He then turned to the witness stand. "And Mister Brovartey, as for you. I believe you'll be sleeping in Mister Batiste's cell this evening. Bailiff, the attorney from Mississippi is all yours."

"That won't be necessary Your Honor." Conroy spoke up from the back of the courtroom. "The FBI is taking Mister Brovartey into custody."

Katie now gave me a confused and slightly angry look as the FBI agents stepped forward to handcuff the sobbing attorney. Katie had her heart set on being the one to prosecute Brovartey. The FBI's arrest also crumbled whatever plans Brovartey had in mind to discredit Spenser's testimony against him. I was satisfied to have protected my boss in the mess over the shootings and was relieved that Junior Hauser would hold Spenser and not Katie or me accountable for his attorney being delivered into the hands of the FBI.

Chapter 45

Uncle Felix unexpectedly stopped by Strada Ammazarre for Happy Hour the next day. This was an especially festive one because of the buoyant mood over the arrests of so many people involved in either trying to rig the election or framing Lionel, or both. Even Michael Conroy was there, but this was as much to reaffirm the friendship he needed to restore with Chief Avery as it was to thank Katie for delivering Brovartey into his hands. She was gracious about accepting the gratitude despite feeling the FBI had swiped one of her Christmas presents before she even got to open it. I was going to be hard pressed to find her anything she would like near as much as being the one to put Junior Hauser's fixer behind bars.

"I still say that Louisiana politics need to be reported on the sports page. That way everyone knows what the game is and who is on which team." This was my uncle's favorite thing to slip into a conversation, and I am still not sure if he made it up or took it as his own from someone else. It is the best indicator of the extent of his intoxication. The man can drink like a fish, but he can still be a barracuda when royally drunk. "Katie, my dear, tell me about this nonsense my nephew hauled you into."

The three of us moved to one of the tall bar tables to have this conversation. Katie wasn't concerned about being overheard, it was just too loud to be heard standing at the bar that was already three deep with regulars and every cop and Fed imaginable.

"A company called Tribal Investments sold their property to a company called CSA Holdings, which is owned by Councilwoman Delia Adams' brothers. Tribal thought they were getting a great deal because the land is on Biloxi's back-bay. Their intention was to build a pair of massive condominium towers. The tract of land turned out to be a protected wetlands and the only way to build on it was to build above the ground in the least obtrusive manner possible. CSA Holdings decided to buy the houses the Make It Right Foundation built in the Lower Ninth Ward and move them onto pilings in the wetlands. It would have satisfied the objections of Biloxi's planning commission, but met with heavy criticism. The credit union insisted they break ground by this Thursday or they would call in the note. CSA would lose its ability to complete the project if they weren't well under way before the next election changed the politics of the city council and county commissioners." Katie paused to take a sip of her champagne and let Uncle Felix digest what was by far the easiest part of the things he needed to understand. "The Batistes resisted being displaced all over again and convinced their neighbors to reject CSA's offer on their homes, too. About that time, Lionel was told he might get a book contract for his story about being in the Convention Center after the storm if he ran for office. Cooter's dad's agent came up with that bright idea. He told Lionel he needed to have a good ending for the book, and channeling his anger at what happened into positive action was the best ending. Nobody imagined Lionel was going to win; he just needed to run to have an ending for his book."

"And that's when everything went sideways," my uncle chuckled. It wasn't like he had not seen variations of what happened in the past. "Every avalanche starts with one small snowball rolling downhill."

"Exactly. Councilwoman Adams ran unopposed in the last two elections and was already facing some guy who just moved here from Florida when Lionel joined the fight. She hatched a plan with her brothers to frame Lionel because he was the one who was most likely to pose a threat."

"How so?" Uncle Felix challenged her. "He was only running to sell his book."

"He and his mother are sort of housing activists down there. They are well known and liked by the people who grew up in the Ninth Ward. Delia has been having to walk a thin line between keeping the pre-storm population happy without alienating the people who have moved into her district since the storm. Those are two entirely different sets of voters," Katie explained, probably unnecessarily. "Lionel gets framed and then one of Junior Hauser's fixers shows up to defend him. Brovartey used to work for the credit union that Hauser allegedly controls. The credit union was who loaned CSA Holdings the money to buy the land that was causing them the problem. Brovartey wrote it into his contract that Lionel had to use his house as collateral to pay his bills if his mystery benefactor decided not to pay them after all. The plan all along was to use that clause to force the Batistes out of their house, with the assumption everyone else would sell if they were gone. Cooter figured it out and we set a trap for Brovartey. He confessed to everything in court and the FBI arrested Delia and her brothers for the conspiracy to frame Lionel. Now it looks like Lionel will win her seat on the Council, whether he wants it or not."

"Nice and tidy," Uncle Felix declared and finished his fourth martini in two gulps. He plucked the pair of green olives from their skewer and popped them in his mouth. He was still chewing when he looked me in the eye. "Then why is the real bad guy still running loose?"

"What do you mean?"

"You two need to go back and follow the money." He reached into his pocket and pulled out a fountain pen and grabbed the last dry napkin on the table. He wrote the names of everyone Katie had mentioned from memory and then focused his attention on her instead of me. "Everyone on this list had something to lose. Where is the person who had anything to gain? Someone made money out of this or it never would have happened, at least not this way. That councilwoman knew she didn't really need to fear Lionel Batiste, so why do something as stupid as frame him for something nobody even believed he did? If you're going to frame somebody, make up a story people will believe. The Indians didn't really think they were going to get their buildings put up, and that house flipper was just trying to cover all his bases. He needed to be on the winning side, but his business was going to keep chewing up real estate no matter who won the council seat."

"So, you think we haven't found the person behind all of this." Katie wanted him to say it in as many words, but we both knew Uncle Felix had a point. Looking at it from his perspective made the case she worked so hard to build look like a house of cards.

The FBI only had Bear Brovartey's testimony that Delia and her brothers were behind framing Lionel. They might find substantiation in the Adam's email and phone records, but I was suddenly very doubtful of that. For one thing, the cost of framing Lionel may well have exceeded any of their abilities to raise that kind of cash. One doesn't write a check to pay for, or borrow, fifty thousand dollars' worth of illegal drugs. The brothers being in a cash bind was what brought this on, so they didn't have that kind of money lying around and Delia likely didn't either. It wasn't like she could use campaign funds to buy meth without someone noticing. There was still some question of just how tightly they could be connected to Brovartey. Surely Delia was not in Junior Hauser's pocket.

Katie and I were left feeling a lot less festive when my uncle excused himself and went to order another free martini and schmooze the regulars. He was always in need of a new client and another favor to call in.

Uncle Felix's rebuke that an unseen puppet master eluded justice bothered me enough that I could not get to sleep that night. Late night television wasn't enough to bore me to sleep, so I decided to try using the financial reports and other odds and ends in Tulip's folder. I was chagrined to realize my sister had already provided an answer to the question that was keeping me awake. I drove to Katie's house and debated my new suspect with her until nearly dawn. She believed my first solution to the case, so she was understandably more argumentative this time. It was fortunate that SAC Conroy really liked both of us just then, because the probable cause Katie had for the stack of search warrants it would take to prove or disprove my thin theory was thin. Most of them were for phone and email records she could get from the parties' carriers without alerting the target of my investigation. The financial records were going to be a lot harder to get from the credit union without sounding alarms in Junior Hauser's house. I was once again relieved that the FBI would be the target of the crime lord's anger and not Katie or myself.

Chapter 47

Tulip and I attended Lionel's first campaign rally at Reverend Sharpe's church the following Saturday. Their Christmas nativity, with its Black figurines, filled the former department store's display window. Reverend Sharpe was doing everything he could to mend his fences with the new front runner in the race for the council seat from which Delia had just resigned. He made sure the media was there in force and that he and Lionel were seen together as much as possible. Reverend Sharpe presented us with T-shirts bearing a slogan taken from the house I pointed out to Gavin on his way to meet Lionel the first time. *CAN'T STOP THE FUNK* struck me as being the perfect banner and platform for an upstart politician from the Lower Ninth Ward.

I was still wearing one of the T-shirts when I returned to Strada Ammazarre early that evening. Katie was waiting for me at the bar, being regaled with more of Ryan Kennedy's saucy stories from his days, and nights, as a catering manager in the French Quarter. I politely disentangled her from his company and we headed to my apartment so I could change clothes for dinner. Owning the place doesn't mean I don't have to show the table manners my mother beat into me as a child, and a t-shirt at the dinner table isn't alright.

I came to an abrupt halt when I spotted Alex Boudreau sitting with an older couple at a table in the far corner of the dining room that was just beginning to fill with dinner reservations and walk-in guests. I gave Katie's hand a tug and moved across the dining room.

"Alex, you sly dog." I grabbed his shoulder as I invited myself to sit down. Katie quietly took a seat from one of the nearby tables and sat in the aisle, certain she was going to get a good show.

"Am I under arrest?" He didn't sound very concerned about that prospect.

"That's not why I am here. I just came by to commend you on a well-played game. You almost got away clean with all of this. I never once thought to see who hired you as an intern while you were a law student at Tulane."

"It wasn't my job to tell you everything, detective," he said with a smirk I was now determined to wipe from his face.

"But, if you had, I might not have dug nearly so deep that I found what Katie turned over the FBI. You have a lot more to answer for than just what your attorney pal accused you of the other day." I left this hanging between us to see just how nervous Alex was about keeping his world intact when so many others were already on a road to ruin.

"The FBI already contacted my attorneys. I have promised to cooperate, but I am interested to know what you think you can hang on me." He was fishing, and it would take him a while to realize what he was reeling in was the weight of the damning evidence our digging and the FBI's search warrants turned up.

"Do you mind?" I asked Katie. Alex had barely looked at my companion, but he was deeply unsettled to find one of the assistant state attorneys at his elbow.

"Have some fun." She nodded her head and leaned back just slightly as a thin smile formed on her lips. Alex frowned at her and shifted his attention back to me. His companions had stopped eating and were taking a serious interest in this.

"What links you and Brovartey also links you to Bristol Taylor. The two of you were interns at the credit union your junior year in college, and you both reported to Brovartey. Were you two dating or just enjoying a summer fling?" I was a little disappointed that this didn't get the reaction I was looking for. It surprised me when I found out, and I assumed he would be shook that I was able to make the connection.

"No sex, sorry to disappoint you," Alex chuckled just a bit hollowly. "We had to come up with ways for the credit union to maximize the return on its investments. We both saw commercial real estate as having higher returns than home or car loans, and better collateralization. I came up with the idea of investing in areas that were recovering from major disasters, but Bristol took it even farther. I just saw an opportunity to make higher interest loans on properties that were temporarily assessed below their fair market value. The credit union could not lose money if it had to call in the loan and seize the real estate. Bristol was the one who saw an opportunity to change the economic foundation of entire parts of town in such a recovery. Developers always have a problem moving large populations from areas they want to develop, but a storm like Katrina does that for them. Developers can buy up large tracts of abandoned property and change the entire character of the neighborhood by not replacing the low income housing or small businesses. Her idea was to go back with mid-range condos and trendy shops to kick-start gentrification and then slowly increase the price of each new condo or housing development."

"And which of you came up with finagling the property values by financing the sale of your own buildings?"

"That was me," Alex shrugged modestly.

"You owe me five dollars," Katie spoke up. Alex turned his head back and forth between us in mild confusion.

"I thought Brovartey figured out how to launder

money that way." I shrugged and passed the money to Katie right under his chin.

"I'm not laundering money," he protested.

"You have a laundromat of almost Biblical proportions. The FBI agents I gave this to say it was evil genius at its best. That's pretty high praise." I wanted to remind him of the FBI's interest in his operation. It wasn't just me scouring his background any longer.

"That's not even the worst thing they are going to want to talk to you about. You tried to steal a seat on the city council, and you almost pulled it off."

"I don't have to sit here and let you embarrass me in front of my parents," Alex hissed and began to wad up his dinner napkin. It was a grand performance, but he wasn't leaving the table.

"Oh, these are your parents?" I smiled cordially. "Man, are they going to hate you."

"Why would we hate our son?" his mother's indignation was nearly as perfectly acted as her son's.

"Because your son pulled you down with him," I said in a tone that implied what I was saying was obvious. "See, he must have known someone would look at his bank accounts when this was all done. It would look bad if he somehow made a profit from either Tribal or CSA losing their deals, but nobody was going to look at *your* accounts. You made a mistake when you made an offer to the credit union on a half dozen pieces of prime property CSA owns the day before Lionel was framed for dealing drugs. Whoever put the frame around Lionel knew it wouldn't hold, because they were also the ones who were going to prove he was innocent. That entire frame job was a way to damage the councilwoman and her brothers by framing them for having done it, and Lionel as well if possible. Someone knew those properties were going back on the market when CSA went bankrupt in the midst of the bad press, and told your parents to get their offer in. Dumb move, folks."

Katie turned towards the appalled pair and gave them a reproachful shake of her head. Their son may well have just cost them their own fortunes. It was out of her jurisdiction, though, and she was still mad about that.

"That wasn't all they found," I continued down my path of destruction. Alex apparently didn't want to make the now crowded dining room into a courtroom by defending himself, but he saw a lot of legal trouble was headed his way. "You used your work teams and shell companies to make illegal campaign contributions to both Celia Adams and that ringer you brought in from Florida to run against her."

"I don't know what you are talking about," Alex finally raised a hand in objection. "I never told anyone to make any campaign contributions, and I have no idea what you are talking about when you say I know Donald Ursin."

"I didn't say you told anyone to do so. Your accountant made all of the contributions in their names without their knowledge, or at least every one of them Katie questioned seemed more willing to swear they had no knowledge than they were to go back to prison. As for your buddy, did you think re-using Neighbors for a Good Neighborhood wasn't going to ring some bells? You two scammed a legit developer out of his project in Pensacola ten years ago by using a fake neighborhood preservation group to turn the city council against the poor guy so you could swoop in and take his building, after he did the most expensive part of its renovation. Then you turned it into high end condos instead of the affordable housing he planned for the building."

"I don't remember doing anything of the sort," Alex huffed, which has never been a very effective defense in or out of court.

"Well, the Florida Bar Association remembers censuring Mister Ursin, and the News Journal even ran a picture of the two of you together when they printed the expose that got you kicked out of town. Was it your idea to have him go by Don instead of Eugene when you brought him here?" Evidence like this wasn't something I was supposed to have found if Alex's eyebrows were any sort of indication.

"Cut to the chase. My food is getting cold," he said and pushed his plate away. He turned and glared at me, as if to say he didn't give Katie and me near the credit we deserved for knowing where and how to dig in his past.

"It was the bikers that blew it for you," I said to explain how I discovered the key to everything. "I didn't catch what bothered me for the longest time. A bunch of Black bikers should be headed to Houston for a weekend of fun and not Biloxi. They all evacuated to Texas during Katrina, and that is where they still have family and criminal ties. The Black Knights shouldn't have any interests in Biloxi anyway. That is Junior Hauser's back yard and the Dixie Mafia has never embraced job equality for every race. But, it is also true that Junior has always wanted a piece of the pie in New Orleans, and Hurricane Katrina might have offered a chance at one."

"How so?" That question was miles from a denial.

"Everything got upended. Everybody left town, most of the businesses the local mobsters were still holding onto were closed, most permanently. Their rackets got disrupted and everyone was looking at making a fresh start whether that's what they wanted or not," I elaborated. The table had grown very quiet. I noticed a couple of tables nearby had taken an interest in our conversation as well, so I lowered my voice just a bit. They would have to wait to read all of this in the paper someday. "Junior must have seen his chance to move in. Thing is, he couldn't just send his people over and set up shop or cops here or there would notice. He had to peel off some business nobody was all that attached to, like supplying Black heroin dealers while he expanded the credit union's money laundering operation. He probably had to learn to bite his good old boy tongue when he dealt with the Black Knights, but they were his opening. All Junior needed to get started in New Orleans was a face nobody in law enforcement over here was watching for as criminals began coming back to town. Junior looked in his Rolodex of grifters with no criminal record and came up with your name."

"You think I work for Junior Hauser?" Alex tried to force a laugh, but neither the accusation nor being publicly exposed as Junior's pawn were particularly funny.

"It doesn't matter what he thinks. What matters what can be proved in court," Katie reminded both of us. Alex spun to face her, having all but forgotten she was present until then. He came to the realization he was boxed in. "I'd say he has given us quite a bit to work with, though."

"Your money laundry is a pretty simple business model. You buy a bunch of houses grouped close together on the cheap and remodel them all at the same time, creating a flurry of invoices that makes it almost impossible to sort out what it cost to renovate any one house. Then you sold pieces of the rehabs as investment properties. Most of your buyers turned out to be investment shell companies, and most of those turned out to be registered overseas. You rented the properties in a disproportionate number of cash transactions. I think Katie said the Feds think about five million dollars a year slipped through the cracks, isn't that about right?"

"Something like that," Katie agreed. We hadn't actually heard from her own investigators, but they would have a lot easier time finding the money if this conversation compelled Alex to start moving Junior's money in ways they didn't normally do so.

"And all those new rich kids in the neighborhood meant new bars and restaurants could afford to open up, and new retail shops as well. Junior's credit union financed some of them, and his goons leaned on all of them for his protection in such a rough transitional neighborhood. Junior even used some of the places to move stolen goods. You were nothing more than his key to the lock of the New Orleans kingdom." I was past the point of speculation, but the way Alex was fidgeting told me that my degree in economics and taste for finding bad guys had me headed in the right direction. "I don't imagine Junior asked you to be the guy to bring the Black Knights into the fold. No, that was probably Brovartey and he blew the deal somehow. Worse, he even tried to bully them and that really didn't work. His guys killed two of their prospects and drove them away."

"Why do you think this Junior guy had anything to do with a bunch of Black bikers? I thought you said he was a racist," Alex was fishing again. He was going straight to Junior with the details of this conversation, and that might be the last really dumb thing he lived to do.

"I finally stopped to consider how Brovartey's two idiot henchmen crossed paths with those dead Black biker prospects. It wasn't by accident. I think the Black Knights went to Biloxi to negotiate with Junior to be their heroin supplier. They didn't like the deal, so they left. Junior told Brovartey to lean on them, so he had his guys kill two of the bikers' prospects. Killing their prospects was meant to scare the bikers, but that didn't work. Brovartey must have thought implicating the bikers in the frame up on Lionel would bring them back to the table, figuring I might take an interest in them and cramp their style. I started to put the pieces together when it turned out Brovartey's guys planted the dope on Lionel."

"None of that was my circus," Alex shrugged. I suspected my revelation held a lot more trouble for the two brothers and the attorney than it would Alex once he shared our conversation with Junior. That trio could link Junior to the Black Knights. Both of those parties might want to see the three men dead to keep that a secret.

"Junior saved you for the big work. You were supposed to deliver a city council seat to him this time around. You had your bases covered until Lionel jumped in. Your guy Ursin would win if you could find a way to force Delia out of the race, and Ursin made Delia feel vulnerable enough that she played into your hands. Junior was going to control the seat no matter who won. Going after Lionel managed to take Delia Adams down, but Ursin is about to get forced out as well when his connection to you, and what you've been up to, makes the paper. He owes you, not Junior, but he probably won't take any of the rap for you this time. How happy will Junior be that you just handed the city council seat to a Black kid who is going to make cleaning up his neighborhood his first priority?" I was done. I had nothing more to poke Alex with, and it was going to be a while before the FBI or the State Police kicked in his door and hauled him off to face whatever charges they could make out of everything I had just accused him of doing.

"I guess you'll have to wait to find out," Alex tried to shrug it all off. If I wasn't arresting him, he had to ask himself how much of what I had just spelled could ever be proved.

The answer was the FBI had the evidence to prove *all* of it. I was content to let others take the credit and spend all that time in court. I didn't want to spend my quality time with Katie in a courtroom. I had already kept her from dinner for too long this evening.

"Yes, he will," she conceded. "I suggest that you call your accountant and see whether or not your accounts are frozen. But, then, why should you worry? It's not your money anyway, right Alex? Oh, you can also expect a visit from Tulip. Lionel is suing you for defamation instead of Delia. That ought to tie up all your legal bank accounts."

Alex was already dialing a number into his phone by the time she set the chair back in place and took my arm. We left the trio, with their unpaid check, to find their own way out of the restaurant and out of Junior's reach.

I doubt Alex's folks imagined they might lose everything to a mobster's bank because of an investment tip from their son. Alex was going to have to decide whether to spend the rest of his days in witness protection or prison before they were drastically reduced in number by whoever Junior had next in line to clean up his messes.

But, to borrow what Alex Boudreaux had just said, this wasn't *my* circus any longer.

Acknowledgments

Thanks of the highest order to my wife for her unflinching
support of my dreams and ambitions.

Only in New Orleans would there be two investigative
reporters with the same name. Special thanks go out to
Jason Berry for his political coverage and Jason Brad
Berry for his reporting on housing and political problems
in the wake of Hurricane Katrina. I also need to give a nod
to my friend George 'Loki' Williams and his Humid City
blog for keeping me informed about the dilemmas short-
term rental property have added to life in my beloved city.

OTHER BOOKS BY
H. MAX HILLER

Cadillac Holland Mysteries
Blowback
Blue Garou
Ghosts & Shadows

https://www.indiesunited.net/h-max-hiller

ABOUT THE AUTHOR

H. Max Hiller's first taste of New Orleans was as a cook on Bourbon Street at the age of seventeen. His resume now includes many of New Orleans' iconic dining and music destinations. These jobs have provided a lifetime of characters and anecdotes to add depth to the Detective Cooter 'Cadillac' Holland series. The author now divides his passions between writing at his home overlooking the Mississippi River and as a training chef aboard a boat traveling America's inland waterways, and is always living by the motto "be a New Orleanian wherever you are."

CPSIA information can be obtained
at www.ICGtesting.com
Printed in the USA
LVHW110728100721
692195LV00021B/1169